PRAISE FOR JENNIFER PROBST

"For a sexy, fun-filled, warmhearted read, look no further than Jennifer Probst!"

—Jill Shalvis, *New York Times* bestselling author

"Jennifer Probst is an absolute auto-buy author for me."

—J. Kenner, *New York Times* bestselling author

"Jennifer Probst knows how to bring the swoons and the sexy."

—Amy E. Reichert, author of *The Coincidence of Coconut Cake*

"As always, Jennifer Probst never fails to deliver romance that sizzles and has a way of tugging those emotional heartstrings."

—*Four Chicks Flipping Pages*

"Jennifer Probst's books remind me of delicious chocolate cake. Bursting with flavor, decadently rich . . . very satisfying."

—*Love Affair with an e-Reader*

PRAISE FOR *LOVE ON BEACH AVENUE*

"Probst (*All Roads Lead to You*) opens her Sunshine Sisters series with an effervescent rom-com. The characters leap off the page, the love story is perfectly paced, and an adorable dog named Lucy adds charm. Readers will eagerly await the next in the series."

—*Publishers Weekly*

"The perfect enemies-to-lovers, best-friend's-brother romance! I laughed, smiled, cheered, cried a few tears, and loved Carter and Avery!"

—*Two Book Pushers*

"*Love on Beach Avenue* is a three-layer wedding cake of best friend's brother, enemies to lovers, and just plain fun. Another yummy confection by Jennifer Probst!"

—Laurelin Paige, *New York Times* bestselling author

"I could feel the ocean breeze on my face as I turned the pages. *Love on Beach Avenue* is chock-full with magic ingredients: a dreamy seaside, a starchy hero with a tiny dog, sparkling wit, and fabulous female friendship—a must-read romance!"

—Evie Dunmore, author of *Bringing Down the Duke*

"*Love on Beach Avenue* is the perfect enemies-to-lovers romance with well-developed characters, sexy banter, and so many swoon-worthy moments! Jennifer Probst knocked it out of the park with this book! Looking forward to the rest of the series!"

—Monica Murphy, *New York Times* bestselling author

"Fantastic start to a brand-new series from Jennifer Probst! *Love on Beach Avenue* is beautifully heartfelt and epically romantic!"

—Emma Chase, *New York Times* bestselling author

PRAISE FOR *ALL ROADS LEAD TO YOU*

"Funny, sexy, emotional, and full of scenes that make your heart swell and the tears drop, *All Roads Lead to You* is a beautiful story set in hometown America and one you will want to read again and again."

—*A Midlife Wife*

"Harper's story was everything I wanted it to be and so much more."

—*Becca the Bibliophile*

"Ms. Probst has a way of writing that I can't help but be 100 percent invested in from the first page!"

—*Franci's Fabulous Reads*

"Jennifer Probst expertly blends humor, sexiness, and emotion, keeping the reader delightfully addicted. She entwines these elements, evoking a hope that fate will align and bring love and happiness between two characters that seem to be at once perfect yet ill fitted for one another. I enjoyed this story; its plot, backdrop, characters, and romance gave me the warm fuzzies."

—*TJ Loves to Read*

"Jennifer Probst shines when she talks about her animal rescues in real life, and the saying is true: write what you know, and it will always be the best story. The same goes for this one; it's one of her best stories to date."

—*AJ's Book re-Marks*

"JP writes beautiful words, and I just loved this story. There was enough action, adventure, passion, and swoon factor, not to mention romance."

—*The Guide to Romance Novels*

"A read that will not only fill your emotional romance need but will fill your heart with the fulfilling need to care for a goat that needed to be hugged and be besties with a horse to feel safe."

—*The Book Fairy*

PRAISE FOR *A BRAND NEW ENDING*

"*A Brand New Ending* was a mega-adorable and moving second-chance romance! I just adored everything about it! Run to your nearest Amazon for your own Kyle—this one is mine!"

—*BJ's Book Blog*

"Don't miss another winner from Jennifer Probst."

—Mary from *USA TODAY's Happy Ever After*

PRAISE FOR *THE START OF SOMETHING GOOD*

"The must-have summer romance read of 2018!"

—*Gina's Bookshelf*

"Achingly romantic, touching, realistic, and just plain beautiful, *The Start of Something Good* lingers with you long after you turn the last page."

—Katy Evans, *New York Times* bestselling author

Forever

in

Cape May

OTHER BOOKS BY JENNIFER PROBST

The Sunshine Sisters Series

Love on Beach Avenue

Temptation on Ocean Drive

The Stay Series

The Start of Something Good

A Brand New Ending

All Roads Lead to You

Something Just Like This

Begin Again

Nonfiction

Write Naked: A Bestseller's Secrets to Writing Romance &

Navigating the Path to Success

Write True

The Billionaire Builders Series

Everywhere and Every Way

Any Time, Any Place

Somehow, Some Way

All or Nothing at All

The Searching For . . . Series

Searching for Someday

Searching for Perfect

Searching for Beautiful

Stand-Alone Novels

Dante's Fire

Executive Seduction

All the Way

The Holiday Hoax

The Grinch of Starlight Bend

The Charm of You

Our Italian Summer

Forever

in

Cape May

JENNIFER PROBST

 Montlake

Published by Montlake, Seattle

www.apub.com

Amazon, the Amazon logo, and Montlake are trademarks of Amazon.com, Inc., or its affiliates.

ISBN-13: 9781542017855
ISBN-10: 1542017858

Cover design by Caroline Teagle Johnson

Printed in the United States of America

For Kristi Yanta . . .
You have dragged me from the brink many times,
always reminding me I have the talent to get to the end.
I cannot thank you enough for your support,
cheerleading, tough love, and belief in my work.
I have loved sharing this Cape May journey with you.
Thank you.

Prologue

"Dude, that was weird."

Taylor Sunshine and Pierce Powers were lying in the twin bed in Taylor's dorm room. The party had been the usual—loud jocks, giggly girls, and too much alcohol. Taylor had lost at beer pong—God, that game sucked—and had been pretty tipsy when she'd left. Of course, Pierce had spotted her and insisted on walking her back. He'd gotten her to the bed and then turned to leave, and her hug/lunge ended up bringing him down on the mattress next to her. After a good laugh, she'd looped her arms around his neck to pull herself up, he'd leaned closer, and they'd . . .

Kissed.

She'd waited for fireworks and the shattering knowledge that he was the one. Her sister Bella had met the love of her life in junior high school and said she'd always known they'd get married. But other than the softness of Pierce's lips and his familiar scent that always comforted rather than aroused, Taylor felt a pleasant hum and then . . . nothing.

He groaned into the red plaid pillow. "This isn't happening. You are not telling me my kissing was weird."

"That's not what I was saying! I said the *kiss* was weird, not your specific kissing style. Did it feel a bit like incest to you, too?"

He let out a noise into the pillowcase and climbed off the bed. "I'm outta here."

"No, I'm sorry." She caught his hand and pulled gently back. "Stay. The room's still spinny, and I'm afraid I'll get sick."

She refused to feel guilt at his concerned expression. She needed to have him close tonight: the boy she'd grown up with and the man who knew her best.

He sat back down with a frown. "Do you need water?"

"Not yet."

"You need to breathe slow and focus. Want me to put on the TV?"

"In a minute. Look, I'm really sorry. We swore we wouldn't do that again."

His face tightened with irritation. "We were fifteen, Taylz. It was a miracle we didn't end up playing doctor earlier."

Her nickname softened the rough edges of his statement. "That's my point. We both felt nothing and promised we wouldn't muck up our relationship with crap like feelings and sex, and here I went and attacked you. It wasn't fair."

He laughed and she relaxed. Thank God she hadn't hurt him. They'd met freshman year in high school, when they'd been assigned as lab partners. He was an A student; she was a C. He'd ended up tutoring her all semester, scared shitless she'd tank his grade, and a friendship had immediately bloomed. Other than that one experimental kiss, they'd been best friends who'd had each other's backs, all the way past graduation. She got accepted into Monmouth, and he attended Montclair a short distance away. They'd been able to hang out on a regular basis and keep the same closeness from high school.

"You should be studying poetry, not performance art," he said with a roll of his pale-green eyes. "I swear, you're nothing like the other girls I know. And I'm not sure that's a compliment."

She fluffed up the pillows, leaned back, and motioned him closer. "Come sit next to me, and you can insult me all you want. I deserve it for sticking my tongue in your mouth."

"We didn't get that far," he muttered, still obviously annoyed by the whole scene. But he took his place next to her, his arms crossed in front of his chest.

A relieved sigh ballooned into her lungs and then softly out. Warmth flowed in her veins from the alcohol, and the darkness masked the shabbiness of her tiny, cluttered room. She leaned her head against his broad shoulder—beefed up from lifting weights and boxing—and breathed in the scent of cotton, soap, and tequila. His jean-clad legs were crossed at the ankles. She'd seen a ton of girls checking him out at the party and knew he never lacked for a date or anything else he wanted. Pierce was a good-looking guy. Unfortunately, many of his partners talked, and talked loudly, confiding all the yummy details she didn't want to hear, so she also knew he was good in bed.

Still, she knew she got the very best of Pierce Powers, the part that no one else could ever claim.

Loyalty. Friendship. Trust.

"You forgive me?" she asked softly, nudging his shoulder. "I'm a bit drunk, and Will just broke up with me. I think I was feeling sad and kissed you on impulse."

He snorted. "*You* broke up with Will, and we went out specifically to celebrate your freedom, remember?"

She scrunched up her nose. "Oh yeah."

"You're hopeless." But his words were softened with humor again, and she knew she was in the clear. "But I forgive you. Unless you think we should try once more in a few years? Maybe third time's the charm."

"Doubt it. Besides, it would be awful if we ever hooked up. If we had a fight, who would I call? It couldn't be you."

"Your sisters?"

"Ugh, I never tell them anything. I love them, but they chose life-styles I despise. Bella's having a baby, and she's so young! And Avery is going for her PhD, which is boring as hell. No, thanks."

"Okay, how about we make one of those marriage pacts? If we turn thirty and we still haven't married, we marry each other."

"I'm not getting married at thirty! Maybe thirty-five."

"So we'll make it thirty-five."

She pulled lightly at the crisp hairs on his arm. "Nah, that's so tropey, like that movie *My Best Friend's Wedding*. Best friends always vow to marry when they get super old. We should do the opposite."

"What do you mean?"

The idea hit her, and she nodded with satisfaction. "We vow to each other that no matter how old we are, or how tempting it is to have sex, we never hook up. We swear friends till the end—nothing more, nothing less."

Pierce shifted his weight and shot her a funny look. "What if we change our minds? Hell, what if we want to have sex one day? Or decide to become fuck buddies?"

She glared. "We won't—we're better than that crap! We tested it twice already and know we're safe from the spark thing. It will be a way to protect our relationship forever. What do you think?"

He cocked his head. His long dark hair had escaped from its tie and now fell loose against his cheeks. "Never thought about it like that."

"Let's do it. Make it official." Taylor jumped up and grabbed a safety pin from her desk. "Stick out your hand so we can do a blood pact."

"You're freaking me out. We're not the kids from *IT*. I don't want a scar on my hand."

She grabbed his hand impatiently. "I'm just going to prick your finger."

He raised his thick dark eyebrows, which gave him an adorable Groucho Marx look. "Why are we doing this again?"

"Because you're important to me, Pierce. You're my best friend. My ride or die. I never want us to jump into bed on impulse and ruin the best relationship I've ever had. Okay? Are you with me?"

His features softened. "You're such a dork," he said with affection. "Be gentle."

She made the strike short and quick, then repeated the move on herself. They lifted their index fingers in the air, pausing a few inches away.

Their gazes met and locked.

The air shimmered with a current of energy.

They said the words together, their voices melding in perfect harmony.

Then touched their fingers together.

A hot bolt of fire shot through her body, crackling into a shock like she'd just touched a wet electrical outlet. She gasped and jerked back, her finger throbbing.

He yanked his hand away, glaring at her. "Hey, I told you not to hurt me!"

"I didn't." She stared at him, cradling her wounded hand, but when she shook it out, there was just the tiniest dot of blood from the safety pin. The air in the room eased, and she breathed deep. Probably the alcohol. She was imagining things. "Sorry, I must have pressed harder than I thought. I'm still tipsy."

His face relaxed, and he grasped her wrist loosely. "Come on, let's sleep it off."

They cuddled together on the bed, fully clothed, her head tucked in the crook of his shoulder. "Pierce?"

"Yeah?"

"Where are you going after graduation?"

His heart beat steadily against her ear. "I want to get into photography, so maybe I'll take on an assistant position. Learn some stuff before I branch out and do my own work. What about you?"

"Anywhere but Cape May," she murmured sleepily. "I want to travel. London, Paris, LA. I feel like the entire world is out there ready for me to explore and conquer. Do you feel that way?"

He was quiet for a while. "Not really. I like Cape May; it's my home. I wouldn't mind settling back there if I had a place and work that was all mine."

"Not me. I'm never going back."

She drifted off to sleep with big dreams swimming in her head, the future mapped out like an adventure with buried treasure at the end of every path.

Until a few months before graduation, when her mother called.

Bella's husband had been killed in an accident, leaving Taylor's sister alone with a newborn baby. Things had fallen apart, and she was needed.

So she went home and learned that some dreams weren't meant to be.

Chapter One

"We have a problem."

Taylor turned to the frantic MOH—maid of honor—and knew this was going to be bad. They were already well into the reception, and everything had been running smoothly. Had she really believed they'd get through this evening unscathed?

Dammit. It was Friday the thirteenth. She'd known it would be bad luck to book a wedding, but her sisters had laughed at her superstitions and had practically bullied her into taking it on. Her stupid sibling pride had once again overridden her good sense. Next time, she'd stick to her beliefs, no matter how her sisters teased her.

She arranged her face into the fake calm that was critical to keeping panic to a minimum. "I'll take care of whatever it is. Tell me."

The MOH, dressed in an awful pink fluffy dress that had been chosen specifically to make her look uglier than the bride, mashed her fingers against her poppy-pink lips. "Susan found her husband banging one of the waitresses in the bathroom and is going apeshit. They're over there." She pointed out a small circle of three people at the back of the room, near the wedding cake. "I don't know what to do!"

Taylor's brain flickered past the endless scenarios that all spelled F-U-C-K-E-D. "Where's the bride?" she asked.

"Over by the bar."

She'd taken this one on alone, so she had no assistant to lean on. She mentally ticked off the top three actions of the wedding planner creed:

Contain the problem.

Keep the wedding couple blissfully unaware.

Smile and don't panic.

"Patty, I need you to keep her at the bar. Do shots. Tell jokes. Anything you need to do to keep her attention. Okay?"

The MOH gulped, nodded, and took off.

Taylor stopped by the DJ and instructed him to start the popular coordinated dances. In seconds, most seats were empty, guests enthusiastically dancing to the "Cha Cha Slide."

With determined strides, she headed to the knot of people consisting of an emotionally distressed wife, a guilty husband caught with his pants down, and a nosy bridesmaid with a satisfied smirk. She pegged the problem right away: meandering cheater hubby had previously nailed the bridesmaid. The cheater looked a bit like Chris Hemsworth and probably liked using his hammer with different partners. Susan was young—Taylor estimated her age to be around twenty-two—and emanated shocked hurt.

Halfway there, Taylor caught Pierce's gaze. He lowered his camera from taking candid shots of the dancers and mouthed the words *All okay?*

She shook her head and gave the thumbs-down signal for code red.

His expression matched hers. God, they'd just wanted an easy evening so they could get home at a decent hour, crack open a couple of beers, and shoot the breeze for a bit. He tucked his camera under his arm and headed over.

"Why would you do this to me?" Susan asked in a broken whisper. "At my friend's wedding?"

"Baby, I didn't do anything! I had a stain on my pants, and she said she could get it off with seltzer. You are completely overreacting."

Taylor's fingers automatically clenched into fists. God, she wished she could deck him. But she kept her cool, smoothly inserting herself between the couple. "Susan, I think you need some space and privacy. Why don't we go into the bridal room and discuss?" she asked in a low voice.

"I think that's a good idea," Fake Thor said. "Let's not embarrass ourselves."

The nosy bridesmaid—Willa—gave a sneer. "You can't talk yourself out of this one. I knew you'd get caught again one day, and Susan has finally had enough of your filthy lies!"

"Stay out of this, Willa," Fake Thor warned.

Pierce appeared like a Prince Charming and smiled at the cheater. "Hey, why don't we take a short walk and get out of the spotlight?" He slowly walked forward so Fake Thor was forced to back up. Taylor did the same with Susan, and a few precious feet were finally put between them.

She could do this. Get them to the private room, where they could blow up or break down. As long as it wasn't in front of the wedding couple and their guests.

Susan stiffened, her gaze swiveling to lock on Willa's. "What do you mean 'get caught again'? Did you know he'd been cheating on me?"

Willa flinched. Two spots of red flushed her cheeks. "I suspected."

"Shut up, Willa," Fake Thor hissed. "You've always been jealous of Susan. Always been trying to break us up. Come on, baby. Let's go talk alone, and I'll show you there's nothing to worry about. You're the only woman I love."

"Liar," Willa mumbled. "You've said that to everyone."

"Yes, let's go talk, this way," Taylor said, gently guiding Susan another step away.

Susan shook off her arm, her voice strengthening. "I want to know right now what's going on! Who else did he say that to?"

"No one!" Fake Thor swore. "Just you."

"Willa, did you sleep with my husband?" Susan demanded, her hands shaking. "Tell me now. As my friend."

Tears gathered in Willa's eyes. "It was before you got married, I swear. He said he'd always been interested in me but was afraid to back out of the wedding and hurt you. But he lied, to both of us. I found out later he was sleeping around with someone else."

"*She's* the liar, Susan! I'd never cheat on you with her—she's jealous," Fake Thor proclaimed.

Ah, shit.

Taylor shot a look at Pierce, and they recognized it was like trying to bail out the *Titanic*, because the entire wedding was at risk of going down with this sinking ship.

Pierce grabbed Fake Thor's arm. "Let's go before you get into more trouble, buddy," he said in a man-friendly tone, like a co-conspirator. "You'll have time to explain. This way."

Fake Thor followed, apparently realizing that shutting his mouth was a good idea.

Taylor put her arm gently around Susan, her trembling body evidence of the traumatic event, which elicited a flare of sympathy. "Come on, let's go where it's quiet. It'll be okay." She murmured a litany of useless words meant to soothe Susan and get her moving. Taylor shot a deadly glare at Willa to remain there and not follow.

The bridesmaid began to sob dramatically. "I'm sorry, Susan. Please forgive me."

It happened just a few feet away from the door of safety.

A warrior cry burst from Susan's lips, and she dove for Fake Thor. He jerked out of Pierce's grasp as she tackled him, and in slow motion, Taylor watched them both crash into the table, collapsing it on one end.

The three-tiered chocolate buttercream cake with cherry-soaked rum sponge slid off the pedestal.

Taylor and Pierce both dove for it, and for a brief shining second, she believed they'd catch it midfall, just like in those wedding rom-com movies her sisters loved to watch.

But this was Friday the thirteenth.

The cake splattered to the ground.

Susan and Fake Thor lay on the floor in a twisted tangle of limbs.

Willa began to scream.

And Taylor swore she'd never be dumb enough to get married.

♥ ♥ ♥

"Well, that was fun. Why do you have Michelob Ultra in your fridge? Please tell me you're not on some kind of diet."

Pierce laughed and took down a bag of pretzels from the cabinet. "Carter wants to lose a few pounds before the wedding, so he switched beers. Your Raging Bitch IPA is on the door section."

"Thanks. God, I hate wimpy beer. It should be illegal." Taylor grabbed a bottle for her and a Goose Island for him, using the refrigerator magnet to flip off the cap. Then she handed him his beer while she dropped onto one of the padded stools by the high granite countertop.

Pierce's house was like her second home. She liked the no-nonsense decor of black and muted gray with pops of red for color. The leather sectional was oversize, worn, and reclined; the television took up an entire wall; and the kitchen had an open concept with bar seating and a generous counter so she never had to sit at a real table. He was a minimalist, but the real beauty was the collection of photographs that hung on the walls—gorgeous shots of Cape May beaches, vibrant sunsets, wedding couples in the throes of love, and the occasional moody ocean shot that made people ponder their life choices.

"I can't believe Carter is worried about looking good for the wedding. I thought it was just Avery." Her oldest sister and future brother-in-law planned to marry in October, just four months away.

Pierce ripped open the bag and sat across from her. "Avery wants to lose five pounds. Carter tried to talk her out of it, but she's stubborn, so he decided to join her and lose weight, too."

She shook her head. "He's so damn sweet. She'll never make it a week without a chocolate croissant. Speaking of pastries, I've never lost a wedding cake before. Have you?"

"Nope. But technically, it didn't happen to me. I'm just the photographer."

She crunched on a pretzel. "I'll never live this down," she said glumly. "Susan asked if I knew a good divorce lawyer, like I keep business cards to distribute after I plan perfect weddings. We're going to get killed on reviews for this one."

"Not necessarily. You replaced the cake pretty quickly, so they were able to cut something. Hell, the bride even smooshed it in the groom's face. I got a great shot."

She groaned and took another slug of beer. "Thank God Pretty Tasty Cupcakes had a huge inventory. Saved my ass."

"It was good thinking in an emergency." His gaze lifted, and his familiar sea-green eyes met hers. "It'll be a huge loss for your sisters when you go."

She stiffened, refusing to feel guilty. She'd promised to help run the family business until they were on a solid foundation, but her goals had never included wedding planning. Now that Sunshine Bridal was booming, she was off to pursue her own dreams soon. It was finally her turn. "Trying to make me feel bad?" she asked sharply. "You think I should stay?"

The muscle in his jaw ticked, a telltale sign he was annoyed. "No. I'm trying to tell you how much you're valued here. That you've made a difference."

She softened and reached across the table to squeeze his hand. His fingers wrapped around hers, and the familiar strength and weight of his grip washed through her. Pierce had always been her safety in the storm of her usual unruly emotions, and the only man who'd ever been able to put up with her. "Sorry. It's just that . . ." She trailed off, not sure how to express her thoughts.

He cocked his head. "What?"

"Ever since I booked that art show in Paris, you've been acting weird. I can't put my finger on it. Are you mad at me?"

He jerked back. "No, of course not. You need to live your life. I just found it interesting I was the last to find out."

Taylor caught the slight bitterness in his tone only because she'd been listening to every nuance of his husky voice since high school. Regret washed over her. He was right. When she'd made the decision, she'd told her family and Gabe—her coworker and Bella's boyfriend—but not Pierce. Hell, she'd tried to tell him, but each time she'd thought about bringing it up, her stomach lurched and she made up an excuse to delay. "I apologized for that. Don't take it personal."

Pierce lifted a brow. "It *was* personal. I had to hear from my friends that you were leaving—I felt stupid. Don't try to pretend it was nothing."

This time, she bowed her head and spoke from her heart. "You're right. I freaked out. It was easier to tell everyone else because I could still pretend it wasn't real." She threw her shoulders back and faced him, her gaze locking with his. "I'm really sorry, Pierce. You've always been my person. I figured once you knew, I'd have to deal with the reality of completing a series of paintings for other people to judge. I got scared."

He let out a breath, and the firm set of his mouth relaxed. He reached out and touched her cheek, somehow knowing the contact would ease the awful vulnerability she tried desperately to avoid. It was another reason he was so important to her. He sensed exactly how to deal with all her moods and accepted her as is, wholeheartedly. "I get it. And I forgive you."

"Thanks."

"How's the work going? How many pieces do you have left to do?"

"Too many." She ate more pretzels, savoring the salt. "I only have eight weeks left to get three more paintings completed. But the worst part? I'm not even sure what I have is good enough. Something seems lacking."

He gave a snort. "You always say that. The first few you showed me were amazing. When can I see the rest?"

She hesitated. Finally being able to show her work to an audience was a dream, but the reality was terrifying, especially if she failed. Usually, Pierce was the only one she allowed to see her paintings, which had always been intensely personal. When she confronted a blank canvas, she came alive, and all those messy emotions that got her in trouble in life became valuable. But these new projects were going to be seen by industry experts and strangers. They had to be better than her previous work, which had developed from a beloved hobby. They had to be good enough to launch her into the esteemed world of art.

Would Pierce be able to tell her the truth if they sucked? He might be too close to see the missing elements, and fake praise could be detrimental. "I don't know."

"Why?"

Taylor sighed. "Because I'm afraid you'll be too soft on me. You may not be objective enough."

Instead of protesting, he seemed to think seriously about her statement, then nodded. "I hear you. I've always been honest with you, though, Taylz. And this is business. I promise to tell you my true opinion, if you're brave enough to let me see. I mean, I'm no art critic, just a layperson. In fact, I think you should let Carter see them, too. He has experience with the art world and what's considered good. Plus, he got you the gig."

She shook off the doubt and finished her beer. "Yeah, you're right. This week, then. What are your plans?"

"I have appointments every day but Wednesday. Then weddings both days this weekend. Sometimes, I hate summer."

"Me, too. Hey, why don't we play hooky on Wednesday? We can go to the beach."

"Don't you need to paint?"

She stuck out her tongue. "We'll only stay for a few hours. We haven't hung out in a while."

"Because you always have a date." His mild tone contradicted his judgy eyes.

A strange discomfort flitted through her, which only pissed her off. "Just because you've been a monk doesn't mean I need to be a nun. What's up with you lately? I haven't seen you with anyone in weeks. Are you experimenting with a dry June?"

"Very clever. Nah, I'm just focused on work lately. Thinking about doing something different."

She raised her brow. "Really? You never mentioned this. Are you getting tired of photographing weddings?"

Suddenly, his gaze locked with hers. A weird sensation of falling washed over her before it quickly passed and she was steady again. "It's time for me to make some changes, too."

Curiosity stirred. Pierce was a man who loved his routines and stability. Making any type of change was a big deal for him. "Like what?"

"I'm not sure yet. But I'll let you know when I figure it out."

She nodded, tipping her beer bottle in a mock toast before drinking. They sat in companionable silence for a bit while she studied him, wondering what had recently changed. It wasn't as if he was distant, but there was an assessment in his searing green eyes when he looked at her that hadn't been there before. As if he was trying to figure her out.

The thought made her inwardly wince. She wasn't big on opening up. Pierce was the only man in her life who knew the real her—the bad and the good—and she never felt judged. So what was he trying to get from her when she'd already given him everything? Or was the fact that she was finally leaving their hometown causing some aftershocks?

The idea of not seeing him every day was unthinkable. He was a thread interwoven in the fabric of her life.

Her gaze appraised the man across the counter. He'd always liked to wear his hair long, and tonight it was held back at the nape of his neck, the blue-black strands gleaming like silk. His face was a mishmash of strong features that didn't seem to fit individually, yet when put together, they gave him a rough edge that was definitely sexy. Scruff clung to his jaw in an almost-goatee. Sharply angled cheekbones, a Roman nose, and a high brow set off those amazing eyes that seemed to peel off every surface layer to get to the core. It was a talent that made him an amazing photographer—the ability to see hidden emotions.

She loved his landscapes, but his portraits were legendary. One shot seemed to capture a person's soul. She wondered if his new direction would include expanding his photography business. Of course, she could never see him leaving Sunshine Bridal or Cape May. This was his home and his heart. He'd always dreamed of settling into their childhood town and making a name for himself. He'd accomplished everything he'd ever wanted.

Now, it was her turn.

She spun on the stool and lightened the mood. "As long as you don't quit to become a politician. The world will stain your innocence."

"I'm surprised you think I have any left after years of hanging with you."

She stuck out her tongue again. "You'd be bored without me. I'd better get going."

"Hell no. You're not driving tonight. It's too late, and that has a high alcohol percentage." He plucked the empty bottle from her hand and took it to the sink to rinse.

She blew out a breath. "It's only a five-minute drive. Trust me, I still feel like I'm highly caffeinated. These night shifts are brutal."

"I don't care, you're staying."

She regarded him closely before relenting. He was impossible to argue with when he was in this type of mood—a mule looked easy to handle in comparison to Pierce when he made a decision on something. "Gonna make me do the walk of shame?"

"Like you'd care. But you have your sweats and T-shirt here from the last time. I washed them and put them in the top-left drawer."

"Thanks. Should have told me before—I hate wearing these clothes. Since I'm staying, pop me open another beer, okay? What are we gonna watch?"

His groan echoed through the hallway as she walked into his bedroom. "I'm too tired. We need to sleep."

After closing the door halfway, she listened to him rustle in the kitchen while she quickly tugged off her too-stiff clothes and replaced them with her comfy ones. "Don't be a loser!" she shouted back, deciding to steal a pair of his socks. "Did you finish *The Witcher* without me?"

Silence condemned him.

"Bastard! Now you're gonna have to watch it again!" She hopped on one foot, slid the other sock on, and met him back in the kitchen, glaring. "I told you not to skip ahead."

"Then stop going on dates," he said, walking over to hand her an open beer. "If you leave my ass stranded, I get to watch an episode."

She rolled her eyes and made her way to the couch before flopping down and setting her beer on the glass table. "Fine."

"Use a coaster."

"You're so twitchy lately," she huffed, resetting the bottle on the designated space and then grabbing the remote. "I'll set it up. Go get changed."

She clicked on the television, then settled in with a happy sigh. Funny, she was always dealing with her itchiness to be on the move, out socializing, working, anything that would soothe the wild restlessness inside her she'd been born with. But whenever she was in Pierce's house, the beast inside her settled. The thought of being alone in Paris caused a trickle of worry to leak through her. So many things were about to change. Would she be truly ready? To take on the world without her best friend at her side?

Ugh, why was she acting like Eeyore? It would all work out. No need to torture her brain by spinning imaginary scenarios.

She grabbed her favorite slate-colored mushy throw pillow, propped it under her cheek, and got ready to watch Geralt kick some monster ass.

Chapter Two

Pierce stripped and changed into sweats and a tank, then spotted Taylor's messy pile of clothes on the floor. Typical. She termed herself "casually messy," like it was an artistic phrase.

He shook his head and scooped up the black skirt and white silk blouse, neatly folded them, and put them on his dresser. Her scent drifted up to him. Musky, a bit exotic, and always a contradiction. Just like the woman.

A strange ache hit him in the gut, which he tried to decipher. It felt a bit like loneliness. Probably the knowledge he'd be losing his other half in a few short months, and nothing would ever be the same. Hell, how was he going to get used to not having her around? She slept over at his house more than any woman he'd ever dated. How many nights had they crashed together because one of them was too drunk or too tired to go home?

But finally, her dream was coming true. She'd be out of Cape May and launched into the world of travel and art. A world away from him. Sure, she'd come back for occasional visits and holidays, but he knew nothing would ever be the same.

It was time to begin dealing with it.

He dragged in a deep breath, reset, and headed back to the living room. "You'd better be ready for spoilers," he warned. "You know I suck at hiding things, so don't blame me when I tell you the end of—" He stopped, gazing down at the figure sprawled under his Phillies baseball fleece blanket.

She was asleep.

Shaking his head, he walked around the couch and clicked off the TV; retrieved her beer, rinsed the bottle, and placed it in the recycling bin; then carefully pulled the rest of the blanket over her, moving her legs so she was stretched out.

She murmured something and smiled in her sleep.

He stilled, studying her relaxed features in slumber. She'd always been beautiful. Pink hair like cotton candy tucked under her chin. Finely plucked arched brows and thick black lashes. Those Bambi-brown eyes were filled with a fierceness that always seemed too big to contain in her five-foot-seven frame. Her face was rounder than her sisters', with a natural sulk to her full lips. Her nose held a diamond stud, and he knew every marking on her body—from the flock of sparrows tattooed on her nape, to the mole at the top of her right breast, all the way to the ugly bump on her little toe that she despised.

He smiled, enjoying being able to study her without her squirming or pushing him away. Her appearance didn't properly reflect her personality, even with the nose stud, pink hair, and multiple tats. He'd never known anyone who could match her sharp wit and droll humor—able to deliver a stinging one-liner without thinking. She was hell on egotistical men who thought they could mansplain something when she'd asked a serious question. He liked to pretend he didn't know what was going on, just so he could watch her tear assholes apart with the weapon of her tongue.

The woman was hot.

Too bad they weren't sexually compatible. Or maybe it was a good thing. Sometimes, when he looked at her, an awful longing overcame him, as if his soul cried out that she was meant to be his. But logically, he knew they were a terrible fit. She wanted to fly, and he wanted to roost. She didn't believe in marriage or having a family of her own, and he dreamed of both. As friends, they were perfect. As lovers?

Disaster.

Taylor was his confidante, his partner in crime, and the only person who knew who he truly was, all the way back to their youth. Sometimes, he dreamed they could share a life together without the pressure of sex, but Taylor embraced her sexuality wholeheartedly and made no apologies. That was another thing about her he admired, even though he felt as if her partners were barely scratching the surface of what she really needed. Lately, her face seemed to reflect an emptiness after her encounters, as well as a glint of frustration in her eyes. As if she'd hoped for . . . more. Was she seeking a partner who could offer additional qualities rather than only sexual satisfaction? Maybe once she left Cape May, she'd slake the restlessness in Paris, or Italy, or wherever she ended up.

But it wouldn't be with him.

Ever since they'd met, he'd been struck by her obsession to discover what was around the next corner, as if she was consistently searching for an answer to all the questions that buzzed in her creative brain. It was the biggest difference between them. He was happy with a beer in his hand, the ocean at his front, and his feet on the familiar, crooked sidewalks of home.

At least, until lately.

Something had stirred inside him—his own sense of restlessness that he couldn't figure out. He kept coming back to the work front, wondering if it was time to try something different from photographing weddings. His own creative muse was itching to investigate a side path and see if it would help smooth the sudden rough edges.

Change was seeping into the air. With every breath, he sensed it might be best to embrace it rather than fight it.

Pierce smoothed back Taylor's hair, took one last lingering look, and headed to bed.

Jennifer Probst

♥ ♥ ♥

Taylor propped her iPad in front of her, sipped her dark-brewed coffee, and tried to muster some enthusiasm. God, she hated Mondays. They were stripped of any fun, and the morning conference meetings at Sunshine Bridal reminded her how jam-packed their summer wedding calendar was.

She gave a half nod to her sister Bella, who was already sitting with her folders neatly out, a zen smile on her face. Her blonde locks were caught up in a loose ponytail, and she gave off a calm, focused aura. Taylor knew she'd been up since five a.m., gotten Zoe off to school, and completed her morning run. Yet she looked ready for a long day ahead.

A minute later, Avery walked in, the oldest of the three. "Good morning, everyone! It's going to be a great day," she practically sang, her energy and enthusiasm more potent than a double espresso. She headed to the conference table with her usual coffee and chocolate croissant, but Taylor noticed this time that it was cut in half. She smirked. Guess those five pounds were more serious than she'd thought, if she was sacrificing half her favorite pastry. Not that her sister needed to worry about her weight. She'd always been a bit envious of Avery's curvy body and wildly curly hair. Her own body reminded her a bit of a boy's—small breasts, straight hips, thin frame, and long limbs.

Taylor shook her head. "Aren't you tired of being chipper all the time?" she grumbled, picking at her scarlet-painted thumbnail. She dragged over the other chair and stretched out her black combat boot–clad feet. She may be forced to wear a boring work uniform for weddings, but for conferences or appointments, she preferred her own wardrobe—namely, loose, cool clothing with a bit of a personality. Today, she sported a black T-shirt with #unimpressed on the front and had paired it with olive-green cargo pants. When she dressed like a bit of a badass, it gave her some extra pep.

22

Avery grinned and sat down. "Nope. I find if I'm focused and positive in the beginning of the day, it sets up the rest for success. Don't you agree, Bella?"

"I agree," a male voice boomed out. Gabe, the fourth member of the Sunshine Bridal crew, entered the conference room. He set down his espresso and walked directly to Bella. Handing her a coffee, he then pressed a kiss to her lips, his dark eyes lit with a male possessiveness that could have made Taylor swoon if she'd been the romantic type. "Hi, sweetheart," he murmured.

Bella smiled with a sweetness that tagged her as completely smitten with her new love. "Hi, baby."

Avery sighed. "You two are just the cutest thing ever. I'm so glad I made you work Adele's wedding together."

Taylor arched a brow. "Excuse me? That did not get them together. It was my wise counsel that made Bella finally see the light."

"You wish," Avery sang, clicking on the keyboard.

Gabe laughed and took his normal seat next to Avery. "You were all responsible for us getting together," he said. "We couldn't have fought our own demons without your support."

Gabe had started as Avery's full-time assistant, then had moved to take on his own client list. He'd been in love with Bella since the moment he'd laid eyes on her, but it had taken three years for Bella to finally realize he was her soul mate. It had been a rocky journey, but seeing her sister and Gabe so happy and settled now made her feel even more confident about leaving in a few months. With Avery's wedding to Carter coming up in October, nothing was holding Taylor back from leaving. Both her sisters would have men who loved them to walk by their sides. She couldn't ask for anything else.

God knew, that'd never be her path. She didn't believe in marriage or declared love or any type of thing in life that imprisoned with good intentions. The idea of being tied to someone who got a say in your life filled her with distaste. She imagined her future filled with travel, adventure, art, and big experiences.

"Well, I'm just glad you did," Avery said. "Now, let's go over our schedule. July is pure insanity, and we need to make sure everyone's tasks are tight as a drum."

"Like you?" Taylor teased.

Avery surprised her with a wink. "That's what my fiancé says."

Taylor let out a hoot. She loved how Carter got Avery to relax and let go a bit. Before she'd met him, she ate, slept, and breathed Sunshine Bridal, but she'd been getting a bit obsessive. Taylor gave her thumbs-up approval while Bella and Gabe laughed.

"Where's Nora?" Taylor asked. They'd recently hired a new assistant for Avery to help with the boom of business. Everyone hoped she'd move into Taylor's position at the end of the year.

"She worked back-to-back events with me this past weekend, so I let her have the morning off. Don't want to burn her out too soon," Avery said.

"Is she working out well?" Gabe asked.

"Definitely. She's extremely organized, color-codes her files, and seems to be one hundred percent focused on work."

"In other words, she's a mini you," Taylor said with a smirk.

"Exactly! Isn't it perfect? Kind of like having a piece of Gabe back. You guys like her, right?"

Bella nodded. "She seems a bit shy, but genuine and sweet. I hope we don't scare the hell out of her. This family is a bit intense."

"Speak for yourself. I'm totally normal," Taylor said.

Avery sputtered out a laugh. "Okay, Miss Normal. Let's start with you. Give us the status on the Rodriguez–Murphy wedding."

Taylor opened up her spreadsheet, even though she'd memorized everything. "Three weeks till D-Day. I'm confirming all final appointments, but this one has been smooth."

"They booked that eighties band to play, right?" Gabe asked.

"Yep. Of course, we're also doing an eighties-themed party following the formal reception, so this will be an all-nighter."

Bella shook her head. "Plus, you're back for the Sunday brunch! You'll be exhausted. Are you sure you won't need help?"

"If one of you is on standby, I'll be fine. Every part is organized, my vendors are the best, and Pierce will be there."

"Great. Should we make sure a cake is on standby, also?" Avery asked.

Taylor jerked and shot her sister a look.

Avery burst into giggles.

"I knew I wouldn't live this one down," Taylor muttered, taking in the hidden mirth from Bella and Gabe. "Go ahead. Let's get it over with."

"I can't believe you lost the cake!" Bella finally burst out. "How bad was it?"

"Bad," she said with a sigh. "I'm talking a physical brawl right in front of me. I'll forever have dreams of watching that cake slowly topple and Pierce diving to get it. The good news? No one-star review yet. The cupcakes saved the day, and a few of the guests said it was the best time ever because they finally had something out of the ordinary to talk about."

"What an awful thing," Avery said.

"I found a cheating couple once in a closet," Gabe said. "It freaked me out because his wife was a bridesmaid."

"What did you do?" Bella asked.

He shrugged. "Told them to put their damned clothes back on and not get caught or it'd ruin the whole wedding."

Bella bit her lip. "That's so sad. Weren't you tempted to tell the bridesmaid her husband was a cheating asshole?"

"Sure, but by the end of the night, he was drunk enough to tell her himself. Accidentally, of course. I heard she ended up leaving him, but at least it was after the wedding."

"I'm starting to think I should carry divorce attorneys' business cards with me," Taylor said.

"Don't you dare!" Avery said, stabbing her finger in the air. "It's bad juju."

She threw her hands up. "I was just kidding. Kind of."

"How did you not inherit the love gene?" Bella asked. "I mean, our family has been in the wedding business for years. Don't you ever think that one day you may want to be in love and get married?"

Taylor looked around the table and saw three hopeful faces. Three faces madly in love, so it was easy to believe. Or maybe they'd found love *because* they had all believed. It was kind of the "chicken or the egg" theory, all mixed up. "Well, to be honest . . ." She trailed off and sighed like she was about to confess something epic.

Bella and Avery leaned forward.

Gabe cocked his head.

"Nope," she said with a big grin. "But I'll do my job, and I promise not to lose any more cakes."

They groaned and threw out teasing insults, then got back to work.

Chapter Three

Pierce left the photography studio and headed into his office. He dropped into the red leather chair behind his desk and looked around.

What a mess.

Usually, his inner sanctum was a place of artistic energy and harmony. The ceilings were high, with crisscrossed wooden beams, and the light spilled from endless oversize windows. He preferred a minimalist look, but the metal-and-silver chandelier gave him pleasure. It was a sculpture itself, with lanterns stacked in tiers. The stark white walls displayed some of his favorite photographs. But today, he saw only the endless piles of work he was behind on.

Papers and folders littered every surface. The message light on his phone blinked madly. A glance at the screen showed that his in-box was full. Was it time to take on a full-time assistant? A receptionist? He'd hired a college girl to work on filing and administrative tasks for the summer, but he needed to look at his business seriously and decide what changes he wanted to instill.

The real problem was, he didn't know. He liked to think of himself as a man of focus and direction, but lately, he'd been floundering.

He'd known in college that photography was his passion and would be his future occupation. It had been an easy choice to return home and put his talents to use at Sunshine Bridal. The Sunshine family was like *his* family. He'd spent just as much time at Taylor's parents' house as at his own home. He'd quickly taken on a few jobs and, before long, realized it would be smart to open up his own business. He'd found this space out in West Cape May dirt cheap—it had been a failed market-place, then a bike shop, and then it had remained sadly vacant. He'd seen the beauty of the place immediately and had friends help him renovate. Within the first year of returning, Taylor took her place as a planner with her sisters, and he'd opened up Powers Studios, quickly booking local weddings.

He never expected both of their businesses to explode. He was well known in town and the first person to be recommended for an event. Now he couldn't keep up with the assignments and could easily expand. The real question lay with his direction. Did he want to continue book-ing strictly weddings, engagements, and parties? As much as he loved immortalizing a couple's love story, lately he'd been a bit itchy for more. When he was in school, studying during an internship, he'd thought about creating more of an art form and selling his photographs rather than strictly doing work for hire. But that was a bigger risk, and when the money was steady and you didn't hate your job, was it wise to make a change?

He spun around and looked at the giant canvas on the wall behind his chair. He'd always hung one of Taylor's paintings there so it could be on full display. Carter had seen the previous one during a photo appointment and had bought it. He evidently saw the same type of raw passion and fresh perspective in Taylor's work that Pierce did.

The painting he looked at now showed a woman falling off a cliff, her nude body poised in the air, half-twisted around, so it wasn't clear if she'd fallen or dived. Her eyes were closed, but her lips curled upward in a sneer, as if she were rebelling against God himself. Beneath her, the ocean roared, and a dark shadow of a man stood hidden in the waves, barely noticeable unless you studied the painting. It was a piece of art-work that fascinated him and challenged his mind to look deeper than what was presented. He wondered many times who Taylor was thinking of when she'd painted it. When he'd asked, she'd just shrugged and said it had poured out of her, with no deep, analytical story to share.

He felt poised on the edge of that cliff. If he pulled back from weddings, where would he want to concentrate his efforts? His summer was double-booked, but he could begin turning down new clients to give himself some breathing room. He needed time to figure out what he really wanted to photograph.

He glanced at his watch and jumped up, realizing he was late for his next appointment. He hurriedly locked up and got in his truck to make the drive out toward the lighthouse. One of Sunshine Bridal's clients, Octavia, had begged him to take her baby's pictures. He found babies to be delightful but difficult to work with, but he couldn't say no to her. After he'd sat down with Octavia and her husband to go over their wedding pictures, she'd burst into tears of gratitude and made him pinkie swear that when they had their first baby, he'd be the one to do a portrait session.

Pierce never broke his promises.

He pulled into the driveway of the cheerful yellow Cape Cod, walked to the wraparound porch, and knocked.

Octavia greeted him with her daughter hitched on her hip. "Pierce, it's so good to see you again. Come in."

He stepped through the threshold, admiring the sunny, open space, the bright and beachy colors, and the comfortable furniture. A quick glance around showed no sharp edges, no breakable valuables on display, and endless baskets filled with toys, folded-up blankets, and carefully constructed play areas. "I love your place," he said with a smile. "And this must be our princess of the day. Jasmine, right?"

"That's right. Let's just say I'm surprised I booked you for baby pictures so soon. The honeymoon worked fast."

He laughed, and the baby stared at him with fascination, a bit of drool dripping from her open mouth. Wide brown eyes, a cute tuft of fine, dark baby hair, and chubby legs that pumped against her mother's ribs. She was dressed in a frilly red-and-white polka-dot dress that made her look like a sweet baby Minnie Mouse. "Twelve months, right? You look great."

Octavia snorted. "I've never been so tired in my life. Sleep is more precious than diamonds right now. Mel came home on his lunch hour yesterday just so I could nap for forty minutes."

The idea of that type of love hit him right in his solar plexus. "He's a keeper," he said. "I've heard some new dads go for a drive to get milk and come home hours later."

She grinned and walked into the kitchen. "Can I get you water? Soda?"

"No, I'm good, thank you."

"Okay, tell me what you're thinking of as a setup."

"I know we discussed a more casual than formal portrait, which I love. So right now, I'm going to bring in some of my equipment, and I just want you to relax and get her comfortable with seeing me. Do what you'd normally do right now in your routine."

"I put on Baby Einstein for half an hour while she's in her playpen, but that doesn't sound very photogenic."

"You'd be surprised. Don't worry, we'll get what we need. Trust me."

Octavia shook her head. "You don't know Jasmine."

He laughed again and began unloading his equipment, analyzing the space, and setting up some possibilities. "Do you have a beach blanket to lay outside for some shots?" he called to her.

"Sure." She handed him a worn bright-yellow comforter, and he prepped a pretty spot under a large oak tree, half in the shade, half in the sun.

He stopped at the playpen and made funny faces at Jasmine, who seemed to easily take to strangers and gave him a toothy grin. With the handheld, he got comfortable with the light angles and caught various expressions on her face as she grabbed for his equipment and determinedly tried to climb out of her netting prison. After a while, she let out a shriek of frustration.

"I'll move her to the play mat," Octavia said. "Just let me know whatever you need, Pierce."

"I will, but I don't want you to worry about posing, or if she cries. This is just a natural extension of her environment. We'll have plenty of shots to choose from."

Octavia visibly relaxed. Pierce figured her new-mother drive to get the perfect shot was stressing her out more than him.

Jasmine immediately went for her basket of toys, loudly banging and pulling them out one by one. Each had an interest span of about two minutes.

"Octavia, why don't you sit down with her and just play."

"Okay."

He got some great shots of mother and daughter, and he marveled at their strong bond. He loved watching Bella with her six-year-old daughter, Zoe. Those were the times he was reminded that one day he wanted a family and ached to experience that type of emotion. But for now, capturing the moment on film was like a superpower. His job reminded him daily that he was an important part of the most special days in a person's life. Knowing that Octavia trusted him in her home, to photograph her child, humbled him.

Pierce spent the next hour chasing Jasmine's expressions while she went about her day. Octavia changed her into different outfits, each cuter than the last. They took her outside for a few attempts at shots, and he grabbed one great candid of her staring up at the sky after hearing a bird screech. The light was good, but his skin itched with the knowledge that he hadn't gotten the money shot. Not yet.

He'd learned early on in his career that one perfect shot was more important than various average ones. He was looking to grab a piece of the person's inner being—even a tiny glimpse. That unique something inherent in everyone but hard to share, which was usually easier with a baby, who had nothing to hide.

They went back inside. "She'll need her nap soon," Octavia said. "Do you think you got enough?"

He did, but not the one he wanted. He hesitated as Jasmine gnawed on her hand. "We're good," he reassured. "Why don't you go get ready to put her down, and I'll watch her?"

"Thanks, I'll be just a minute."

She disappeared, and he turned to Jasmine, who began to whine, obviously ready for a rest. She crawled over to the empty basket and began hitting it, trying to topple it over in toddler fury, then reached for her cup of Cheerios on the coffee table. It had slid to the middle, and her chubby arms couldn't get to it, so she let out a shriek.

He laughed. "I'll get it for you; calm down. You and Taylor would get along perfectly."

He took a few steps forward, and his heel caught on the edge of a LEGO block with wheels. In seconds, he knew he was going down, so he automatically cradled his camera and hit the floor with his ass. The carpet cushioned the blow, but the surprise of it took him a moment to register the embarrassment of a fall. At least no one saw. Well, except . . .

The burst of baby giggles exploded in the room. His gaze met Jasmine's wide brown eyes, filled with glee and mischief, and he hurriedly brought up his camera and began snapping. "Thought that was funny, huh?" he asked, grinning, while her delighted expression filled his lens.

"What's going on out here?" Octavia asked, walking in and laughing. "Oh, you got a good laugh from her. What'd you do—stand on your head?"

He winked at Jasmine. "Something like that."

Octavia scooped her up and pressed kisses to her fat cheeks. "I'd better get her down."

"I'm all set here. I'll grab my stuff and let myself out. I got some great shots, so I'll call you by next week."

"Thanks, Pierce. This meant a lot to me."

"Me, too. Bye, Jasmine. Thank you for allowing me to make you laugh. I think it was the highlight of my week."

"Hey, she's here anytime you want to babysit!"

He laughed, packed up, and headed home. His head buzzed with the anticipation of developing the new shots. Hopefully, he'd gotten what he wanted, and Octavia and her husband would be happy. It would hang on their wall—a flash of memory forever frozen in time for both of them to always remember.

Yeah. His job was pretty fucking cool.

If he could just fine-tune exactly what he was missing, everything would be perfect.

Chapter Four

Taylor headed down the crowded sidewalk, weaving her way in and out like an expert. It was a beautiful summer night in high tourist season, and people flocked to dine and shop. She waved to Emily, standing outside the Fudge Kitchen and giving out samples with a fitted plastic glove. The small arcade blasted noise and flashed brightly, strollers bullied their way through long lines, and families slurped double scoops of ice cream from Uncle Charley's.

The sounds and sights of Cape May flowed over her, both bitter and sweet when she thought of how long she'd wanted to escape, only to find herself right back home. Now, with her trip looming, she gazed at the town with more forgiving eyes, and admitted that her heart still recognized the only place that contained her memories and shaped the woman she'd become.

She cut past Congress Hall and headed to the Rusty Nail. She'd almost canceled tonight to paint, but her muse was being a cranky little bitch, so she figured a cocktail, an appetizer, and a handsome face might help. Rick was hot, with giant steroid-type muscles, but a bit simpleminded. Usually, she stayed far away from the type, but he was just entertaining enough for her to spend a few hours with him. She hadn't taken him to her bed yet, but the possibility was there if things felt right.

The music lured her closer, and she nodded to the hostess while she made her way toward the tiki bar. She scored the last stool in a corner and surveyed the place. The cool Caribbean band played Bob Marley while some people danced around the firepit. A group of men played a lively game of boccie on the side lawn, and picnic tables were packed with platters of fish and fried delights, set off by island-style cocktails with more visual appeal than alcohol.

She settled in with a sigh and ordered a sauvignon blanc.

"Aren't you supposed to be painting?"

She swiveled her head around. Pierce held the neck of a beer bottle loosely by his fingertips. His grin flashed a set of perfect white teeth, courtesy of two years' worth of braces.

She shook her head. "I needed a break. Are you here with Carter and Gabe?"

"You just missed them. They cut out early, but I figured I'd stay." He motioned subtly behind him.

Her gaze focused on the woman who was glaring at her with angry dark eyes, obviously waiting for her prince to return to his chair. She wore a white designer dress with too-high sandals that must have been hell on the sand. Heavy silver jewelry cuffed her neck and wrists. "She's trying too hard. Who dresses like that for a beach bar?"

"She's used to the city, that's all."

Taylor snorted. "If she's jealous already, you got issues."

One shoulder lifted. "Not gonna marry her. She's a corporate-finance wiz. CEO of a bank. She's smart."

Taylor deliberately waved enthusiastically at his catch of the night and blew a kiss. The woman stiffened, her demeanor going ice-cold. Definitely not used to being in the passenger seat.

Pierce groaned and nudged her with his hip. "Cut it out. Thought you told me I needed to loosen up and go on a date."

"Yeah, but with someone cool."

"Are you here alone?"

She shifted in her seat. "Meeting Rick for a quick drink to clear my head."

Disapproval shot from his eyes. "He's a meathead."

She couldn't help the laugh that burst from her chest. "No, he's not. He's just a bit obsessed with lifting weights."

"You think? How can you stand the way he talks?"

"What do you mean?"

"He's got a high, shrieky voice. Sounds like Mickey Mouse."

This time, she mashed her hand against her mouth to keep from snorting. "Stop! You don't judge my date, and I won't judge yours."

"Fine. Same signal if we need to bail?" Back in college they'd created a way to ask for help from the other if a date was in a crash-and-burn situation.

Taylor gave him a look. "Don't you think that's juvenile? We're adults now."

His sea-green eyes suddenly filled with intensity. "I will always be your wingman, Taylz."

Pleasure flowed through her. "Back atcha. Fine. Let's hope we don't need to spontaneously erupt into a coughing fit and ruin our chances at a good time. Now, hit the road. Rick is here."

He drifted away and rejoined Finance Girl, who seemed thrilled to have regained his attention.

Taylor smiled as Rick greeted her with a kiss on the cheek. "Hey, pretty lady. I'm really glad you called. Was wondering when I'd see you again." He was dressed in a tight T-shirt that was lovingly molded to each impressive muscle. His arms were tree trunks, but he was on the short side, so she could pretty much stare him right in the eye. His head was smoothly shaved.

"Been busy," she said. "It's the height of wedding season."

He snapped his fingers. "That's right. How's the true-love business?"

"Same. How's the personal-training business?"

He lit up. "Got a few more clients and thinking of starting my own protein-shake company."

"Ambitious. I like it. Tell me everything."

He ordered a drink and filled her in on his plans. She listened with genuine interest, always happy when someone decided to take their business to the next level and seemed passionate about their work.

They—mostly he—talked for a while, and by the end of his beer, he'd moved close and had his arms wrapped casually around her waist. His touch felt good. She leaned into it, hopeful that she could satisfy the restless ache in her gut that seemed to be stuck there. She craved to lose herself in a man's arms and connect, at least until dawn.

The bartender asked if she wanted a refill, but before she could answer, Rick waved him away. He whispered against her ear. "Why don't we have a drink at my place?"

She knew it was more than a drink invitation. His hands were warm over her thin shirt and spanned her stomach. His dark gaze met hers, and she took a moment to probe and search, looking for a nameless thing to guide her and confirm that this was what she wanted. In his eyes, she found hot male eagerness and a flare of lust. That had never been a problem. She recognized what most men wanted when they weren't involved in a relationship, and she'd made peace with what was enough for her long ago. No, it was the lack of other emotion that made her pause. An emptiness inside that told her she was just a body to him. He'd enjoy her and what they did, but when he walked away, there'd be nothing to remember.

Slowly, she moved his arms away. "Sorry, not tonight," she said easily, softening the rejection with a smile. "I have a bitch of a day tomorrow."

"I can make it better. Come on, Taylor, don't break my heart. I want to spend more time with you."

The false words confirmed her decision. "I'm flattered, but I'm sure your heart is safe. I'll have one more drink with you here, though."

His easygoing manner frayed, and his face tightened. "You really going to play this?" he asked quietly. "I thought you were different."

She cocked her head. "Excuse me?"

His eyes turned a shade colder. "I didn't think you were a game player. This is our third date, and it's obvious what you've been putting out. I'm not stupid. You like to tease? Rev a poor guy up and leave him hanging?"

Fury shook through her, but she forced herself to pretend she was taking his feedback to heart. "Oh God, I'm sorry! You're right—you took some precious time telling me all about your business and shakes and clients and dreams. Of *course* that entitles you to sex! I'm such a bitch, Rick. I forced you on three whole dates and gave you nothing. How can you forgive me?"

Confusion skittered over his features. He took a step back and frowned. "That's messed up. I didn't mean it like that. I just thought we were connecting, and I was looking forward to spending some quiet time with you."

The fight drained out of her. She'd been silly to think she'd find what she needed in Rick's arms. She'd be better off in her workroom, throwing all her emotions onto the canvas. At this point, she only wanted to retreat. "Forget it. Let's just call it a night."

"No, come on, let's have another drink together. Talk a bit. Settle down."

Damn, he was in the fix-it mindset, actually thinking he might still have a chance. She really had no choice.

Taylor took a deep breath and began to cough.

Loudly.

She bent over, hacking away, feeling the dryness in her lungs while Rick stared at her with unease.

In seconds, Pierce was at her side. "That bad, huh?" he murmured under his breath, patting her on the back.

She didn't even bother to answer.

"You okay?" Pierce asked her, stepping in front of Rick.

She grabbed her purse and moved away so she'd have a clear escape path through the crowd. "Yep, I'm fine. Rick, this is my friend, Pierce. Sorry, but I'm not feeling too well. I'd better get out of here."

"I can walk you!" Rick started, but Pierce blocked him with his arm, allowing her to hurry through the crowd until she'd made it out the front door. She knew Pierce would delay him and give her the time to be halfway home.

Hell, she hadn't even gotten to order the crab fritters! At least she'd stuck the jerk with the bar bill.

She turned down a side street, enjoying the cover of darkness as she walked. The salty ocean air teased her nostrils. Away from the chatter and crowds, she let her mind drift, wondering why she felt unbalanced. She'd always embraced sex and the freedom to choose, refusing to get caught up in the hurtful terms that kept women from their power. She liked who she was and how she looked, and she chose men to share her body with who attracted her. But lately, she'd been looking for more.

The last few weeks, she'd turned down every invitation from men she'd normally deem worthy. Maybe they weren't, though. Maybe her instincts were kicking in at her older age, or maybe her standards were rising, because if she'd once imagined Rick as a man she'd willingly invite to her bed, she would've made a terrible mistake. The whole icky way he'd blamed her for not giving him sex was one of her hot buttons. It was a good thing she'd gotten out of there before she let her temper explode.

Suddenly, footsteps echoed behind her. She stiffened and whirled around.

"Hey. I think we should talk. I think we had a miscommunication."

She stared at Rick, a bit wary. Those huge muscles were intimidating, but he was standing a few feet away from her, his body language relaxed. She quickly took stock of her surroundings. A good scream would wake up a few houses, but he'd managed to catch her in a more deserted section by a condo parking garage. Dammit, she wasn't in the mood to deal with this.

"I don't appreciate being followed," she said coldly, going for the assertive approach. He'd never acted aggressively, but she didn't know him very well. "If you want to talk, you can call me, but I really need you to back off now."

He lifted his hands in the air in a surrendering gesture. "Crap, I'm not going to hurt you! I'm just frustrated that we had something good going on, then I said a stupid thing and you ran away. I didn't imagine our night ending that way."

She raised a brow. "Oh, I know how you imagined it ending, and that's not going to happen. Look, Rick, I'm tired and I want to go home."

He moved in a few steps, his hands still lifted as if he were approaching a cop. "Can't we just talk? I'm really sorry I said shit like that. I didn't mean it."

"Apology accepted." She slipped her phone out of her pocket and flashed him the keypad screen. "Now, please stop and don't come any closer, or I'm calling 911."

"Why are you acting like I'm a violent criminal?" he practically whined, taking another step closer. "I want to get back to the way it was." He had a pleading look on his face, caught in this weird urgency to be near her, and that freaked her out.

"It's too late, Rick. Please stay there, or I'll have to do something."

Frustration shimmered from his aura. "Taylor, come on." He took another step and would have loomed over her if he'd been a little taller.

She didn't wait for his next move. Cursing her choice of footwear—she wished she'd worn her favorite combat boots and not sandals—she lowered her knees to gather power, then exploded into a jump, aiming her heel right at his crotch.

She hit her target.

Rick screamed and grabbed his privates, curses blistering from his lips. He staggered, giving her enough time to move around him and run toward the safety of the well-lit sidewalk, where the chatter of people rose. More pissed than scared, she muttered a litany of expletives that was more original than Rick's had been and then rammed straight into Pierce.

"Taylor? Are you okay? Oh hell, did he hurt you?" His hands were gentle, as if checking her for broken bones, his gaze a bit frantic.

"Yeah, I'm okay. Gym Rat got a bit too close for comfort. I got nervous, so I hit him in the groin."

Rick was just beginning to recover, stumbling a bit toward them. "Why did you have to do that?" he cried out, his eyes full of agonized pain. "I told you I wasn't going to hurt you!"

"Well, excuse me for not trusting a muscled, sexually stimulated half stranger who stalked me on a deserted road! Are you serious? I mean, I can't believe—Pierce? No, don't. He didn't do—ah, crap."

Sinking down to primate status, Pierce jumped toward Rick and then socked him in the jaw.

Taylor shook her head. "Really? I don't need a knight. I already slayed the dragon myself."

"You ever touch her again, I'll find you, and I'll make you pay," Pierce growled, shaking his fist in the air.

She raised a brow. "Impressive. Can we go home now?"

"Want me to call the cops?"

Rick was groaning, now cradling his injured jaw and his privates. She figured he looked the part of brute but didn't get into many fights, since he'd dropped pretty fast.

"No. He got the point. Let's go," she said.

They had just stepped onto Beach Avenue, where people were scattered, talking in groups and enjoying the summer night, when Pierce was suddenly whirled around.

It happened too fast to do anything.

41

Rick punched him in the face.

Pierce stumbled back, his hands cupping his injured eye.

An animal shout exploded out of Rick's mouth as he shook his finger at them with fury. "I wasn't going to do anything!" he yelled. "I wanted to talk, but this isn't worth it. Shit, no woman is worth this type of trouble. Go ahead and keep her, but stay the hell away from me!" He took off at a half run until he'd disappeared around a corner.

Taylor spun around. "Are you okay?"

Pierce groaned. "I can't believe he surprised me like that."

"Here, let me see." She carefully removed his hand and studied his swollen eye. Oh yeah, this was gonna be a bad one. "Do I look blurry to you?"

"No, but I have a feeling I'm not going to win the Beach Bachelor contest, like Gabe did."

She laughed, smoothing his hair back from his cheek. "Let's go put some ice on it to get the swelling down. Do you want me to call the cops and report him? Ron could be here right away."

He shook his head. "Only if you think the asshole will bother you again."

"I doubt it. He'll know we're all watching him, and I have a sense he really was harmless. Just stupid."

"Then let's get out of here so I can nurse my wounded pride in peace."

She linked her arm with his. "I think it was sweet that you tried to defend my honor."

He shot her a glare. "We're not going to tell anyone about this. Right?"

"Right. Do you have frozen peas at home?"

"Will corn do?"

She laughed. "Yes. Hey, I thought you were hooking up with Finance Girl."

"I watched him leave and had a bad feeling. Decided to follow for a while and make sure he was going home. Had to dump Finance Girl."

"I'm sorry, Pierce. I appreciate it, though. Thank you."

He ruffled her hair and slung his arm around her. His familiar scent enveloped her—a mix of clove from his cologne and freshly washed cotton from his T-shirt. For a few moments, the disaster of the evening faded, and she treasured a simple walk with her best friend, the man who'd followed her to make sure she was safe. The man who'd punched a guy who could have hurt her.

Maybe she was becoming so picky with men lately because no one would ever live up to Pierce.

The thought teased her mind before she firmly pushed it away. Pierce was like a brother. He was better than a lover because he'd be hers forever, instead of someone with a time stamp, waiting to end in disaster. Sex changed everything. That was the main reason they'd agreed to never, ever get tangled up in that mess and ruin an ideal relationship.

Thank God they were better than that.

Chapter Five

Taylor tried to be cool as her future brother-in-law studied the five paintings hanging up in her workroom. She'd sworn she'd take the criticism like a professional and not get depressed. After all, she wasn't classically trained, and this was her first attempt at putting a body of work together.

Thanks to Carter's contacts with many international bigwigs from his hacking career in Washington, DC, she was set to show her work in a Parisian gallery, along with two other brand-new artists. It was an introductory show that would give her exposure to the international art scene and potentially provide financial backing to help her build her new career. Taylor had to keep reminding herself that even with a personal contact, if her art sucked, Luis would have politely sent her away when she'd shown him her samples. He owned popular galleries in Paris, Milan, and Switzerland and had a talent for discovering and launching the careers of new artists. Luis would have never taken her on if he hadn't thought he could sell her work. She had no time for impostor syndrome or doubting herself. If she did, she'd lose her golden opportunity.

She refused to let that happen.

"Well?" she finally said, picking at her thumbnail. "Just be honest. Give it to me straight."

Carter turned toward her. His dark hair was neatly brushed, and his blue-gray eyes were serious. He wore cream shorts, a short-sleeve linen shirt, and canvas shoes. His wardrobe was conservative, practical, and subtle, just like his personality. He held a tiny Yorkshire terrier named Lucy in the crook of his arm. Lucy regarded Taylor with solemn judgment. The dog's pink, glittery collar and matching bow were a testament to how much Carter adored her. It had taken Lucy a while to warm up to Avery, but now the two of them were tight.

Taylor? Not so much.

She motioned toward Lucy. "Um, should she be in my workroom? What if she pees?"

A deep frown crossed Carter's brow. "Lucy would never urinate where it wasn't proper," he said with a touch of irritation.

She pressed her lips together. "Sorry. Go ahead, tell me what you think."

He refocused and spoke in a slow, thoughtful tone. "This first set is exquisite. I love the way you've shown this woman's development over the series, giving us a bit of intrigue and investment. It makes me want to see her progression. The angles are sharp, and you've used color in a way I haven't really seen before. The blues and greens are so vivid, it almost jars the viewer when you pair it with the muted shades of the woman."

She nodded, glad he recognized her technique. "Do you remember the movie *Schindler's List*?"

"Of course, it's a classic."

"I loved how Spielberg used the little girl dressed in red throughout the movie. Everything was black and white but her—she was the only spot of color. I tried to incorporate the same type of technique with this canvas. I wanted to play with making the character fall into nothingness while her environment takes over." She gave a self-conscious laugh. "At least, that was my intention. I know art can't have a narrator ready to explain, so I don't know if it's good or bad."

"It's good, Taylor, very good. You have a way of making me care about this woman. It's like she's embroiled in a series of heartbreaks and pain that's going toward . . ." He paused, tapping his finger against his chin as he studied the paintings again. "Not happiness. I wonder if she can get there. Maybe self-peace?"

Relief flooded through her. Oh God, he understood! Her subconscious had been obsessed with a woman who haunted her dreams. She saw her everywhere—on the cliffs, on the beach, on the road, in the kitchen. But there was pain and brokenness and a restlessness that made Taylor wonder if she could ever find peace. She hoped the last paintings would reveal some type of closure to the woman's journey, but Taylor had no idea how they would turn out. She never knew until she began painting.

Pierce had spent the entire time in the background, quietly reflective. She waited for him to speak, but he just kept gazing at her work, his expression hard to read. He owned one painting from the series that she'd painted a while ago and then had given to him for his office. Unease trickled. Did he not like them? She figured he'd be the most vocal, since he was usually so supportive.

She refused to prod, turning her attention back to Carter. "What about the other two?"

"Something's missing."

Taylor stiffened. Her gaze swept over the last ones she'd been working on. Dammit, she'd sensed something was off, and now Carter had confirmed it. "Yeah, that's why I wanted you to look at them before I moved on. Do you know what it is?"

"Emotion," Pierce said suddenly.

She tilted her head and stared in surprise. "Really? These two were focusing on heartbreak. I figured I'd nailed that part."

The paintings were a dual set in black and white. In the first canvas, the woman was dressed in an evening gown, her silhouette in the doorway while she watched from across the room as a man and woman danced. The inside of the ballroom was in color, and the background faded to shadow. In the second, she was framed in the bedroom watching the couple make love. A silent, pained voyeur, frozen in time.

Carter made a noise in the back of his throat. "Interesting assessment. Technically, it's a visual feast. But there's something on her face that doesn't resonate with the rest. Her expression is . . . lacking."

She squinted and analyzed each feature of the woman's face. Taylor had tried to evoke the agony of losing the one you loved, but apparently it hadn't hit. Was she missing something basic? Was it a technical issue or something deeper? She'd been blocked for a while and hoped she'd pushed through, but obviously she'd failed.

"It looks forced," Pierce said. Regret flickered in his eyes. "Not as true as the others."

"No matter," Carter said, swiping his hands together. "You're right on track. Play a bit with these two and see if you can tweak them. You should have no trouble getting the others done in time—remember, I need them shipped by the end of next month. You're taking the one from Pierce's office, right?"

Pierce laughed. "She can borrow it for the big art show, but I hope it doesn't sell. I've gotten attached."

"Hmm, you'll need to pay her a hell of a lot more, then."

"It was a gift!"

Carter threw up his hands. "I'm not her manager, but Luis may insist she sell it with the set and paint you a new one."

Taylor pushed her disappointment away and reminded herself she still had a solid foundation. She needed to paint two more pieces to finish the Woman and the Cliff series. Then she'd go back to these and see if she could figure out what had gone wrong. She wouldn't rest until she knew they were perfect. "Don't worry, I'll paint you another naked woman as a replacement."

Pierce gave a snort.

"What happened to your eye, man?" Carter asked. "Looks wicked."

"I walked into a door."

Carter turned to her with a questioning look, clearly not buying it.

"Pierce was defending my honor from an overeager admirer. He got caught in a surprise attack."

Pierce glared at her. "I thought we were keeping that to ourselves."

"Carter's family. He doesn't care."

"No shit?" Carter asked. "I haven't gotten into a fight in a long time. Who won?"

"Pierce did," Taylor said.

"Actually, Taylor did," Pierce muttered. "Kicked him in the balls and took him out. I punched him for good measure, but the asshole jumped me."

Carter looked at her with pride. "Nice work. The Sunshine sisters know how to take care of business. Did you tell them about your encounter?"

"No."

He shook his head. "They're gonna want details. I have to tell Avery I saw the shiner, so just prepare yourself."

She groaned. "Great. I'll get another lecture about safety. They're worse than Mom."

"No, they're not," Pierce said. "Your mother is plain scary. Remember when she canceled your phone account because she caught you sneaking out at night? You didn't have any way to text, check Facebook, or watch YouTube for a week. She doesn't yell. She just gets even."

Taylor shuddered. "Yeah, she does have those cruel tendencies. Remember when she caught you smoking?"

"Hell yes. She told my mother and suggested if I was old enough to smoke, I was old enough to do all the chores in the house. They worked me from six a.m. to late at night. I was falling asleep in school."

She laughed. "I remember. My mom was always advising your mom about the worst ways to punish you. It's kind of nice they're both in Florida together."

Carter grinned. "I love hearing stories about you guys growing up. Not all of us were lucky to have childhood friends who are like family." He hitched Lucy up higher in his arms. "I'd better get back to work—I'm on break. You're doing great, Taylor. Call me if you have any further questions, but I think you're on the perfect path. You'll rock Paris."

Her heart softened. "Thanks, Carter." They said goodbye and watched him walk out. Then she let out a groan. "They're lacking emotion, huh?"

Pierce came up beside her and stood close. Their shoulders touched, and they spent a few minutes studying the series of paintings in silence. "With all of your other work, my gut gets twisted up. My senses are engaged. It's a total package that reminds me how much raw talent you had even when you were sketching out those awful graphic novels sophomore year."

"They were good. Better than some of the stuff you read at the time."

"A quartet of superhero witches has some merit, but they were always beating up men."

She blew out an annoyed breath. "Because the men were all bad."

"All of them? I don't know, I got depressed. I needed to believe in a good guy."

"Now you know how women have felt for centuries reading about men all the time."

He winced. "Yeah, you're right. Sorry."

"It's okay. I'll just have to find a way to fix it."

Those heavy brows drew down into a fierce frown, and his lips pursed. It was his thinking face. She used to tell him it made him look like he was sucking on a lemon, but then he'd gotten pissed, and she hadn't mentioned it again. "Maybe it's because you don't know what that type of heartbreak feels like," he said.

She jerked back. "I know what heartbreak is," she said hotly. "I've had my heart broken before!"

"Not like that. Not like your entire soul is being ripped out of your body. Not the way you want to express how that woman feels, because she realizes the only man she ever loved will never be hers."

Shock barreled through her. Her gaze narrowed. "I've never thrown myself off a cliff, either, and I painted about that," she said, a bit annoyed. "You don't have to experience everything you illustrate."

"You're right. But I think you've gotten in touch with other emotions in that series. Wanting freedom. Confusion about the future. Sifting through your innermost thoughts to find who you really are. But love? You always said you don't believe in it—not the 'happily ever after, get married' kind. Maybe you need to look there first if you want to tweak."

The depth of his answer threw her off. Suddenly, she felt vulnerable, as if he were seeing her naked and making a judgment. It was odd, because Pierce had always been her safest ally. She decided to deal with his comments later. "I'll think about it."

He shrugged. "Or don't. I told you, Taylz, I know nothing about art. I'm just slinging around some high-concept theories I read on the internet."

She relaxed back into easy camaraderie. "At least you don't have an online photography degree."

"Not a bad idea. I could offer classes and make some big money."

"Speaking of work, you're with me Friday night for the big bachelorette party, right?"

His face told her he was not enthusiastic. "Yeah. I'm rarely asked to capture someone's last shot at freedom, but these girls are photo crazy and don't want to be tied to their phones all night. They want the whole thing documented—even the strippers. It's going to be painful."

"Hmm, tipsy, attractive women dressed in skimpy clubwear all riled up? Yeah, sounds like a real drag."

He glared. "It is. It's not like I'm going to find a quality woman to date there. Cassie is only twenty-two, and so are most of her friends. That's practically jailbait for me."

She sighed. "You are so set in your ways. Don't worry, I'll cover for you. I have a long list of itinerary items to keep them occupied and make your job easier."

"Good. I'd better head out, too. Catch you later."

After he left, Taylor wandered around her workroom, trying to psych herself up to attack a new canvas, her mind already clicking madly through a range of images that had been haunting her. But Pierce's words resonated with a warning she wished she could ignore.

Was her work lacking because she wasn't allowing herself to open up?

She bit at her thumbnail. Emotion had always been difficult for her. She was different from Avery and Bella. For a while, she'd wondered if something was wrong with her whenever she watched her sisters scream happily on Christmas morning or sob over breaking up with a boy. Even her mother had consistently lectured her on opening up more, as if she was afraid that Taylor would never experience joy.

But she did. Quietly. Inside.

She hated saying mushy things or feeling vulnerable. She liked a certain amount of control where she felt safe. Humor and sarcasm were her favorite tools. She made witty jokes and mocked open affection to hide the fact that she was different. Ever since she was young, she'd looked upon the world through a strange filter—a glass wall that kept her separate from the ups and downs of people flinging themselves into intense relationships in the quest for love. But she'd never ached with that type of need to connect.

Why was it so difficult for her to be vulnerable? To be as connected with the world as her sisters were? To crave a lasting love and children and a stable home? Why did she have to be so different?

The questions consistently puzzled her, especially when her emotions were easier to get in touch with when she was dialed into her muse and working on her art. Allowing her fingers to guide a brush opened up the vault of innermost fears, dreams, passions, and heartbreak she spent her waking hours trying to wrestle. It was the way she made sense of things.

Connecting with her creativity allowed all her barriers to crash down.

She just couldn't do it with another person.

She blew out a breath and frowned at the blank canvas, her thoughts still skittering like a kitten chasing a ball of yarn.

Her sisters and parents had often claimed surprise at Taylor's ability to sketch something that made them feel a certain way, and they always encouraged the pursuit. But when she went to college, she'd still looked at art as a beloved hobby, not a career. She'd never thought she could make a living of it, so she'd taken some classes and studied technique mostly from books and YouTube, keeping her formal studies to more practical pursuits.

Now, after spending years at Sunshine Bridal, she understood that she had a special opportunity with this art show. Yes, Carter had used his contacts to help her get her foot in the door. But what she did with that opportunity was the crux of what mattered. Carter could only get her so far.

She needed to do the rest.

Frustration nipped at her nerves. Ah, hell. She was done analyzing. She needed to do one thing now.

Get shit done.

Taylor got to work.

Chapter Six

Pierce watched the sexy blonde raise her beer bottle in the air and gyrate on top of the bar. The bartender, Mike, shot him a pleading look, but Pierce just shrugged and lifted his camera to capture the shot. Dancing girls were not allowed on the bar, but this group seemed to have taken over by sheer enthusiasm and dedication to the art of partying.

God, he was getting too old for this.

Harry's was their second stop of the night. At least the evening wasn't too muggy, and they could enjoy the outside bar, which over-looked the beach. He watched Taylor work the room, making sure all the girls were accounted for and having fun. They'd started with sig-nature martinis concocted specifically for the bride at Iron Pier, then made the walk to Harry's. The band was a mingle of rock and pop, the perfect accompaniment for a casual Friday night.

The bride, Cassie, wore a veil and a cropped wedding dress. The bridesmaids wore tacky rainbow dresses. Taylor had spearheaded a "worst dressed" contest and had them all parade in front of the crowd in a mockery of a wet T-shirt contest. Everyone seemed to love it.

With her pink hair, slim black pants, sequined tank top that declared "Den Mother for Drunken Bridesmaids," and her favorite combat boots, Taylor looked young enough to be one of them. Of course, she'd rather die than put a ring on before thirty. Or even forty.

Pierce doubted she'd ever get married, with all her big plans and goals, unless she really fell in love.

The idea made his nerves tighten and his skin itch. He couldn't imagine another man in her life. She'd always belonged to him.

He took a few pictures of the group doing shots and hugging each other, their emotions close to the surface from both the event and the alcohol. As the band began to play slower songs, he sensed the mood changing, and on cue, Taylor jumped in.

"It's time to go to Carney's!" Taylor shouted, holding up her shot glass, which he knew contained only water. "Are you ready for the scavenger hunt of the century?"

The girls whooped, jumped, and followed her like baby chicks who were a bit wobbly. They attracted a crowd as they walked down the busy, crooked sidewalks. People pointed and laughed at the dresses and the revelry vibe. By the time they'd reached the bar, they'd picked up a small group of partyers who wanted to join them.

There was no one else more capable than Taylor with a boisterous, impulsive crowd, but Pierce kept his gaze sharp at all times as he worked. He always felt Cape May was a relaxed, less douchey setting than some of the other places that encouraged major hooking up and getting falling-down drunk. Cape May was mostly known as a family beach town, and just about everyone knew to keep the party fun but relatively clean.

Until they went back to the booked hotel room to see the strippers.

He shuddered at the thought.

Taylor took over from the DJ and made her announcement to the bar. "Listen up! We have a bachelorette party in town, and we want to give them a warm Cape May welcome!"

Everyone roared in approval. Pierce laughed, enjoying Taylor in her element. She liked her events action oriented and took a strong lead. She was also great at improvising and had proven it at many disastrous weddings. Hopefully, they wouldn't have another one like the cake debacle for a long time.

"In order to get to know everyone a bit better, I decided to send our bride and her crew on a little scavenger hunt. All items will be returned to you at the end. The winner will be declared the Cape May Queen and get a free shot of her choice. Are we ready to play?"

A cheer rose. Cassie jumped up and down with excitement. Taylor passed out the list to her group and gave them a few minutes to go over the items. Gasps and giggles hinted at some of the naughty activities he bet were on there.

Lord, help him. He couldn't believe he was almost thirty and still doing this. Sure, it was fun to let loose, but he'd outgrown recording these kinds of parties. He craved more serious work, and this was just another sign confirming that his instincts were right. He needed to find another niche.

"Go!" Taylor commanded into the microphone. "The first item is a man's sock."

The women scurried, looking for males without sandals and eventually stumbling to the stage in hysterics while the patrons cheered them on. Taylor kept careful score, encouraging the bridesmaids who fell behind, and the DJ put on Beyoncé's "Single Ladies" to get them motivated.

Pierce snapped pictures at random. They ticked off a lady's ring, a pic of a guy's tattoo, a signed bar napkin, any item that was blue, and a bra. By the time Taylor had come to the last item, the entire bar was involved in the game, picking their favorites to win.

"We are on the last item, which gets double points, so this could be a game changer," she purred into the microphone. "But this item is a little naughty. We don't have any children here tonight, do we? Or objections?"

It was already midnight, so Pierce doubted there were youngsters here. The enthusiastic response from the bar confirmed they were safe.

She paused, drawing out the tension. "The last item is a pair of men's underwear. Go!"

He grinned, watching in amusement as the girls raced around and scurried past random men, pleading their case. And then he was staring straight into the bride's frantic hazel eyes.

"Pierce, I need your underwear!"

His jaw dropped. "I can't, Cassie! I'm the photographer."

She jumped up and down in her wedding dress and began begging at the top of her lungs. "Please, Pierce, I want to win this so bad. I won't look!"

Multiple gazes pinned him in place. A fine sheen of sweat beaded his brow. "It's not professional," he said in a low tone. "Here, I'll help you find someone else." He motioned to the packed table near him, which held a quartet of dudes. "Guys, help my bride out, please. She needs underwear."

The guys hooted. "Sorry, man, I'm just here to watch. But if you're her photographer, you should be helping your bride out."

"Oh, please, Pierce! Look, we'll cover you," she cried out. "Who has a jacket or blanket?"

One of the dudes tossed her a giant hoodie.

"Thank you!" She shook out the hoodie and then held it up in front of him for blockage. He suddenly felt like he was a toddler at the beach while his mother shushed him and told him to change behind a towel. "Get against this wall. Hurry, please!"

Shock froze him in place for a few seconds, but then the chant began. "Take it off! Take it off! Take it off!"

He didn't move, and Cassie's lower lip began to tremble. "I can't lose at my own bachelorette party," she whimpered.

Fuck.

He placed his camera down beside him and toed off his shoes. With quick, jerky motions, he tore at his jeans and began to strip. "Do *not* let that slip until I get my pants back on," he warned Cassie.

"I won't, I promise! Thank you, Pierce. I'm not looking!" She closed her eyes halfway.

Yeah, she was totally lying. She was looking.

Gritting his teeth, he stepped out of his boxers, turned around, and hunched over to hide as much as possible. Then he shoved the underwear into her open hand. "Here. Give me one more second." He began to get his jeans back on, hopping a bit on one foot, and almost stumbled. Cursing, he gripped the wall for balance, and that's when it happened.

The hoodie dropped.

A cold breeze touched his flesh.

"I got it!" Cassie screamed at the top of her lungs, shaking his boxers madly in her fist. "I have the underwear."

In slow motion, he realized with unfolding horror that the entire bar was staring at his naked ass.

Taylor's voice boomed over the microphone. "Our bride, Cassie, is the winner!"

Hoots and shouts drummed in his ears, and he hurriedly yanked his jeans up, zipped his fly, and faced the music.

The guys at the table were cracking up. "Dude, that was epic!" the guy with the hoodie gasped. "My girlfriend got it on Instagram!"

He swore he wouldn't blush. He was too much of a man for that, and proud of his ass. But damned if his cheeks didn't heat up as he took in the approving, appraising looks of the bridal party.

"And now, folks, a round of applause for the hottest rear in Cape May. Pierce Powers—take a bow!"

He glared at Taylor, but she just blew him kisses, humor dancing in her golden-brown eyes. As the applause rose to a crescendo, he shook his head, realizing that by making it a joke the entire crowd had been involved in, she'd taken the real heat away. Once again, she'd known instinctively how to do the right thing in a crisis.

Especially with him.

He took his bow and mouthed the words to her across the bar: *You are so gonna pay.*

♥ ♥ ♥

"I'm not tired," Taylor declared.

They stood in the hotel parking lot after they'd dropped the bridal party off at their suite. The stripper had done his thing, and Taylor had walked him out, officially done with the evening. She'd chatted with the young man, who was putting himself through college by dancing for women, and she'd tipped him extra while Pierce rolled his eyes. Bella was known to own the mushiest heart of the group, but Taylor had a soft spot for people sacrificing to follow their dreams.

Plus, he'd done an excellent job.

"Me, either," Pierce said. "Do you have a wedding tomorrow?"

"Nope."

"Neither do I. Let's go to karaoke for a few drinks. I need to bleach out certain parts of the evening."

She patted his very fine ass. "I think most of the women in the bar don't want to forget."

"Real funny. Did you tell Cassie to come over to me?"

She gasped. "Of course not!"

He stared into her eyes and cursed. "Hell, you did! That's low. You're buying the drinks."

"Fine."

He locked his equipment in his car, and they headed to the Boiler Room. The dimly lit tavern was in Congress Hall and housed in a cellar. The combination of rich wood, concrete floors, and casual vibe was perfect for hanging out and kicking back. Neon signs blinked **BAR** and **LOUNGE**, and they were able to grab two seats right at the bar. The band had retired after their set, and karaoke was now in full session.

They ordered two beers, but the munchies had set in hard, and Taylor craved something with cheese badly. She directed her question to Winona, the bartender. "Any way to get a pizza?"

Winona shook her head. "Sorry, kitchen's closed, hon."

Pierce leaned over the bar. "I know we're being pains in the ass, but I've just finished the bachelorette party from hell. Can you beg Ed to do me a solid?"

Taylor watched as the woman practically melted. "Aww, those type of nights suck, don't they? Hell, I got you covered. Ed owes me one. Want anything else?"

"Just the pizza will do. You're the best, Win."

The bartender's smile showed her clear devotion, and she left her spot to go back in the kitchen.

Taylor shook her head.

"What?" Pierce asked.

"You are something else, dude. I swear, I don't know how Gabe keeps getting picked for Beach Bachelor. There's no one in this town who wouldn't do anything you asked."

He shrugged and took a sip of beer. "Been here my whole life, just like you. Part of the perks."

She studied his profile in the dim light. "Yeah, but it's more than that. No matter where you go, you fit in."

His gaze narrowed, suddenly intense. "So do you."

She opened her mouth to protest, then shut it. It was too deep to get into at this hour, especially while listening to karaoke. So she nodded in agreement and turned toward the makeshift stage.

They listened to bad renditions of popular songs and drank their beer. The spike of adrenaline eased, and she slowly began to relax. Winona came back with a pizza to share, and they hungrily feasted until it was gone except for the remnants of crust Taylor always left behind.

He shook his head and ate her leftovers. "Why do you leave the crust? It's the best part. I know you're not afraid of carbs."

"I don't like it. And you're wrong: the cheese is the best part. Why do you like brussels sprouts?" She made a gagging noise.

"If you roast them with olive oil and seasonings till they're almost burnt, they're delicious."

Her brow shot up. "Dude, you've made them in your kitchen?"

He concentrated on his crust. "No, I had them at Iron Pier, but if I wanted to cook them, I could."

She laughed. "You always rag on me for not knowing how to cook, but you're just as bad. You'd die without Uber Eats."

"Good thing we'll never get married. We'd either starve or go broke."

She knew his response was meant to be a jab, but her brain caught on the word *married* and gnawed on it. "You want to get married?" she asked, suddenly curious.

"Of course." He pushed his empty plate toward Winona and nodded in thanks.

She knew that. He'd always been as vocal about settling down with a bunch of kids as she'd been about running in the opposite direction. Hell, even now, Winona was staring at him with flirty eyes, just waiting to pounce on a date invite. "I guess I'm surprised you haven't met anyone yet."

He gave her a look. "Taylz, I'm not even thirty. I've got time. It's women who begin to panic."

"You never really told me what happened with Jill," she said. "After you broke up, you were pretty closemouthed about the whole thing, and then Jill started avoiding me like I had cooties."

"She was jealous of you. It was becoming problematic."

Her jaw dropped. "Are you kidding? Why didn't you ever tell me?"

Pierce shrugged as he lifted his hand and got them another round. "It didn't matter. Why upset you? She was too jealous for me. I want someone who knows me. A woman not afraid to give me her full trust."

A strange satisfaction settled over her, followed by a sting of guilt. She felt terrible she'd messed up a prospective relationship for Pierce, didn't she? Then again, if Jill wasn't the right woman, then things had worked out for the best. It would kill her to watch him settle down with a woman who couldn't appreciate him. "Well, I agree, you deserve that. Can you imagine the dirt I can give to your future wife?"

He snorted. "I can do worse. I know you a hell of a lot better than you know me."

"Excuse me? Not even close. Try again."

He tilted his head. "Yeah? Wanna bet?"

Temper stirred at his cockiness. "Hell yes."

A strange look of satisfaction flickered over his face. She refused to think of it as a warning, positive she'd show him up in no time.

Pierce slowly smiled. "Good. Let's play."

Chapter Seven

Pierce called Winona over. "Can you line up some shots of tequila for us, please?"

Taylor shuddered. She and tequila didn't mix so well, and he knew it. "What are you doing?"

He pushed over the wedges of lime and the saltshaker. "Proving I'm right. We each ask the other a question. If you get it wrong, you take a shot. Last one standing wins."

The challenge stirred her blood. God, she hated to lose. She'd always been a competitive cutthroat. Once, she lost a Monopoly game to Avery and threw the board across the room, calling her a cheat. She'd been locked in her room for the rest of the weekend in punishment. "Fine. I go first."

He waved a hand in the air. "Go ahead."

Oh, this was going to be fun. "What's the name of the guy I lost my virginity to?"

He rolled his eyes. "Like I'd ever forget bumbling Bill Hayderson."

She tried to hide her surprise with a breezy tone. Remembering names was not one of Pierce's best skills. "Very good. That was just a warm-up. Go."

"What was the word I missed in the state spelling bee competition?"

She tried not to smile smugly. "Piquant. You spelled it with a *kw* because you never even studied the list they gave out for practice."

Annoyance skittered over his face. "No need to expound on the answers. Your turn."

"Whose invitation did I turn down for prom?"

"Riley Vanwigner. Are you really going to keep asking me name questions, or will this get more interesting?"

"As you've mentioned, no need to expound on answers. Just go," she shot back.

"Fine. Why did I get punished and forced to miss the Foo Fighters concert?"

"Easy. You skipped first period to go to McDonald's for breakfast, and your mom found out."

He smiled slowly. Then pushed the shot in front of her. "Drink."

She blinked. "What do you mean? That's what you told me!"

"It's because she was cleaning my room and found my stash of weed and nonfeminist magazines."

Taylor gasped. "That's not fair! You lied to me, so I didn't know the real truth!"

"If you didn't know I'd lied, you don't know me well enough. Drink."

Irritation nipped at her nerves. He wanted to bend the rules? Fine. She could play dirty. Taylor snapped back the shot, licked her salt-laden hand, and sucked on the lime. Hard.

Ugh. Tequila was evil. It was time for revenge.

"Why did I have to ditch you at the beach party on Memorial Day weekend senior year?"

His smug look made her want to scream. "You got your period."

She pointed to the shot glass. "Drink."

"What? Why would you lie about your period?"

"Because I wanted to hook up with your friend Nate, and I knew you'd be pissed if you found out."

His jaw dropped. "Are you kidding me? You both lied to me? That's messed up."

"Ask if I care. Drink."

He glowered and took the shot. A sizzle of energy hummed between them. They leaned toward each other, challenge sparking the air. "Nice to finally learn the truth. Who knows what else I'll discover tonight?" he drawled, gaze narrowing on her face.

She gave him her famous shark smile that usually scared the hell out of everyone, including her sisters. "Bring it," she said softly.

"I will."

The questions fired rapidly between them. The stakes rose as they began to dredge up ridiculous details and various occasions on which they'd lied to each other. Nothing mattered except beating the other.

Another round of shots disappeared, but Taylor refused to admit she was past tipsy and now tried desperately to focus. "Let's switch it up. I'll say a statement I believe is true. If it is, you drink. If it's not, I drink."

He signaled for more tequila. "This is the final knockout round. Winner takes all."

It was her turn. She tried to think of the worst thing her best friend would want to hide. "You weren't able to give Penny Rickerson an orgasm the first time you had sex."

She sensed victory when his skin paled. He muttered a curse, glared, and took a drink. Taylor tried not to scream with glee. Three left.

"When you came in second place for the division championship in girls' track, you locked yourself in the bathroom and cried, even though you denied it multiple times."

The frustration at losing by a second to the bratty Brianna, prom queen who was voted "most likely to succeed," still poked raw. She'd sworn on a thousand Bibles that she didn't care. Damn, she should've known he'd suspected she'd sobbed in a women's stall for a solid fifteen minutes.

Taylor refused to say anything. She just took the shot.

It was time to go all in. Blinking rapidly at his fuzzy image, she licked her lips and took the risk. "You've had a dirty sex dream about me."

His quickly indrawn breath gave her a savage sense of satisfaction. She'd always wondered, but now the truth lay out there, naked and raw for all to see. Taylor wondered if she'd regret asking the question, then quickly dismissed the worry. What could possibly happen between them? They were rock solid, even with this competition.

For a few moments, Pierce did nothing. Just sat on his stool, staring at her with an odd expression, but it was probably the tequila messing with her vision.

He took the third shot.

Anticipation tangled inside as she waited for the final takedown. Nerves exploded in her belly. She needed to win this. Being able to gleefully claim victory in the "who knows the other one better" game would be a trophy for a lifetime.

"You worry you'll never be able to love a man the way your sisters do. All in. Heart and soul." He hesitated, as if he was almost fearful of pushing it too far, but the alcohol and the bar and the shadows didn't allow it. "You're afraid something's wrong with you."

She jerked back. Her hand knocked the last shot glass over, and she watched as the tequila slowly spread across the bar. Their gazes met and locked.

Some woman was singing Adele's "Hello" and trying to belt out the high note, but it sounded like a sick animal dying in the woods. The lights flashed, and Winona made the announcement of last call. Someone was vaping—illegally—and the sweet smoke drifted in the air, turning Taylor's stomach.

Her thoughts flickered in random, crazy patterns as she tried to process the truth of Pierce's statement. Somehow, he knew. Knew about the dark, awful secret she kept locked deep inside and swore to never share with anyone.

Not even him.

With a trembling hand, she righted the glass and opened her mouth to ask Winona to refill the last shot because he'd won fair and square.

Pierce's hand shot out and grabbed her wrist. His thumb pressed at the base of her palm, and her pulse rocketed under his touch, the familiar feel of his warm, rough skin settling all her jagged edges.

"I withdraw my statement. You win." Regret glimmered in his sea-green eyes. He was giving her the out.

She shook her head hard. "No. You're right. I need to drink."

He motioned to Winona for the bill. "I don't know what I'm saying, Taylz. The tequila is kicking my ass, so let's call it a draw. Okay?"

She wanted to protest, but her tongue couldn't seem to form the words. "'Kay. A tie, then. Need water."

Winona slid over the bill along with two giant glasses of water with ice. They gulped both down greedily. When Taylor eased off the stool, the world tilted a bit.

"Wow. Tequila costs a lot of money," Pierce said with a slight slur.

"We had lots."

"Glad you're footing the bill for this one. You agreed to buy the drinks, remember?"

"Bastard." She glared. "You tricked me."

"Just pay. And leave her a good tip."

It took her a while to get out her credit card, sign her name, and get it back in her purse. Funny, everything was in a beautiful hue of soft colors and light. When was the last time she'd gotten this tipsy? Not in a long time.

Stupid tequila.

"Come on," Pierce said, grabbing her hand. "My place is closer. Let's crash there."

"You guys okay to get home?" Winona asked. "Do I need to get you an Uber?"

"Gonna walk," Pierce mumbled. "Thanks."

Taylor gave Winona a thumbs-up. "Good for you for checking. We're walking."

"I said that already," Pierce said, leading her out the door.

"I did, too. Oh, it's nice out! Look at the stars! They're so shiny!"

He laughed, and they began walking home, trying to navigate crooked sidewalks in the darkness as they ventured away from Beach Avenue. She babbled on about the crescent moon, which was a cool yellow orange, and pondered the reasons why each time they walked another block, the moon didn't seem to move. This made Pierce crack up, and they needed to take breaks for him to stop laughing before they could continue their journey.

Finally, they reached his house and stumbled through the door. "Gotta pee!" she announced.

"I'll get more water."

She relieved her bladder, washed her hands, and squinted at her blurry reflection in the mirror. Ugh, her makeup had smudged, her hair stuck up on one side, and her work clothes were all wrinkly. She quickly splashed her face with cold water, scrubbed at her racoon eyes, and smeared off the lingering red lipstick.

Already feeling better, Taylor wandered into the bedroom, pulled off her clothes, kicked them to the side, and grabbed shorts and a T-shirt from his dresser drawer. Thank God she didn't feel sick.

"Taylz! Come get your water!"

She headed to the kitchen, where Pierce was leaning against the counter and had just chugged another full glass. As she took in his appearance, she began to giggle.

He frowned. "What?"

"You look as bad as I do. Why is your right eye twitching?"

He rubbed at his face self-consciously. "When I drink too much, I get this weird tic."

She drank her water, then wiped her mouth with the back of her hand. "You never got it before."

"I'm getting older, and more shit is happening to my body." His gaze narrowed at her outfit. "That's my favorite shirt. I was gonna wear it tomorrow."

She shrugged. "Wear another shirt."

"Did you leave your stuff on the floor again?"

She gave a long-suffering sigh and bent over with drama. "Why are you always so anal? Live a little. Make a mess. Wear a shirt not on your daily calendar. Eat expired yogurt."

"I just don't like dirty clothes on the floor when there's a hamper a foot away. And anything with sour milk will not enter this body. Stop moving."

"I'm not. We need Advil now, or we'll be in trouble tomorrow," she said.

They began laughing, both seeming to find the statement hysterical.

After tracking down the bottle of meds and popping two pills each, she crawled into bed while he went to the bathroom. Taylor gave a sigh of deep contentment as she lay upon the down comforter with navy-blue and white stripes. She loved his bedroom. It was masculine and cozy, with clean, bold lines and mahogany furniture.

Snuggling into the pillow, she slowly closed her eyes. Then shot up. "Pierce!"

He stumbled from the bathroom in his black boxers. "What?"

"I got the spins." She hiccupped, cursing under her breath. "Dammit, you know I freak out when the world becomes a teacup. Help me."

"Okay, give me a minute."

He finished in the bathroom, then went to his dresser and pulled on a pair of sweats. Her focus wasn't too good, but she did catch a glimpse of his fine ass as he bent over.

Pierce's body was something to behold in a bathing suit or in boxers. She remembered when they'd met how he'd been all awkward, with braces, gangly limbs, and a chest without any muscles. Now? His pecs were well defined, and he owned washboard abs. He was nicely built, without overkill.

"You got hot," she said as he climbed into bed beside her.

He laughed. "You're drunk."

"I am, but I tell the truth." She moaned and held her head when she tried shutting her eyes again. "Oh, I hate this. Make it go away."

"Best thing to do is focus on something else." He used the remote to click on the TV and found an old episode of *Friends*.

"You're staying up with me, right?"

"Of course." He plumped the pillows against the headboard and propped himself up. "Concentrate on your breathing and relax. Slow and steady."

She did what he said, and the dizziness began to fade. But then she gasped. "Oh no! It's the episode where Ross cheats on Rachel and breaks her heart. I hate this episode."

He gave a snort. "They were taking a break. It's ridiculous for her to think the poor guy wouldn't hook up with a hot woman after she'd told him she wanted space."

"You suck. All men suck. If we were in a relationship, had a fight, and decided to take some time to think and ponder, would you jump into bed with the first woman who was *hot*?"

"Oh, for God's sake, Taylz, you're getting all riled up. No, I wouldn't. Just watch it and go to sleep."

She huffed out an annoyed breath. "I don't know if I can believe you now. You'd cheat on me."

"Only if we were on a break. Now, shush. I'm exhausted."

She muttered under her breath but obeyed because she was getting tired, too. The mattress steadied underneath her. Pierce's bare shoulder pressed against her arm. Her little toe touched his. She went to jerk it back, hating that awful bump, but then relaxed when she remembered that Pierce didn't care.

The final scene flickered on the television, when Ross begged Rachel to forgive him, praising her arms, her face, and all the things he loved about her.

Taylor's throat tightened. The desperation on Ross's face as he looked at Rachel shook through her. Suddenly, she wondered if living a long, lonely life was going to be as fabulous as she'd believed. What if, when she finally fulfilled her dream of traveling, she still felt there was something missing? Why hadn't she fallen in love like everyone around her had? Was it the lack of quality men that held her back? Or was it something worse—a lacking deep inside her?

Had Pierce been right?

Tears burned the backs of her lids, and suddenly she wasn't tired anymore. She sat up, pressing her fists to her eyes in an attempt to block off the strange surge of emotion rising up inside.

"Headache?"

She shook her head, refusing to answer.

"Hey, you okay?" His hand was gentle as he stroked her back. Her shoulders shook, and then he was pulling her arms to her sides so he could see her face. "Taylz, what's the matter?"

Her voice broke. "Do you think it's true—the final question at the bar? Is something wrong with me?"

He swore. "No. There is nothing wrong with you. Don't you ever question that again. You haven't met the right guy, and guess what? You don't need a man to complete you anyway. Remember?"

She choked out a pathetic laugh. "But what if I want to love someone the way other people do someday, with all that cavity-inducing Valentine's Day stuff?"

"Then you will." He cupped her cheeks, tipping her head back to force her to meet his gaze. His thumbs rested on the curve of her lower lip. She looked deep into his sea-green eyes, flaring with a mixture of raw emotion. "When it's the right man, and the right time. But for now, you have bigger things to do. Can you imagine what a clusterfuck it would be to meet Mr. Right before you take off to Paris?"

She nodded, trying to gather her composure. "I guess. It's not like I dream of falling in love—I don't even know if I want to get married! But my whole life, something inside me has felt different. It's why I've always wanted to travel. Not just for my art, but to see if maybe the problem is that I've been stuck in one place most of my life. Why do I always want . . . more?"

"There's nothing wrong with wanting more." His voice was fierce. "You're still figuring shit out. We both are. And as for being different, that's a good thing. You're careful with your heart. It's not going to just anyone. One day, when the right guy comes along and you open up, that lucky bastard is going to strike gold, Taylz. You're a treasure."

Tears clogged her throat. Her insides shifted at his words and cracked open. She felt on the verge of a crying jag. God, she was falling apart.

Damn tequila.

"Come here," he said, pulling her close.

She sighed, her head resting against his bare shoulder, his arms wrapped tight around her. The scent of spicy male and mint filled her nostrils. His leg tangled with hers. He stroked her hair, murmuring soothing words, and she sank into a blissful state of comfort.

Until it suddenly turned.

She realized her breasts were pressed against his chest, and her nipples tightened into hard points, easily felt through the thin cotton of her shirt. His arms tightened, and his caresses changed, becoming more like those of a lover than a friend as he trailed his fingers down her spine and lingered over the curve of her buttocks. Deep shivers shook her. He grew hard against her thigh. Her mouth dried up, and her head spun, but this time it wasn't from the tequila shots.

This time, it was from him.

Her brain madly tried to grab on to sanity and the million smart reasons to pull apart and laugh. They were still drunk and half-naked together in bed, and even the most reasonable of couples would find themselves tempted. It was simply a physical reaction.

Except, she'd never felt this way about Pierce before.

And they weren't laughing.

"Taylz?" He breathed her name in his familiar husky voice, but this time it reeked of an intimacy and question she didn't know how to handle.

Dragging in a deep breath, she raised her head, determined to get back on track.

Her gaze stumbled on his.

Fierce, fiery heat lashed out at her. His hand fisted in her hair, tipping her throat back as he studied her face with a strange longing, as if the civilized barriers between them had crumbled to ruins, and all that was left was the fragile line between primal want and the easy friendship they'd shared for years.

Her heart beat madly in her chest. She licked her lower lip, suddenly wary, and that wolfish gaze followed her gesture, his body slightly shaking. And in that stunning moment, sure that sanity would rule and she'd be able to ease back, Taylor did something that would forever change their course.

She leaned in and kissed him.

Chapter Eight

He'd lost his mind.

Pierce felt as if he was in a strange place between dream and reality, where every action had no consequence or worry. When he'd glimpsed the sadness on Taylor's face, his entire insides twisted in pain, and he only knew he'd do anything to make her smile again. He'd regretted his stupid, drunken statement about her love life at the bar the moment he'd uttered it, but seeing how deeply he'd cut her had broken him.

Over the years, they'd embraced a hundred times. Hell, a thousand. There'd never been anything sexual between them, so he'd been comfortable holding her close, stroking her back, soothing her worries. That's what he'd always done.

Until his body had betrayed him.

The moment had turned so quickly that he couldn't slow it down. Suddenly, his dick was hard, and her soft, warm body was melting against his. Her nipples tightened and pressed into his chest. Their bodies tangled together. He'd struggled with the sudden urge to kiss her, blaming the weakness on alcohol, and for a few seconds, Pierce believed that his mind had won. He'd been ready to pull back and save them both.

Until she'd kissed him.

And he kissed her back.

God, he had no choice. Once her mouth covered his, he was lost. Her lips were soft and sweet, clinging and responsive to every movement, every bite and lick, driving his hunger higher and harder.

His fingers twisted in her hair when she parted her lips with invitation.

Pierce wasn't a saint. With a groan, he dove in deep and explored the slick interior of her mouth. He tasted the sting of tequila, the tartness of lime, and the unique flavor of a woman he'd loved since he was in high school. His senses swam as they kissed each other with a ferocity that overtook rational thought and drove him to press her back into the pillows, his teeth tugging on her lip, swallowing her throaty moan in satisfaction.

Her hands were everywhere—tugging down his pants to cup his ass, scraping her nails against his chest, slipping downward to squeeze his erection with hot hands that pushed him straight to the edge.

He cursed, chanted her name, and stripped off her clothes with rough, clumsy motions. She lifted her hips, helping him divest her of the black lace thong, then parted her legs to his questing hand.

"You're so wet," he growled, his fingers plunging into her pussy, loving the way she tightened and pulsed around him. "God, you feel so fucking good."

"More," she demanded, arching and rotating her hips against his hand. "I want you all over me. Inside me."

"Yes, me, too." He curled his fingers and thrust harder, his thumb teasing her hard clit.

Her body jerked in response, and a rush of wetness leaked down her thighs. Her teeth sank into her lower lip and she moaned.

"You like that?"

She nodded, slowly opening her eyes. He fell into those golden-brown depths, filled with lust and heat and a want that drove the breath from his lungs.

He feasted on the long length of her body—her small breasts tipped with rosy red nipples, the slope of her belly, the curve of her hip—all so familiar yet now all his to appreciate and worship. His palm covered one breast, tweaking her tight peak, caressing every bare inch of skin his gaze fell upon, craving every cry from her lips.

But Taylor would never be a passive partner. Her ankles hooked around his leg, and she stroked his calf with her foot. Her hands were restless, touching him everywhere—his hair, back, stomach, ass—her nails an occasional sting that drove him half-mad. They fell into each other and took their fill until he was throbbing, on the edge.

"Condom," he commanded. "Top drawer."

She fumbled with the knob, yanked it open, and threw a few packets at him. He laughed as he ripped one open and began to sheath himself, but she took over, teasing him with every inch she rolled up, her wicked chuckle telling him it was on purpose.

He lifted her knees and parted her thighs. Her gaze was locked on his. He searched briefly for any hesitation or regret.

"For God's sake, take me now, Pierce."

Her sexy, drawling demand drove away any thought to stopping.

He drove into her sweet, wild body with one hard thrust.

She not only took his whole length, but she gripped him like a tight, wet fist, dragging him deeper. He leaned down and sucked on one hard nipple while he eased back and forth, inch by inch, making sure she was completely ready. Then, guiding her hands to the headboard, he wrapped her fingers around the spindles and began to fuck her with everything he had.

Each stroke made him want to weep with pleasure. She was crazed underneath him, her hips arching to meet him thrust for thrust, broken cries spilling from her throat as she urged him faster and faster.

He gritted his teeth and gave it all to her, reaching his thumb down to stroke and tease the hard bud of her clit, then watching her face as she orgasmed.

So fucking perfect.

He had little time to savor the gorgeous, open expression of her pleasure, because his balls drew up, and with a shout, he came. His body jerked in violent response, the raw mixture of carnality and bliss washing over him.

He fell on top of her, pressing a kiss into the damp skin of her neck and sinking his teeth into the sensitive curve of her collarbone. She shuddered, linked her arms around his shoulders, and then rolled on top of him.

Spread over his chest, her pink hair falling wildly around her, she fell asleep immediately.

So did he.

♥ ♥ ♥

Taylor rubbed her dry, itchy eyes and lifted her head.

Light pricked at her vision like tiny stabbing knives. She groaned and carefully dropped back onto the pillow. What had happened last night? She gingerly searched her memory, allowing wakefulness to come gently so she could take stock.

First, she was in Pierce's bed. His scent surrounded her, along with another muskier fragrance she couldn't place.

Second, she'd finished the bachelorette party. As far as she remembered, it had been successful. There was a scavenger hunt and a stripper. Cassie was happy. Nothing to worry about there.

Third, she'd drunk tequila afterward. A lot of it. Shots.

Half-formed pictures floated in her head of Pierce and her facing off at the Boiler Room. Stumbling home. Then collapsing into bed.

She uttered a sigh of relief and relaxed back into a light slumber. She had nowhere urgent to be this morning, and other than having a hangover, she felt pretty good. Her body was a bit sore, but that was normal after a long night of working a party.

A snore erupted beside her. When Pierce drank, he tended to be a noisy sleeper. She nudged him with her knee and made contact with a hard, naked thigh. Hmm, odd he wasn't wearing pants. Then it slowly hit her.

Neither was she.

The blissful state of semiconsciousness snapped. With a gasp, she sat up in bed and looked down at her naked breasts.

Oh no. Oh . . . no.

Memories surfaced. Pierce's tongue in her mouth. His hands on her body. His gaze holding hers as he pushed inside her. The sense of completion and rightness with each delicious, hard thrust. The tumble into orgasm. Her nails digging into his shoulders. His name on her lips.

Oh shit.

She'd had sex with Pierce.

For a few seconds, she sat still in shock. Then she did something automatic after committing an act that freaked her out.

She told her best friend.

Taylor shook him awake, half hoping her memories were a dream and he'd laugh it off, saying nothing had happened. "Pierce! Wake up, now!"

He grunted and tried to push her away. She shook him hard until his eyelids snapped open. He glared at her like a grouchy bear not wanting to leave his lair in the dead of winter. "What? You said we could sleep in. My head hurts like a bitch."

"Mine, too, but you need to wake up. I think something terrible happened." She clutched the sheet to her bare breasts, still hoping this was all a hallucination. "I think we did something. Together."

"Yeah, drank too many shots. Why are you looking at me so weird?" He propped himself up on an elbow. Slowly, his gaze seemed to clear as he noticed her nakedness. A frown creased his brow.

Maybe it was okay. Maybe he'd have an explanation. Maybe they'd laugh about the whole night, go have breakfast, and get back to normal. Maybe—

"Oh fuck!"

Maybe not.

A mixture of shock, guilt, and something deeper swirled in those sea-green depths as he met her gaze head-on. "Taylor."

Her name was a plea and a confirmation of her greatest fear. "We had sex last night."

"I think so," he said.

Temper flew through her. "You think? Or you know?"

He groaned and rubbed his hands over his face. "I know. There are two empty condom wrappers here."

"Two!" And then it came back to her. Oh God, the second time. Slow and sweet, she rode him, and he rocked her gently to orgasm. Heat flooded her cheeks, which made her angrier. How could she have done this?

How could *they* have done this?

She refused to lie naked in bed amid the evidence of their biggest mistake. She jerked off the sheets in rebellion, then yanked on the shorts and T-shirt in record time.

Had he politely averted his gaze? Already, things were starting to crumble. They couldn't even make a bad joke together.

She turned to face him, safely clothed. "How could we have let this happen? We've been drunk before! Hell, we've slept in the same bed on and off for years and never had the urge to rip each other's clothes off!"

"I don't know." He threw up his hands in a half plea. "All I remember is you getting upset. I went to comfort you, and I guess we got caught up."

She glared and stabbed a finger in the air. "Are you trying to blame this on me? I don't need sex as comfort, dude!"

"I'm not blaming you, Taylor. For God's sake, I'm just as much to blame. I'm sorry."

"Don't apologize! That makes it worse!"

He growled and glared back. "What do you want me to do? I'm pretty damn scrambled myself here, okay? If I took advantage of you and don't remember, I'll never forgive myself."

That did it. She yelled with frustration. "I had two orgasms, you idiot! You didn't make me do anything I didn't want to. Oh God, we broke the pact!"

"What pact?"

She began to pace, shaking her head. "The pact we made in college—the pact to never ruin our friendship by having sex! We swore it in blood, and you don't mess with that juju or things go really, really bad."

"Oh yeah, I remember."

A tortured moan spilled from her lips. "How could we have forgotten our vow? Oh, this is a nightmare."

"Come on, people do blood pacts all the time and break them. That's what you're worried about now?"

"Yes." A strange sense of foreboding washed over her, like a shadow eating up the light. Nothing would ever be the same. The knowledge teased her consciousness. She shivered, rubbing her arms up and down for warmth. "We tested fate and now we pay."

His laugh echoed in the air. "That's just superstition. Don't get all witchy-witchy on me. Listen, we need to take control of this situation. Let's have some coffee and talk. I think we both need some caffeine and more aspirin."

She dragged in a shaky breath, trying to calm down. They'd be fine. They'd get past this. Plenty of friends had sex and moved on without a blip. They were strong enough to get through anything. "Okay."

"Good." He rolled out of bed and stood naked in front of her. He reached for his pants, and she stared at his hard, tight ass and muscled legs, and suddenly the memory attacked her.

"How can you feel this good?" he whispered over her breasts, his breath teasing her tight nipples.

She reached for more, pulling him tight, her thighs easing open for anything and everything he wanted to do. His familiar body was suddenly new, and she couldn't get enough, exploring every hard crevice with her hands and mouth. "Need more."

"Yes. Me, too." Green eyes burning into hers. "Always more."

Taylor jumped, suddenly frantic for distance. She couldn't do this. Couldn't sit across from him at breakfast and have a rational conversation about how they'd had sex. Not with so many strange emotions bubbling up like a witch's cauldron.

She had to get out of here.

Pierce headed to the bathroom, and she backed up to the bedroom door. After shoving her feet into the flip-flops she always kept here, she grabbed her purse and phone. They'd talk later, when she was calmer. Better to gain some perspective, so when she faced him, she'd be her old self.

Tying her hair into a quick ponytail, she quietly eased out the front door. On her way home, she shot Pierce a message saying Bella had texted that she needed help with Zoe. Taylor promised she was okay, and they'd talk later. She'd even inserted a funny GIF to make sure he knew she didn't blame him and that she hadn't run out of his house in a panic.

In other words, she lied.

She couldn't tell him the truth. Not yet. Not until she got her shit together.

♥ ♥ ♥

Pierce read the text a few times before shooting back a casual reply. He even added a few emojis so she wouldn't think he was upset that she'd run out of his house like he was a cheap one-night stand rather than her best friend.

In other words, he masked the truth.

Because he was scared shitless.

Cursing, he filled his coffee mug and sat alone at the counter. The night kept resurfacing in flashes. The way she'd looked, abandoned to the moment and naked underneath him. The breathy whisper of his name as she begged. The way she touched him, setting fire to his skin and a need in his soul he hadn't realized was there until he'd claimed her. This was no ordinary, casual fuck encounter.

This was so much more.

He groaned, burning his tongue on the hot brew and welcoming the pain. He had to stop thinking like this. He'd count himself lucky if they could put it on the shelf and laugh about it one day in the future, when thoughts of her in his bed, all sweetness and spice, finally wouldn't matter.

He refused to ruin something sacred, even if last night had been the best sex of his life.

She'd gotten spooked and then had to run. He'd allow her the space to get her thoughts in order, then agree with however she wanted to handle it. As long as she didn't keep avoiding him.

Yes, she was leaving in September, but their relationship was too special to fracture, not even with a few thousand miles between them.

And definitely not with one drunken night of sex.

He'd make sure of it.

Chapter Nine

Taylor regarded the two men who sat holding hands across from her at the conference-room table. When Jose had asked if they could meet today, she'd jumped at the opportunity. She hadn't been able to focus on her art or do anything but replay images of last night. Plus, they were her favorite clients, and planning their wedding was more like an honor than work.

Jose Rodriguez and Marcus Murphy had met on a blind date, had hated each other, and then had spent the next few months trying to avoid each other at social functions. When they both attended a mutual friend's wedding—the one who'd set them up—they ended up sitting at the same table and were forced to converse. Soon, they both realized that the other had been too quick to judge, and they spent the evening dancing and chatting. At the end of the night, they set up another date.

A year later, they were engaged.

Jose was the polar opposite of Marcus, even in looks. Jose was short, energetic, and ready to plunge headfirst into any idea that looked interesting. He loved loud colors, loud music, and loud laughter. Marcus was tall, reserved, and classically handsome. With ink-dark eyes, designer suits, and his sophisticated, seductive voice, he reminded her of Idris Elba. Planning their wedding had been a challenge, since they both loved different things, and she'd worked hard to combine their different visions into one complete experience that they both loved.

"What can I help with?" she asked, genuinely concerned. "You sounded upset on the phone."

Jose glanced at Marcus, who nodded. "We're having a bit of family drama. Originally, we planned for each of us to walk our mothers down the aisle. We wanted everything fair so no one would play the blame game. Lord knows, they're all experts at that."

Marcus sighed. "If only my family could play spades as well as they do the 'who harmed who' contest."

Taylor smiled. "I know a few experts in that field."

"I bet," Jose said. "Unfortunately, it seems our mothers are battling over their dresses. There was an epic fight—each accused the other of stealing her original idea—and now they have almost identical outfits, and neither is backing down."

"My mother says there's no way she's walking down the aisle on my arm when there's a copycat wandering around free," Marcus said with a shake of his head. "And since Dad died, there's no one in the family who's managed to calm her down."

Jose let out a long litany of Spanish, and none of it sounded good. "Try talking my three sisters out of getting our mama all riled up. Taylor, I'm really worried. They don't want to sit next to each other now, and Marcus's family refuses to come to our eighties party." He shook his head, his dark eyes filled with worry and pain.

Her heart ached, but before she could comfort him, Marcus had taken control. "We will not let them ruin our wedding," he said calmly, squeezing his lover's hands. "I promise you. And even if it's us at that eighties party all alone, it will be the best one ever. I'm talking Samantha Fox, Cher, and Prince."

Jose choked out a laugh. "Thanks, babe." He gave Marcus a quick kiss, then seemed to calm down. "Anyway, I wanted to let you know what's happening before it exploded even more, and I just couldn't discuss it over the phone."

"I understand," Taylor said. "I just want you to know that family dramas are part of a wedding. If you had none, I'm sure a friend or colleague would step in to wreak havoc." She coaxed two smiles from them as she mentally sorted through some ideas that had worked in the past. Dueling mothers was a classic problem, and one she actually didn't mind solving. "I may be able to help. First up, if you had to pick one, who's more flexible?"

They laughed, then discussed it briefly. "My mother," Marcus said. "I still may be able to talk her down if I had more time, but the wedding is only a few weeks away."

"Okay, do you have a picture of the dress that caused this epic fight?"

Jose whipped out his phone. "I do." He slid the screen across to her.

Good, the silvery, flowing dress wasn't even specially customized. She'd seen this one before in a few salons, even at David's Bridal, so she knew she could get her hands on something similar. "Does your mom have any favorite color preferences? Did she specifically want a silver or sparkly dress, or did she just like the fit?"

Marcus frowned. "I don't know."

Jose shot him an amused look. "I do. She prefers more neutral colors, but I think she was attracted to this style. Said it was flattering, just like my mama did. They're both busty, so this gives them decent coverage but is enough of a showstopper."

Thank goodness for Jose's fashion sense and tendency to listen to all chatter and gossip. He was a gold mine. "Perfect. Marcus, can you get your mother to meet me at Vera's Bridal on Monday morning? I can show her some other dresses I think she'll love. Then the bigger problem will be solved, and we'd at least have a chance at a truce."

Marcus looked doubtful. "Is there even enough time? She'll probably need it fitted and hemmed. I heard you need to get a dress for weddings months in advance."

"If anyone can do it, Taylor can," Jose said. "That's why she's the most badass planner of the century."

She winked at him. "I'm going to try my very best. What do you think?"

"Definitely. We'll try anything," Marcus said. "Should I send her alone?"

"She's welcome to bring a friend, or you, or anyone who makes her feel good about herself. But I'll take good care of her, so she shouldn't be afraid to come alone. Besides, I've been dying to meet her. I bet your mothers fight so much because they're alike. They raised two amazing men."

Jose blew her kisses, his eyes wet. "I just adore you, Sunshine. Thank you for making us feel better."

She didn't like mushy interactions, so she quickly brushed off their thanks and walked them out. But afterward, she found herself thinking of the two men and their commitment and how nothing seemed to divide them, even their families. Instead, they stuck together. That was the type of partnership that might be able to last a lifetime.

If she believed in it.

She quickly checked her cell phone but found no texts from Pierce. Guess he'd accepted her excuse and wasn't going to push. Then again, he seemed to sense when she needed space, or a shove. As usual, he'd chosen correctly.

Groaning, she trudged back to the conference room, where she laid her head on the smooth, cool table. How should she handle this? Laugh it off and pretend it meant nothing? Insist they never speak of it? The sex was phenomenal, but they'd been drunk. It couldn't be that good when sober. Their first two attempts at kissing had fallen completely flat. She'd never looked at Pierce and craved to jump his bones. What the hell had happened to them?

"What are you doing here?"

She jerked her head up and stared at Avery, who was looking at her with too much suspicion. Crap. She had to keep this thing locked up, or the gossip would be too much for everyone. She forced a careless shrug. "Jose and Marcus had an emergency. I came in to take care of it."

"Oh no, I hope they're okay," Avery said, dropping her large tote and laptop on the purple couch. "Were you able to fix it?"

"They're fine, and I've got a plan. I'm not worried."

Avery smiled. "You never are. Meanwhile, I'm running around like a crazed chicken, trying to lose these damn five pounds. I'm hungry, and I think I'm getting mean."

Taylor frowned with concern. "Listen, babe, you need to stop putting all this pressure on yourself because you're afraid if you don't have a perfect wedding, people will gossip and say you're not a great wedding planner."

Avery gasped and dropped into the seat next to her. "How did you know?" She nibbled at her lower lip. "I just want to look good in the dress."

Taylor softened at her sister's low voice. "You will, because you're gorgeous and already the perfect weight, and Carter loves you. Please don't ruin your moment by worrying over silly things. Bella and I are here for you. We've gone over every detail, and it's perfect. And if something does happen, who cares? We'll fix it, like we always do. Okay?"

Emotion burned in Avery's hazel eyes. "Yeah. Okay. Thanks, T, I needed that today."

"Good. Now, for God's sake, go to Madison's Bakery and get a chocolate croissant. And tell Carter to eat one, too. He deserves it."

Avery laughed. "I will. How did your bachelorette party go last night? You were out drinking late, huh?"

She stiffened. "How did you know?"

"Gabe said he ran into Winona at the coffee shop. She told him you and Pierce were doing shots all night. What brought that on? Did Cassie drive you insane? Were the girls too crazy?"

Relief poured through her. "No, the girls were fine. We just needed to blow off some steam."

The memory exploded and took her off guard.

His lips slid over hers, teasing. The hot, wet thrust of his tongue as it dove in, gathering her taste. His teeth nipped as he pushed the kiss deeper, touching the very depths of her inner soul.

Smothering a shriek, she jumped up from the chair. "I gotta go. Stuff to do. See ya later."

She raced out of the room as if she could outrun the memory.

Unfortunately, it followed her—haunted her—and she realized there was nowhere else to run.

She had to talk to Pierce and fix it.

♥ ♥ ♥

Pierce looked down at the sixteen-by-twenty portrait with a sense of accomplishment. He'd gotten lucky and liked a lot of the pictures in the batch, but having one masterpiece was always his goal. He'd found over the years that if he presented a large batch to his customers, they riffled through them like toddlers with too many presents on Christmas. They got distracted. Nitpicky. But when given fewer choices with better quality, they were happier.

He smiled at Octavia and the cooing Jasmine, then turned the framed canvas around. "What do you think?"

Octavia sucked in a breath. "Oh, Pierce. It's beautiful! She's so full of joy!"

He set the portrait on the display and walked over, kneeling in front of his new friend. Jasmine squealed, reaching out chubby arms, and he tickled her under her chin, enjoying her reaction. "It's her natural state, but hard to capture in fleeting moments. I guess I got lucky."

The memory of himself falling poked him, dubbing him a liar. But in this case, it didn't matter. Might as well save his dignity. Jasmine wasn't going to tell on him.

"No, it's more than that." Octavia walked over, studying the canvas. "You captured something within her that shines."

Jasmine was sitting with her legs stretched out, her dress falling perfectly around her, bare feet poking from underneath the hem. As she stared straight into the camera, her giant smile flashed two baby teeth and lips shiny from drooling. Almond-shaped, dark eyes sparkled with a fierce mischief that gave a glimpse into her personality. Energy vibrated around her, barely held within the frame of the camera lens. Her face was a gift to capture.

Jasmine wriggled to get to him again. On impulse, he lifted his arms. "May I?"

"Absolutely."

Octavia handed him the baby, who began immediately investigating his face, finding his rough, shadowed jaw fascinating. Her babbling charmed him. He wondered what went on in her mind. Was she finding out all the things she loved and didn't? Did she dream? Was she at peace as long as she was around someone who made her feel safe? The questions zigzagged in his mind, and a pang shot from his gut, the beginning of a stirring he'd never really connected with before.

He imagined having his own child, created from love for a woman who was still nameless and faceless. Imagined experiencing that level of love and devotion for himself. Pierce wanted it all one day, with someone who knew his heart and soul and would be proud to walk beside him.

The bell at the door tinkled in warning. Most clients waited outside in the waiting room, but he heard the steady stomp of heels and looked up to see Taylor poised in the doorway.

His breath caught.

Her gaze studied him with Jasmine, comfortably cuddled in the crook of his arm, her tiny hand resting on his cheek. For one brief moment, the air caught fire and sizzled. His chest tightened, and need raged from within, overtaking him and throwing him into confusion. What the hell was going on here?

Taylor stepped back, jerking her gaze away. "I'm sorry. I didn't know you were with a client," her husky voice drawled.

"Taylor! It's Octavia—remember me? Avery planned our wedding."

Taylor smiled, walking in to join them. "Of course I remember. It's so great to see you! Is this the new addition?"

"It most definitely is. I had Pierce take some pictures, and I'm knocked out. Didn't he do an amazing job?"

Taylor stared at the canvas thoughtfully. He waited, because he knew she wasn't one to pull punches, though she'd be polite in front of Octavia. He'd know the lie in her eyes, though.

"It's gorgeous," she said. "Then again, look at your daughter. He had perfection to work with."

Octavia laughed.

Pierce shifted the baby in his arms, wondering why the hell Taylor refused to look him in the eye. Hell, she hated it. Was it too generic? Maybe he was wrong to think he'd captured Jasmine's personality shining through. Maybe—

She swung her gaze around, and he froze. So many emotions swirled in those golden-brown depths that they seemed to hit him in the chest all at once.

Admiration. Affection. Respect.

Sadness.

Octavia seemed oblivious to it all. "A few hours in this man's company and my daughter's smitten. Pierce, you're going to make a wonderful father one day. How are you still single?"

He forced a smile but noticed Taylor stiffen. "I guess I haven't met the right one yet," he said casually.

"Well, I'd be happy to help you out. Just say the word, and I'll set you up—I can think of a dozen women who'd be lucky to date you. Did my friend contact you about doing his son's birthday party?"

Pierce nodded. "Yes, but I couldn't take it on due to a conflict."

Octavia sighed. "I'm not surprised. Your schedule must be overbooked, with every couple begging for you to do their wedding. I never realized how intimate photography is until my wedding. To be able to trust someone to capture your most precious memories is special. Cape May is lucky to have you."

He was struck by the beauty of her comment. Jasmine took the moment to coo loudly in agreement, making them laugh.

He glanced at Taylor and saw a smile touching her lips as she took in Jasmine. But shadows danced in her eyes, causing his gut to clench.

She turned around quickly. "I'm going to let you two finish up. Pierce, I'll check in with you later. Octavia, it's always a pleasure to see you." Then she disappeared.

Pierce gave Jasmine back to her mother and finished up the appointment, pleased with the sale. He made a few phone calls, tidied up his desk, and went to go find Taylor.

He made his way toward her house, sensing she'd be trying to throw herself into work.

He rang the bell. When she didn't answer, he used his key and went into the workroom.

No music today. The stark white canvas in front of her held nothing. She was sitting cross-legged on the floor, chin propped in her hands, staring at the wall. She wore frayed denim shorts and a black halter top. Her hair was pinned up, displaying the flock of sparrows taking flight at the nape of her neck. She was barefoot. A silver skull ring adorned her second toe.

Slowly, he walked over and dropped beside her. They were quiet for a while, letting the silence settle between them and fill in all the jagged cracks.

"Still blocked?" he finally asked.

She nodded. Began picking at her thumbnail. Her red polish was scraped off on both thumbs. "I liked the picture of Jasmine."

"Thanks. What bothered you about it? You were looking at me funny."

A sigh spilled from her lips. She focused on her nails. Strands of pink hair escaped her topknot and swung past her cheek, hiding her face from view. "I don't know; some things just hit me. You were so natural holding the baby, and she was really happy. I just pictured you with a ton of kids one day. Even Octavia noticed it. You were born to be a dad. And I realized when that happens, you won't be mine anymore."

He caught his breath. Raw emotion smacked him like a sucker punch. God, he'd forgotten how brutally honest she was. The sacredness of their friendship crippled his words and actions. Normally, he'd reach out and hold her close for comfort. They'd figure it out together. But now, he hesitated, afraid to confess too much or too little.

He couldn't get last night out of his mind. The memories came slow and steady, a tumble of images that reminded him of how much he'd loved having her in his bed. He also knew it had been a moment that they couldn't repeat without veering into dangerous territory. But her confession demanded an honest response.

"I worry about the same stuff with you. That you'll go to Paris and meet all these highbrow art people and leave me behind."

She gasped and looked at him. "I would never do that."

He smiled and tucked her wayward hair behind her ear. "Well, I'd never dump you for a baby mama. We'd change and grow together. All of us."

She wrinkled her nose. "That sounds a bit creepy. Like we'd be a threesome."

Pierce laughed. "Not in that way. I don't know what's going to happen with us, Taylz. We just need to focus on the time we have together and take advantage."

"Oh, I think we took advantage."

He shook his head in amusement. "Yeah, guess we did. But this weirdness between us is freaking me out. We have to talk about it."

"Ugh, I hate deep talks." She rubbed her eyes as if trying to get rid of an image. "I saw you naked."

"Yep."

"And we did it twice. We can't even blame it on a onetime mistake."

"True."

"Want to know the worst part?"

"Sure."

"It wasn't even bad sex. I mean, I expected us to begin laughing when we tried to get physical, like the last times. But it was different. I felt . . . things."

His heart pounded. He tried to sound relaxed, even though his palms sweat. "Me, too. What should we do?"

He tried not to wish she'd suddenly declare they should keep sleeping together and figure things out. That there were emotions between them, lurking, that needed to be dragged out into the light. He wanted time to experiment and see if there could be something more than friendship, because he'd never found that connection in bed before. Not as if parts of him had been found. Which was crazy, because that's how he imagined he'd act if he was deeply in love with a person.

Yes, he loved Taylor. He just wasn't *in* love with her. At least, he always assumed that was the difference between a committed relationship versus a friendship.

Until last night.

The thoughts whirled in his mind, and he held his breath as he waited for her response.

"I think we should move on." Her face reflected a seriousness that told him she'd been thinking about this for a while. "I don't want to pretend it never happened. But one night of great sex shouldn't derail our friendship at this point. If we hadn't been drinking, it would have never happened."

He nodded, ignoring his disappointment. She was right. There was no way they could just jump into bed with one another without consequences. It was best to go back to the way things were. Before last night, things were perfect. "I agree," he said. "You can't be using my body for orgasms whenever you want."

She snorted, but a smile tugged at her lips. "I'm sorry I ran out of your house. I think I freaked a bit."

"Understandable. Seeing me naked can do that to a woman."

This time, she laughed and punched his shoulder. "Idiot. Okay, so we agree to put this episode behind us. You didn't tell anyone, right?"

"Hell no."

She released a breath. "Thank God. It'll be our secret to take to the grave. We good?"

He studied the curve of her cheek, the stubborn line of her jaw, the pert nose. Her lips were pursed in thought as she waited, poised perfectly for his mouth. He remembered the wild, sweet taste of her on his tongue and the way she'd wrapped herself around him like she'd never let him go.

Uneasiness curled through him. No, he wasn't good. He was still tortured by the memory of her in his bed, but he'd force himself to get over it. He had to, or he'd sacrifice their friendship. Taylor needed the reassurance that he'd be able to transition back, and damned if he wasn't going to give it to her.

He nodded. "We're good. Never happened. Moving on."

Relief shone in her big brown eyes. "I'm glad that's over. Thanks for being cool. I'd better get some work done, or I'll never be able to deliver on time."

He stood up. "You'll get it done. Shoot me a text tomorrow with an update."

Pierce left the workroom and stepped back outside. Eventually, he'd get past this stumbling block and fall back into their effortless friendship. He'd bet not many other close friends would be able to talk calmly and make a decision on the best route to take. It just showed that he and Taylor were unbreakable.

Pep talk complete, he swore he wouldn't think about their slipup again.

Chapter Ten

"Aunt TT! We're going to the beach! Wanna come? Oh, please, please, please!"

Taylor rubbed the sleep from her eyes as Zoe charged through the connecting door of their duplex at high speed, skidding on bare feet in front of her. She looked adorable in her Fancy Nancy nightgown, tangled nest of hair, and shiny bright-blue eyes that were so like Bella's. But cuteness wasn't going to get her out of this pickle. "Zoe, what did I tell you the last time you came in without knocking?"

Her niece was smart enough to pretend to think, then clap her hand over her mouth in dismay. "I'm so sorry," she whispered. "I was just excited about asking you to go to the beach with us. I forgot."

Taylor crossed her arms in front of her chest and repeated the question. "What did I tell you?"

Zoe hung her head. "That I'd get punished."

"That's right. I promised your mother if you didn't listen, I'd have to punish you. You have to remember, sweetheart, that this is my private house, and I could have had company."

"Like Pierce?"

Her stomach gave a strange flutter. "Yes, or someone else."

Zoe let out a pathetic sigh that morphed into a whimper. "I was bad. I know. Are you going to punish me, Aunt TT?"

She bit the inside of her cheek and tried to keep a straight face. As if. She'd never punish Zoe. That was what Bella was for—to be the bad guy. "I have to. My punishment is . . ." She trailed off, almost laughing at her niece's obvious distress. "You have to make me a shell necklace."

Zoe blinked. "But then I'd have to go to the beach."

"Exactly. We'll go together, but your job is to collect enough shells and create me a work of art to wear. Deal?"

Zoe jumped up and down. "Yes! I'll make it so pretty, you'll never get mad again!"

Taylor leaned down and kissed her cheek. "I'm not mad at you, silly. Just knock next time, okay?"

"Okay!"

"Zoe Sunshine-Caldwell! Did you come into your aunt's house again without knocking?" Bella stood in the doorway with a frown. "Because if you did, after we keep warning you, I don't know if we can go to the beach today."

"But Mama, Aunt TT said—"

"I said it was a good thing she knocked, or she would've been in big trouble," Taylor interrupted. "And I'd love to go with you. Is Gabe coming, or is he working?"

Bella softened. "Oh, good. Yes, Gabe has a party tonight, but we'll have a few hours. Avery has a bridal lunch, and Carter's working, so they can't make it. Why don't you invite Pierce? I'll pack lunch for all of us, and Gabe can do the cooler."

"Sounds great. Give me an hour to get ready?"

"Perfect. Come on, sweetheart, let's go try on your new pink bathing suit."

Taylor watched her niece skip out the door with a jaunty wave and shook her head. That kid had everyone in the family wrapped up tight, and Taylor didn't even care. Gabe was good for both of them. She knew Bella had been lonely for a long time, and Zoe had been craving a father figure in her life. Zoe adored Pierce and Carter, but having Gabe for a future stepfather was special.

She grabbed her phone and texted Pierce to meet her at the beach. His thumbs-up emoji was perfect. They were finally getting back to normal. Their chat had been reasonable, with no drama or misconceptions. Even though they'd broken the sacred pact, she believed they were strong enough to overcome the curse of the rom-com tragedy by refusing to repeat the mistake.

Friends with benefits never, ever worked.

An hour later, they headed to the beach. Pierce got stopped at the boardwalk by a group of waitstaff from Fins. The man couldn't walk down the street without people asking him to go out, do a job, or just shoot the breeze. He was a beloved staple in town in a way she'd never been. Oh, she had friends and knew tons of people, especially because the family business had cemented their place here. But after Taylor had left for college, she'd begun to disconnect from the beach town. Almost as if she'd already planned to make a home for herself elsewhere.

Who would've believed she'd end up right back where she'd started?

Their feet finally hit the hot sand. The weekends in summer were crowded, but they avoided the bulk of the crowds by picking a spot on the far left, away from the flurry of activity in the center of town. They set up the umbrellas, blankets, and chairs in record time and then walked Zoe down to the water.

Taylor dragged in a deep breath, gazing out at the ocean. Seagulls dove and played in the waves, and big fluffy clouds floated in an azure sky. In the distance, the tips of dolphin fins appeared and disappeared as they frolicked in the surf. The cries of beachgoers rose to her ears as they all followed the dolphins, caught in a moment of simple pleasure and joy that sometimes came too infrequently.

When she left in September, she'd miss the ocean the most. She was raised as a beach girl, and salt water ran in her blood. Tipping her face up to the hot sun, she steeped herself in the present and enjoyed the tickle of cold water nipping at her toes. The roar of the waves washed over her. A smile curved her lips.

All of a sudden, she was ripped from the ground and lifted high in the air. Gasping in shock, she stared at Pierce. A warning growl rose from her throat. "Don't even think about it."

He strode into the waves without pause. "No reason to go to the beach if you're not gonna get wet."

"Drop me, you bastard, or I'll make you pay."

"Fine, I won't drop you."

Her rush of relief disappeared as he swung her forward and back, gaining momentum. She shrieked and clung like a sloth, trying to wrap her limbs around him, but he was too strong.

She flew in the air and hit the water.

The icy temperature stole her breath, and she dove under, gritting her teeth, embracing rather than trying to fight the battering wave that took her for a ride.

Pierce's laugh rang in the air when she surfaced. "Got you good," he said smugly. "You must've been daydreaming. Didn't even hear me coming."

She wiped her dripping face and glared. "Now I have to spend my valuable energy plotting revenge. What are you—five years old?"

He dove in and splashed at her. "Don't be so cranky, Taylz. It's a beautiful day."

"Watch out for the jellyfish."

"What? Where?" He jumped and looked around. He'd gotten stung in high school and said the pain was so bad that he cried in front of everyone. That led to some teasing and ridiculous names, like the "yelly jelly boy." Stupid, yes, but they'd both taken it seriously and had to get in a few fights to regain his reputation.

A laugh escaped. "Gotcha."

His annoyed frown made her feel better, but not for long. He attacked from the side and tossed her again. She went for his legs and hit the back of his knees, then jumped on his shoulders. For the next few minutes, they engaged in a knockout water fight like they were kids, until salt burned her eyes and her nose ran and she was gasping for breath.

The whistle of a lifeguard startled her. She looked up, hoping it wasn't a shark or an accident, then saw the lifeguards pointing directly toward them, shaking their heads. "I think we're in trouble," she hissed, hitting him when he tried to toss her again. "Pierce, stop!"

He squinted at the lifeguards and gave a snort. "Is that Mike and Jorge? What a bunch of babies. Are water fights illegal now? How is anyone supposed to have fun?"

She laughed at his sulky expression. "Aww, you can go build a sand-castle instead, yelly jelly boy."

His gaze sharpened in warning. "You know I hate that name."

"Sorry, just kidding. Oh, wait, let me fix your hair." She reached out, scooped up a load of seaweed, and plopped it on his head. "Much better."

"You're dead."

"Don't let them catch you." She dove away just in time, and they reengaged. Finally, exhausted, she gave up and wrapped her legs around him, holding on as he treaded water. "I need a break. Drag me back—I'm too tired."

He hoisted her around, easily capturing her legs under his arms, and pulled her close. His gaze met hers, his lower lip twitching in amusement. Wet hair fell over his forehead and plastered his cheeks. His dark, lush lashes were spiky with water. Her arms automatically wrapped around his bare, slippery shoulders, and his fingers tightened under her thighs.

Red-hot desire slammed into her. Her eyes widened as she tried to process the change from playfulness to raw want.

His gaze dove deep, recognized her arousal, and responded immediately. He grew hard against her thigh, and his head lowered, his damp, sculpted lips inches from hers.

98

She softened against him, her lips parting with invitation. The memory of his taste and touch weakened her resolve, and suddenly, she didn't care about anything except how badly she wanted to kiss him.

"Aunt TT! Uncle Pierce! I want to play, too!"

Zoe's scream broke the spell. He dropped her quickly and jumped back as if burned, then shook his head like he was trying to clear it.

She treaded water and turned toward her niece's voice. "We're coming to get you!" she shouted, her voice a bit shaky. Refusing to look at him, she began swimming to shore and tried to ignore the sudden awkwardness.

Just a slipup. Some lingering residue from their night together. Nothing to freak out over.

Yet, she'd almost kissed him. In broad daylight. On a public beach. Stone-cold sober.

They reached Zoe, and the girl's delighted giggles kept Taylor distracted for a while. They flanked the child as they jumped waves and pointed at dolphins.

Taylor's skin pruned and her nose burned and still she didn't get out, too afraid to face what reality would eventually show her.

They were in trouble.

♥ ♥ ♥

Pierce finished up his ham-and-cheese sandwich and hid under the umbrella. The encounter in the water had shaken him. One moment, they were goofing around and things were normal; the next, he was ready to make love to her right in the ocean.

Brooding, he watched Bella, Taylor, and Zoe build a sandcastle. His gaze ran over Taylor's tiny black bikini. He appreciated the thrust of her small breasts, the belly ring that gleamed in the sun, and all that endless brown skin on display. The tat of a paintbrush scrolled up her hip. Red dotted the tip, and the gorgeous black scrawl was a work of art in itself.

He'd run his tongue over the design the other night, tracing every detail in a quest to memorize each line.

Pierce shifted in his chair and smothered a curse. He'd seen her in that damn bathing suit for two years now, and not once had he needed to hide his erection. He'd always admired her looks and found her one of the most interesting females he'd ever met. No one could ever get bored with Taylor around. But had he lusted and analyzed every curve?

No. Not since that fateful night.

Zoe ran back and forth to get pails of water while the sisters talked. He would have worried they were talking about him, but he knew Taylor guarded her secrets well.

Gabe crunched on potato chips and dropped in the beach chair beside him. "What's up?"

He shrugged. "Nothing, man. Just enjoying some time off. I'm getting a bit burnt."

"Then put on sunscreen."

Pierce laughed. "No, I mean tired. I'm not feeling my work like I used to."

"Damn, I'm sorry. I guess doing anything over and over can get old, though. Even weddings. What are you thinking about doing?"

He let out a breath and tried to concentrate on the question. "Don't know. I'm not saying I want to quit my bread and butter forever. Just looking to change things up."

"You're really talented, Pierce. I always thought you could do anything you wanted. Would you be interested in heading to the city? Trying to show some of your work?"

"Maybe. I've been drawn lately to natural environments and settings. More interesting candids."

"Is there a market for it?" Gabe asked.

Pierce scratched his head. He'd been poking around doing some research to find the answer to that exact question. "I'm thinking of uploading a bunch of my work to stock-photo sites and see what happens. Maybe visit some local places to display some of my other shots rather than wedding couples."

"Great idea."

"Yeah, we'll see. I need to focus on a new direction." He pondered his thoughts for a while, then added, "Either way, I know gold is captured when someone's not looking for it. I want to be there when it comes up. Make sense?"

Gabe crunched on another chip and nodded seriously. "Nope. But that's okay, as long as it makes sense to *you*."

Pierce chuckled. "If I go that route, I'll need to stop taking on new clients for Sunshine Bridal. Finish up the summer season and then pull back. It will give me more time to explore options."

"Of course. We'll hate losing you, but we understand. Sometimes you gotta make a big change." Gabe shot him a look. "Coincides with Taylor leaving, huh?"

Pierce tried not to stiffen up but avoided his gaze in case any guilt leaked out. God, all this time he'd defended their friendship and had sworn he wasn't hot for her, even when Gabe and Carter had pushed. If they found out he'd slept with Taylor, they'd never believe him again. "Yeah, maybe it's just time for both of us to dive into the next chapter."

Gabe didn't respond. Pierce had a sense that his friend wanted to say something else but was holding back. Had he seen them in the water together? Nah, from that distance it would've just looked like he'd been roughhousing with her.

He thought of their almost-kiss. He'd been caught off guard, that's all. His body was still sensitive to her from their physical intimacy the other night. He reminded himself to just chill. Taylor had probably already shrugged it off.

Gabe finally spoke. "Well, I'm here if you need help brainstorming. Personally, I think it'll be good for you. Broaden your horizons. Meet a hot woman who's not your best friend. You're going through a longer dry period than I was, dude."

Gabe had been crazy over Bella for years and had refused to truly date or sleep with anyone else, holding out hope that she'd one day have feelings for him. Thank God it had worked out, because the poor guy had been knotted up. They'd fought long and hard to get here, but the joy on his friends' faces now was worth it.

The pang came again, deep and hard. The longing for something more in his life. He was content but wondered about real, down-deep happiness. Was it something he'd ever experience? Maybe it was time he did something about it besides sit on his ass and wait.

He got up from the chair and grabbed his camera bag. "You may be right. Gonna take a walk."

He headed down the beach and let his mind wander. Before a shoot, he'd do a quick meditation, opening up his senses so he'd be receptive to the world in a way his clients deserved. This time, he did it for himself, taking in his surroundings. As he walked farther down the shore, the crowds disappeared, and it was only sand and sun and surf.

A brief sense of loneliness cut through him. He embraced the feeling, lifted his camera, and began shooting. Random scenes captured his attention, pulling him deeper into the physical world around him. The rough edges of rock and shell tangled together in the wet sand. The loop and dive of a seagull in its own private dance. The way the sun caught the tips of white on a furious wave and threw out endless prisms of light.

As the time passed, he headed toward the lighthouse, caught up in the search for something simple yet extraordinary. The way nature could reflect a human's emotions fascinated him. He'd just never given himself permission to engage in the chase before.

When he finally surfaced, he realized how late it was. He slid his phone out of his pocket and saw Taylor's text.

You okay? Bailed on us? Heading back home. I have your cooler and camera bags.

He typed quickly back. Lost track of time. See you soon.

He didn't want her to think he'd run away after their encounter. He'd stop by and make sure she knew he was cool.

He trudged back over the sand, thinking about his new direction with his photographs. He'd forgotten how opening himself up to creativity allowed him to get in touch with new emotions—even uncomfortable ones. It was similar to how Taylor experienced her painting by allowing herself to show things on the canvas she'd usually shy away from. Too bad she believed there was only one way to succeed with her art.

Get away from Cape May.

Away from him.

The thought of her desperation to leave secretly stung. Sure, he understood she'd been born with a wanderlust not many could relate to, but he was practically family. Her ride or die. Her damn *person*.

Was it wrong to be a bit hurt that she kept ragging on the small town they'd grown up in together, terming it a prison? Did that mean he was, too?

And once she left, how would it be for him? Carter had Avery. Gabe had Bella. Taco Tuesdays with them would be uneven now—he'd be the odd man out. He had tons of other friends in town he could hang with, but most were either happily married or still into major partying. The previous women he'd been dating had faded in his memory, not worthy of leaving his couch for.

He seemed to be stuck in the middle.

When Taylor flew back from her new, glamorous lifestyle, would she suddenly find him lacking?

Too many things seemed to be changing all at once. Pierce didn't want their relationship to be one of them.

His brain fully accepted the statement as truth, but his gut twisted as if he'd uttered a lie.

Pierce ignored them both.

Chapter Eleven

Taylor returned from the beach and headed straight to the workroom.

Still clad in her bikini, with messy hair and sand in her toes, she stood barefoot in front of the canvas and began to paint. The images swirled around her, clawing to get out, as if her previous block had finally allowed not only a trickle, but a river of ideas to flow.

She chased the faceless woman who consistently haunted her, desperate for her not to disappear again before her muse got what she needed. The background emerged in shadow. The woman reached up from the depths of the ocean, stuck underwater, a silent scream as she lifted her hands to the sky. Another pair of hands broke the surface, reaching out to her.

At first, Taylor thought the woman was trapped and desperate for rescue, but as the pieces came together, she realized she wanted to be there and had chosen her watery grave.

She was screaming against the rescue.

Shaken, not realizing what the hell these images meant, she painted enough to gather the direction and the raw emotion of the piece. As she slowed down, she felt another presence behind her.

Pierce closed the distance between them, standing an inch away. The back of her neck prickled. She smelled the sting of salt water, sweat, and his unique male scent that had always comforted her. But not now. She felt too far away from comfort right now, and she didn't know what to do about it. All she could think about was how good he'd felt pressed up against her, how right it had seemed to just kiss him, as if they already belonged together.

Insane. She was going insane.

"That looks deep." His gravelly voice stroked her ears.

She threw her brush down and wiped the paint off her fingers with a cloth. "I got some crap in my psyche to work out, I guess."

"I didn't want to disturb you. Just wanted you to know I wasn't bailing."

She shrugged and finally faced him. His gaze probed hers. "I know. Gabe said you took your camera. Get anything good?"

"No, but I will. I think I'm going to stop taking on new clients."

She tilted her head in surprise. The easy way he'd said it told her he'd been thinking about this for a while. "What are you gonna do?"

Now he shrugged. "Explore more opportunities. I have a few contacts at some vacation magazines. It may be nice to freelance."

"Sounds good."

The air heightened; the easy camaraderie they usually had ramped up to another level she didn't want but couldn't change.

Taylor cleared her throat. "Well, I'd better get to work."

"We're just gonna forget about what happened in the water, right?"

She jerked at his direct question. God, what was the answer in all this? It wasn't like she wanted to avoid him. She just wanted this chemistry thing to die a natural death and not bother them again. Yet, she couldn't stop looking at his bare muscled arms, or get rid of the sudden impulse to press her mouth against his skin and savor his taste. His presence seemed so much more overpowering than it usually did, as if he ate up the space and breath between them, drawing her in.

She was used to short affairs and one-night stands. She had no experience dealing with relationships that touched her heart, because Pierce was the only man she allowed close. Because he was her friend.

Not her lover.

"I think we should." Taylor forced a laugh. "Let's call it a tiny mistake."

"Probably a lingering effect of Friday night."

"Exactly! Leftover stuff. We didn't mean it."

"Yeah, we didn't mean it." His voice was soft and intimate. Those hooded green eyes suddenly seemed intense and sexy, challenging her to call out whatever this thing was between them. "Even if we did, it would never be as good as that first time."

Her mouth dried up at the idea of one more time. Her fingers curled into fists. "Definitely not. That night was a fluke. We'd probably end up laughing our asses off. Remember when you kissed me in high school and bumped your nose against my chin?"

"Yeah. Got a bloody nose. Real romantic."

"We're a disaster as a couple in that way." Did she sound desperate? Why was her entire body pulsing with expectation, as if their words were a delicious sort of foreplay? "I probably wouldn't even have an orgasm."

"Or two." His jaw clenched, and all those delicious, cut muscles hardened. She practically scented his arousal, and then her gaze dropped and confirmed it. "Maybe we just enjoyed doing something we shouldn't. You always liked to break the rules."

Did he take a step closer, or did she?

Her breath came out a bit ragged. "Every time I did, you followed," she retorted.

"Because it was exciting." His lower lip quirked. "Maybe if we gave ourselves permission to do this, the motivation to actually do it would disappear."

She grabbed on to the theory, suddenly seeing how it made complete sense. What was forbidden was innately craved. It was a human condition. By putting Pierce in the no-touch zone, she'd tricked her mind and body into thinking she wanted him!

Excitement curled through her. Her gaze boldly moved over him, taking in his erection, his gorgeous body on display, and the plain old fact that he wanted her.

Bad.

"So we've set up a situation between us by putting the other off-limits," she said. "How do we solve it?"

One step closer.

"Only one way. Test out the theory. Take the forbidden out of the scenario. If we want to have sex, we have sex. We're adults. Best friends. We know the deal. You leave in six weeks. It can't last."

"The moment we give ourselves permission, we probably won't even want to have sex. Right?"

His gaze narrowed on her mouth as she licked her lips. A low growl rose from his chest. "Right."

"Okay. But if we want to have sex, we should set up rules."

"Agreed. We sleep with no one else, only each other," he said.

"Yes. And neither one of us should feel bad if we don't want to have sex. It needs to be approved by both parties."

He nodded and eased closer. "We keep it a secret. It's no one else's business."

"We don't let it affect our friendship. No silly couple's stuff, or dates, or any of that mushy junk. Just an outlet for sex if we both want it."

"Sounds reasonable. Anything else?" he asked.

They were an inch apart. The room swirled with unbearable tension and need. She stared at his sculpted lips, craving him like a drug. "No."

"Good."

With one quick move, he yanked her against him, cupped her cheeks, and covered her mouth with his. She moaned in approval, tilting her head up to give him full access. His tongue dove deep, swirled, licked, explored. She shuddered, her entire body on fire, her core tight and wet. He lifted her up, and she wrapped her legs tight around his hips. Staggering a few steps, he pressed her against the wall, kissing her like he was dying of thirst and she was the last drop of water. Thrilled with the edgy hunger he displayed, she nipped at his lips, dug her nails into his shoulders, and moved wantonly against him.

"Taylz?"

"Hmm?"

"I want sex. Do you?"

"Yes."

She yanked down his bathing trunks and cupped his hard erection, stroking him with light, teasing motions. Steel sheathed in hot velvet. God, he was big and hard and pulsed in her hands, making her want him with her entire soul.

He cursed. "Ah, fuck, I don't have a condom."

Not stopping her ministrations, she jerked her head toward the desk. "In there. Top drawer. Don't leave me."

He ripped off his shirt, kicked off his bathing suit, and carried her the few steps before dragging open the drawer and grabbing a condom. "Is this stuff organized?"

"Hell no."

"Thank God." He swiped the clutter off the desk, and the junk scattered over the floor. Then, with one twist, he laid her out on the desk. "I wish I could take your picture," he murmured, slowly peeling off her bikini top and bottom. "I wish I could show you how fucking beautiful you are like this."

She was comfortable in her own skin and enjoyed compliments about her body. She'd been called many things during sex, but seeing the raw truth in Pierce's eyes, and the way he savored her with each caress, brought a rush of pride that she pleased him.

He lowered his head to suck on her nipples while his fingers played between her legs. By the time he'd plucked at her clit, she was on fire, desperate to be shoved over the edge. She opened the condom and put it on him, her gaze fierce with demand.

He didn't fight her.

Letting her lead, he allowed her to wrap her legs around him, grip his hard ass, and guide him inside her. Her muscles stretched to accommodate him, the sheer pleasure of his cock pulsing deep inside sending her into orgasm immediately. Crying out, she jerked in his arms as the violent shocks shivered through her.

When she finally opened her heavy-lidded eyes, he was gazing at her with fierce satisfaction. "You're perfect when you come," he whispered, kissing her swollen lips. "Let's do it again."

He moved, hitting her sensitive bud with exact precision and taking her back up with steady, fast strokes. The desk cradled her weight as she arched up, and her fingers stabbed into his long hair, tugging as the need grew like a hard knot inside her, begging for release. His gaze held hers, fierce with focus, his skin damp with sweat as he slid over her. Then he yanked her hips up and slammed into her with one smooth motion, and she fell apart one more time.

He gritted out her name as he joined her, and she reveled in the shake of his body and the intensity of his response. Slowly, he collapsed on top of her, propping his elbows up on either side of her stomach in order to keep from crushing her.

Taylor held her breath, waiting for the regret to hit and anticipating the rush of embarrassment at having Pierce naked on top of her after a sweaty, satisfying bout of intense sex.

"Was it as good for me as it was for you?" he drawled.

And then she laughed, and so did he, and she realized that the sex was just as good as the friendship.

"Better, baby," she teased, batting her lashes. "You are a total stud."

He slapped the side of her ass and grinned at her squeal. "Now I know you're flattering me." His face turned serious. "Taylz, you need to talk to me, okay? If you change your mind, I need to know. I don't want anything to mess up what we have."

"It won't. I think we've both been clear about what we want out of this. We have rules. It's a win-win. I trust you, Pierce, and sharing my body just feels like another step to get closer to you."

His features softened, and tenderness gleamed from his bright eyes. "Thank you."

"Welcome. Now I'm kicking you out. It was a nice booty call, but I got work to do."

"Ouch, you're rough. Okay, I'll see you later." He pressed a kiss to her lips, dressed, and left as silently as he'd entered.

She couldn't help the silly grin tugging at her lips. Her body felt beautifully used. Her soul was light and free. She showered, changed, and fired up Alexa to play some R&B, completely inspired to work the rest of the evening.

She was back on track. Maybe she'd needed great sex all along. She'd read somewhere that orgasms cleared out blockages for both the physical and mental processes. Maybe this new arrangement with Pierce was exactly what they both needed. They weren't dating anyone else. No one would get hurt. And it was a delicious secret that made things a bit edgy and fun.

She already couldn't wait for the next time.

Chapter Twelve

The wedding was held at the Southern Mansion. Jose and Marcus recited their vows before a packed crowd, but their gazes never left each other's. Jose wore a white tuxedo; Marcus wore black. Cocktail hour was served outside, with beautiful white tents shielding guests from the sun. Classical music piped out of hidden speakers. Elegant, sculptured water fountains surrounded by vivid, lush blooms gave off an elegant vibe. Bite-size delicacies such as bacon-wrapped scallops, oysters on the half shell, and puffy brie tarts dazzled endless taste buds.

The grooms chatted and socialized in the gardens, hitting as many tables as possible while they sipped from martini glasses. Taylor oversaw the entire production, making sure the first part of the wedding was exactly how Marcus imagined it. Jose beamed at his side, proud to talk to his new husband's coworkers, friends, and family. She watched with satisfaction as the two mothers-in-law chatted together, the dress war finally tabled. Vera from Vera's Bridal had helped her fit Marcus's mother in a bold new dress that she felt both confident and happy enough in to let the first gown go.

The formal reception was held inside the mansion, continuing with the extravagant classicism Marcus loved. It was out of *The Great Gatsby*, a scene of conservative beauty and culture. A band played old favorites and love songs. Marcus and Jose ate at their own table, enjoying the various speeches confirming that their future had always been meant to be. Taylor barely saw Pierce, who was busy snapping candids. By the time the cake had been cut and ten p.m. approached, Taylor was just beginning to ramp up for the second half of the wedding.

Jose's part.

They moved to another room in the mansion, which was already decorated in a bold eighties theme. A DJ was set up, a glittery disco ball spun merrily, and Taylor had brought in a flashing dance floor. Props were given out to guests, and classic vending machines dispensed candy cigarettes, candy buttons, Dots, Mike and Ikes, and Jolly Ranchers, all with free tokens.

Jose made his entrance dressed like Cyndi Lauper, with a pink wig and tall combat boots, and Marcus had morphed into Boy George. The crowd roared as the music pumped out classic pop, and servers carried platters of cocktails: sex on the beach shots, gin fizzes, and orgasms. Iconic desserts were distributed to tables containing ambrosia, trifles, and upside-down pineapple cake.

Taylor worked the room, bobbing her head to the pop music she'd always had a weakness for. After glancing at her watch, she checked her phone and found the text. Good, Jose's special surprise was ready and waiting in the private room for her. As she headed back, she ran into Pierce.

"Um, I hope you know this, but Cher is here."

She laughed. "Yep, that's a surprise for Marcus. He's a closet Cher fan."

Pierce blinked. "Why would he be in the closet?"

"Because he gets tired of hearing that all the gays love Cher. He likes to buck convention."

"Got it. Well, she looks ready. How's everything going?"

"No disasters as of yet. Personally, this is my favorite wedding I've worked on all year." She cut him a sly look. "Wanna meet her before she does her performance?"

A muscle ticked in his jaw. "No."

A delighted grin curved her lips. "Liar. You used to play 'If I Could Turn Back Time' at full volume in your Miata."

He blew out an annoyed breath. "As if. I was more the Def Leppard type. Now, stop screwing with me and get back to work."

She laughed and watched him walk away, appreciating the sleek cut of his black suit and the way it cupped his very fine ass. Funny, she'd never noticed before how sexy he was. No wonder most of the women at weddings were always following him around and trying to flirt. She'd always taken him for granted, comfortable he'd always choose her over another woman if asked.

Had they been moving toward this evolution in their relationship the whole time? Had their friendship always been an open door to more, but they'd just refused to see it or admit it?

The questions whirled in her mind, but she had no time for answers. She had a show to put on.

Pierce watched the Cher look-alike take the stage. She was dressed in the singer's well-known netlike jumpsuit, her bare ass proudly wiggling and shaking with each belted-out lyric, and the crowd roared. Jose yelled in triumph, and Marcus covered his face in embarrassment. But Pierce caught the joy in Marcus's dark eyes and the way he boogied on the dance floor, hands entwined with his new husband's.

Pierce worked around the couple, taking a variety of candids before fading into the background. He'd gotten plenty of money shots, and it was time for the couple to enjoy themselves without being constantly recorded.

Craving fresh air, he made his way outside. A few stragglers roamed the grounds, and plumes of smoke betrayed the smokers needing a fix. He took a deep breath of the sweet night air and tilted his head up.

The past two weeks, he'd poked around and had begun taking some new photographs around town. Nothing seemed to really excite him, but he'd uploaded a few collections to various stock-photo sites and had crafted some emails to friends in town, asking if he could display his work. Unfortunately, he'd only been contacted for an engagement party and two weddings, which he'd declined. His friend George kept pushing him to do his sister's wedding next year, and Jake down at the Rusty Nail wanted him to recommend that Sunshine Bridal use his venue on a more regular basis.

Frustration flickered. He felt as if he'd been circling around the answer but kept getting blocked. He was spending more time in his darkroom, trying to work out the type of photography he really wanted to explore.

He needed to believe he'd get there if he was patient.

Right now, the only thing that truly satisfied him was the time he spent with Taylor. And she'd be leaving at the end of the summer, so he needed to get himself together and figure it all out.

"Get some good shots?"

The raspy voice startled him. He jerked around, squinting into the shadows, and found an elderly woman sitting alone on one of the benches in the garden. She wore a long black dress, and the shimmery threads of the fabric danced in the moonlight.

He smiled, walked down the steps, and stood beside her. "I did. I'm Pierce Powers. You're Marcus's grandmother, right?"

"Yes, I am. Been secretly watching you. I don't like too many photographers. A lot of them are pushy. So focused on doing their job that they forget they've been invited to be part of a family for a night."

He nodded, liking her insight. "I hope I haven't disappointed, ma'am."

"You haven't. Call me Joss. I may be ninety-one years old, but I still hate being called ma'am."

"It's nice to formally meet you, Joss. Taylor and I agree: this wedding has been one of our favorites to work. Marcus and Jose are special."

"That they are. Harder and harder nowadays to make a marriage last, but they've learned how to compromise, which gives them a head start. Not like my stubborn-ass daughter, who almost refused to change her dress." Joss shook her head and spit out a dry laugh. "Who the hell cares? I kept telling her: no one's looking at you anyway. Not with an extravagant gay wedding and Cher as a guest."

Pierce pressed his lips together, delighted at her candor. Taylor had told him about the near-disaster of battling mothers. "You're right. But I'm sure you've learned a lot of those life lessons from experience." He tilted his head with curiosity. "A part of me always wondered if you stopped worrying about silly things at a certain age. It must be special to see things from that type of perspective. To be clearer about who you are."

He expected her to share some nuggets of wisdom he could use for the future. Or to act grateful for the respectful way he spoke. Instead, she gave an irritated snort and poked her finger in the air. "Why do young people always ask ridiculous questions about old age, like we know the secret to life and just refuse to share it? Let me tell you, boy, growing old is no picnic. You watch your friends and family die. Your body fails you. People treat you like a five-year-old and push you aside. Do you want to know the truth, or hear some fantasy tale? 'Cause what I got to say won't fit in a Hallmark card."

Her words struck him. He was reminded of how every person was judged—by their skin, gender identity, education, past, experiences, and age.

Not wanting to keep looking down at her, Pierce knelt beside her, his camera balanced in his grip. "I didn't mean to offend. And everything you described sounds annoying as hell. I think I was curious about how you look at love now. If it's changed."

Her face relaxed. She gave a cackle and slapped her knee. Her dress floated up, then settled. "A much better question. Love is always changing, isn't it? We get older and more set in our ways. It gets harder to compromise. I was with my husband for forty-two years. It was a good life, but not what you'd expect. We stayed together not as much out of love, but out of respect. Devotion. Commitment."

He hummed under his breath, considering her answer.

Her voice sharpened. "Sound boring to you?"

Chagrined by her response, Pierce admitted he'd been expecting a more magical answer. "A little."

"Good. The harder emotions are what make life happen. Not the passion and stars—that'll drift away after a few good fights and sacrifices. But the friendship? Yeah, that's the heart of it. Because every day my husband came in that door from work, I was happy to see him. You show up for each other, even when it's not fun anymore. Make any sense?"

He slowly nodded. "It does. I never really thought of it like that."

She shook her head. "Young people don't. You're looking for the sex and to feel good in the moment. Sex is good, but someone who really sees you? Really likes you even with your crap? You want that, boy."

Yes. He did. His thoughts flashed to Taylor, but he quickly pushed them away. Things with her seemed too tangled to think about right now. "Do you have regrets?"

"Hell yes. I'm not gonna quote some Maya Angelou poem and say I wore purple and ate the ice cream and claimed bravely not to regret anything. I regret a whole bunch of stuff. Stuff I'm keeping to myself and not willing to share with a stranger—that's between me and God. But I'm glad to have them. If I didn't have any, it'd mean I played it too safe. I'd rather be in it and lose spectacularly than win by default."

Her words sliced through him, probing dark corners and hidden caverns he'd cut off in response to fear. Fear to push, or want too much, or risk, only to be rejected and hurt. But in this perfect moment, Joss was allowing him to truly see what it was to be human.

He cleared his throat. "Can I ask you one last question?"

"Go ahead."

"Can I take your picture?"

She paused for a moment, then studied him with a sharp, razorlike focus.

Had he overstepped? She'd said she didn't trust photographers, so she might shut him down. He hoped not—taking her picture felt extremely important to remember this moment.

Finally, she gave a slow, almost regal nod. "Yes. You may."

Relief cut through him. "Thank you. I just need a few moments."

He got to work, tweaking the settings and lens adjustment until he found the perfect angle. Pierce took a few shots, capturing the silhouette of the flowers and mansion in the background, the poised stillness of Joss, and the layers of emotion and secrets hidden in her dark eyes. She was a beautiful contradiction and complication of a woman closer to the end of her journey, and Pierce felt humbled to be able to immortalize her presence.

"I can send you a copy," he said, straightening up. He reached in his pocket for a release form and pen. "Would you allow me to use it in my collections?"

She laughed. "Of course. If an old lady is ever interesting enough to get you some money, go ahead." She took the pen and scrawled her name at the bottom.

"Thank you."

"Now run along and make sure you do justice to this wedding."

"I will, Joss. It was nice to meet you."

He grabbed his stuff and headed back into the mansion as that old artistic urge rose up inside him, dusty from disuse. It was still there. Buried by too many years of complacency, but something about this encounter had inspired him.

For now, he had a wedding to finish.

♥ ♥ ♥

The rest of the evening flew by without an issue. By the time Taylor had said goodbye to Jose and Marcus, her entire body throbbed from weariness. Damn, she'd been on her feet with no break for eighteen hours. But satisfaction filled her.

This had been her biggest wedding of the season, and she'd pulled it off by herself. Knowing she'd done her part well for Sunshine Bridal soothed her conscience. She may not have wanted to be a wedding planner, but when she'd taken the job, she'd sworn she'd be the best she could. Sure, she wasn't like Avery—a focused, ruthlessly organized leader who lived for the business. And she'd never be the nurturing, calm consultant that Bella was for her clients. Taylor brought her own sense of style, creativity, and fearlessness to a wedding that was unique, like Jose and Marcus's.

For her, it was enough. Her mother and father would be proud.

She finished up with the staff and hobbled toward the exit, where Pierce was waiting for her. They shared a glance, then began laughing.

"Your head or your feet?" he asked.

"Feet. Are your fingers cramping again?"

"Yep. Why'd we decide to get into this gig? Money?"

Taylor snorted. "I wish. At least it was a good night."

"Yeah, it was." He paused, fiddling with his equipment. "You heading home to bed?"

Her body perked up at the question that reeked of hidden meaning. She studied him, noticing his forced casualness and the way he tugged on his ear when he got nervous. God, he was adorable. He wanted sex, but they were still careful about putting pressure on the other.

Two weeks had passed since their sex agreement. At first, they'd tried to be polite to one another and pace themselves. But as another week passed, it became easier to end the day by having incredible, mind-blowing sex together.

She'd stopped analyzing whether this situation was good or bad, or if they were spending too much time together. It worked, and that's all that mattered. The moment either of them was unhappy, they'd change the dynamic.

Easy peasy.

The idea of collapsing in his arms and sharing his bed was too tempting to resist. "I can head to your place, if you promise to give me a foot massage," she threw out.

His head came up. A slow smile curved his lips. "I think I can manage that. Maybe you can give me a hand job." He realized what he'd said and turned red. "Ah, crap, I meant a hand massage!"

A laugh escaped her. She loved it when he got embarrassed—it always reminded her of the slightly awkward kid he'd been in high school. She reached out to brush the hair out of his eyes. "Either one is good for me. Let's get out of here."

They drove to his place. He pulled out their usual postwedding snack menu, and they munched on crackers, cheese, fruit, and leftover pesto pasta.

She pulled back the bowl and glared when he scooped up half the portion in one bite. "Why is it so hard for you to share?" she grumbled, trying not to shove in a big mouthful. God, she got so hungry after these late nights. Amazing that with all the food that was served, she never got to grab much. She was always too busy.

"I share," he said with his mouth full. "You're the greedy one."

"Name one example when I was greedy," she challenged, reluctantly giving back the bowl to prove her point.

He lifted his hand and ticked off each finger. "The time you hid your giant Hershey's Kiss from your sisters so they couldn't ask for a bite. And when you got that new hamper so you could hide your clothes and pretend they were dirty so Bella and Avery wouldn't borrow them."

"Sister examples don't count! No one shares with their sisters."

"Fine. How about when Ms. Finnegan picked you as the winner of the ninth-grade art show and asked if you wanted Deena in the picture for the school newspaper? You said no."

Her fingers squeezed the Ritz cracker until it crumbled. "Are you kidding me? Deena hated me and said I'd never win, so why the hell would I share my moment of glory with her?"

"When you won two fish at the county fair, you wouldn't give me one."

She glared. "I didn't want them to be lonely! Are you still mad about that? You're the one who refuses to share his dessert. You don't even let me have a bite!"

"Because I know you'll end up eating the whole thing."

His calm answers only made her more irritated. She could think of plenty of examples that proved she shared. She just couldn't come up with them now because she was tired. "I don't want to talk about this anymore," she retorted, shoving a grape in her mouth. "I'll just state for the record that I'm extremely generous in the right circumstance."

He gave her a smirk. "Oh yeah? When is that?"

His fingers caressed a grape, and strong white teeth carefully bit it in half. He chewed the flesh slowly, obviously enjoying it. Some of the juice trickled over his full bottom lip. Those green eyes were trained on her, and the sensuality of the act hit her full force. She stared at his very talented mouth, and suddenly she wanted nothing more than to jump him from across the counter.

Her tummy tightened and dropped to her toes. He was still in his work clothes, but he'd ripped off his tie and had unbuttoned his shirt. Crisp white shirtsleeves were rolled up to his elbows, exposing his sinewy wrists and muscled arms. His jaw was clean shaven. Halfway through the night, he'd tied back his hair, but his coal-black strands now hung loose, giving him the sexy look of a pirate.

"Sex," she said.

He blinked. Paused his chewing. "Sex?"

She pursed her lips and nodded. Narrowing her gaze, she slowly stalked him, keeping her gaze locked with his. Already, her body was perked up and ready to play. She stopped in front of him and slowly trailed her fingers down the line of his chest where his shirt was unbuttoned. "Yes. I happen to think I'm a generous lover. Shall we test the theory?"

His muscles clenched, and his eyes filled with a ferocious intensity that made her feel like Wonder Woman and Captain Marvel and Black Widow all rolled up into one. He sat on the barstool, deadly still, waiting for her next move.

She dropped to her knees.

His breath hissed out.

With deft motions, she undid the buckle, slid down his zipper, and took out his hard, throbbing erection.

"Taylz? Um, you don't have to. I mean, you don't have to prove a point. I was just—"

"Shut up, Pierce. Let me show you how well I share." She lowered her head and took him in her mouth.

He cursed as his hands came around to grip the back of her head, his fingers helplessly curling into her scalp. She savored the musky taste of him, the silky-smooth skin encasing steel, and took her time exploring, getting to know him intimately. The floor was hard under her knees, and her jaw ached from his width, but she savored every hot, sexy moment of being a goddess for the man she'd chosen.

He chanted her name and jerked underneath every stroke of her tongue until she took him fully in and sucked hard. With a low roar, he suddenly lifted her up in one quick swoop, settling her on his lap to straddle him on the stool, his breath coming in ragged pants. His face was wild with need, and he took her mouth in a violent kiss that she reveled in, her hands gripping him tight.

"You drive me out of my mind," he muttered against her lips, his hands quickly pushing up her work skirt to her waist. She sucked in her breath as his fingers edged the lace of her underwear aside and dove in, deftly playing with her, his thumb barely brushing her throbbing clit. "My turn."

Her hips writhed under his ministrations. He studied her face with a ruthless intensity, taking in every reaction, tweaking his fingers until he'd wrung out the most intense of responses.

"Go in my right pocket. Get the condom."

She obeyed, thrilling to his rough demand, her entire body trembling as he pressed harder and rubbed in the most sensitive of spots. Sweat pricked her brow. God, she wanted to come so bad; her entire being craved being pushed over the edge, where she could finally fly.

"Now put it on me. Real slow."

She bit her lip as he thrust his fingers deep, hitting her G-spot. "Oh God. Pierce, I want—"

"Know what you want, Taylz." He nibbled on her mouth, sucked her lower lip. "Just do it."

Most men submitted to her in the bedroom. Her dominant personality seemed to spill over to her lovemaking, and she was a demanding partner who expected to be pleased. Right now, Pierce knew she could easily take what she wanted without waiting. But the play was turning her on, the rough demand of him telling her what to do such a sweet relief from always being in charge of every ruthless corner of her life. She loved giving him that type of permission to please her and found even more power by allowing him to take control. No other man had ever given her such freedom.

Her hands shook as she fit the condom on him. His tongue lazily thrust in and out of her mouth, setting up the pace, his fingers slowly withdrawing. She protested the loss, but then he was unbuttoning her blouse, shoving up her bra, and sucking hard on her pointed nipples, driving her slowly insane.

"Put me inside you," he growled, finally lifting his head. "Then ride me."

She shuddered. Then obeyed.

The hot, thick length of him filled her up completely, driving out the memory of any other who had gone before him. There were no longer empty spaces inside her, and she struggled in that moment with the sheer intensity of her feelings, the grip of her channel milking his cock, the feel of her inner thighs squeezing his hips, the press of her forehead against his, the mingling of their breath, the lock of their gazes.

He began to move.

She was lost in sensation. Her eyes slid closed as she gave herself up to him, letting him take her on a wild ride where animal instinct ruled and the only thing that mattered was getting more of him. With each thrust, she arched hard against him, giving her clit the perfect pressure, and then she was coming hard, splintering apart while he held her tight, spinning out of control and knowing she was completely safe.

His body jerked as he followed her over. They spent several moments catching their breath, him still buried deep, her hands stroking his back.

"You win," he finally said.

"Hmm?"

"You get the rest of the pasta. You're the best sharer."

She laughed. "I think I like settling arguments this way."

"Me, too. Can't wait for the next one." He carefully lifted her off to set her on her feet, removed the condom, and brought over a wet cloth to clean her. The tender ministrations made her insides go mushy, each stroke of his hands on her body making her feel treasured.

She undressed, kicked her clothes to the corner of the kitchen, and filled up a glass of water. When she turned around, his brow was lifted. "What?"

He jerked his head toward the pile. "Hamper?"

She rolled her eyes, picked up the clothes, and placed them in the basket inside his bedroom. She grabbed a T-shirt from his drawer and shrugged it on. By the time she'd returned, he'd added ice to her water, since he knew she loved it cold, and had placed it carefully on a coaster. Taylor hid a smile.

"TV? Sleep? Book?" he asked.

She wasn't a snuggler. In fact, she was known to be the runner after a sexual encounter. But right now, she just wanted to hang out under a blanket and relax with him.

"Movie?" she asked.

"Sounds good." He took his regular corner of the couch and stretched out, gesturing for her to join him. She curled up next to him, her head on his chest, and he pulled her favorite afghan over their bare legs. He paused on one of the channels. "Adam Sandler classic?"

"Not in the mood to hear any more wedding singers." She made a face and he laughed. He stopped on the horror movie *The Shining*, and she made an approving noise. "Now, this is a classic. King is a master. I even loved the sequel."

"Me, too. Can't go wrong with good old Jack." He placed the remote down and tugged her closer, their feet intertwined. "Oh, man, it's the creepy-twins time!"

"And buckets of blood. Damn, we should've made popcorn."

"Remember that time you tried to scare your sisters by pretending there were real ghosts in your house?" he asked.

The memory made her chuckle. "Hell, I was good. Bella had to sleep with Mom for a week. I recorded those crazy noises and slipped it under her bed to go off around midnight. Sheer brilliance."

"Until Avery found it, and you couldn't leave your room for a week."

"Still worth it."

They watched the movie unfold, and she relished the parts she'd memorized over years of rewatching. The satisfactory experience was only sweeter next to Pierce, one of the few who understood and appreciated a good horror flick. The added element of their sexual connection allowed her to savor the light stroke of his hand up and down her arm, to breathe in his scent without apology, to melt into his hard body without barriers or worry about crossing the line.

Tonight, there were no longer any boundaries.

Taylor wondered briefly if she'd ever be able to fully go back to being just friends with Pierce, now that she'd experienced having all parts of him, but she quickly pushed the thought away.

Be in the present, she reminded herself. *Just enjoy the now.*

They analyzed the naked corpse in the bathtub and what she symbolized about Nicholson's character. "Did you ever think of making films?" she asked him curiously. "Instead of being a still photographer, I always imagined you on a movie set, being involved in actual storytelling."

His chest lifted in a chuckle. "Nope, but I think you would have pushed me that way in order to meet Joaquin Phoenix."

"I do love him," she admitted. "He's so complicated and deep. A true gorgeous mess."

"Don't get distracted."

"Sorry. So why not movies?"

"They're someone else's stories."

His answer made her angle her head so she could look at his face. "Explain."

She waited while he seemed to think about how to frame his answer. "I don't want the camera's job to narrate a story from a screenplay or actors trying to convey emotion. I'm more interested in what the world can show me in its true, naked form."

Taylor nodded. "Yeah, that's why you've been so good at weddings. You let them tell their story to you."

"Exactly." His brow furrowed with a frown. "I'm tired of chasing the same types of stories, though. I need new ones."

Questions formed that she'd never wanted to bring up, but tonight, lying against his chest, feeling safe and content, she voiced the words. "You never seemed to have any interest in traveling or studying abroad.

And you always seemed so sure of what you wanted to do and where you wanted to end up."

His shoulder lifted in a half shrug. "I did. Why? Do you judge me for not being as adventurous as you?"

"God, no! It's another thing I admire about you. You're so confident about what you want and how to go after it. I guess I'm asking if you ever regret coming back home right after college. I didn't have a choice, but you did. Unless . . ."

"Unless what?"

"Unless you chose to come home to help me."

The moment the words were out, her ears burned. It sounded so egotistical, but she didn't mean it that way. She remembered when she'd decided to go to Monmouth College. Pierce had been accepted to Montclair and NYU, both well known for their communications and visual-arts programs. But he'd immediately decided on Montclair, only a short distance from her school. Once it was confirmed they wouldn't be separated, her touch of nerves about finally leaving home had turned to excitement. She knew the world would be her oyster as long as Pierce was within striking distance.

Funny, she'd never analyzed it before, the way they were always navigating into each other's orbit. But had her sad fortune of returning to Cape May after college been the wrong turning point for her best friend? Had he sacrificed something important for her by choosing to protect her?

"No, Taylz. I made a choice that made sense. I knew I could build a solid business as a local photographer and work with your family for referrals. Mom and Dad were able to give me the loan I needed to start the whole thing. And truthfully, I was homesick. I missed my friends and the ocean and feeling like I belonged somewhere. I loved the security and comfort of knowing where I fit. All the pieces fell into place—how could I possibly say no? I have no regrets." His voice reflected prisms of emotion and truth. Yes, she always knew he belonged here. His words were a simple confirmation.

Relief coursed through her. "Okay, it was something I always wanted to ask."

"I do have a confession, though. I was glad you were forced to come home. Not because Matt died—that was a living nightmare—but that way I didn't have to figure things out alone. We did it together. God, isn't that messed up? Happy I got to keep you for a little bit longer?"

She shook her head. "No. Because I don't think I could have been back here without you. I would have felt the same exact way. So I guess we're both fucked-up and codependent."

"Guess so."

"It's weird, but I've been analyzing pieces of my past lately," she said, kissing his index finger. "Trying to separate where fate and choice intersected. Maybe it's because I'm finally going to Paris for a show, and I never believed in my talent before. It makes me feel . . ." She trailed off, uncomfortable to say it.

"Vulnerable?" he asked softly.

She nodded. "For the first time, I can really spectacularly fail at something that's important. Not that Sunshine Bridal isn't."

"I know. Being a wedding planner wasn't your dream, though, so this has higher stakes."

"Exactly. I keep thinking if the show doesn't go well, I won't have anyone else to blame. Not circumstances, or fate. Just me."

"You won't fail."

She smiled at his confident tone. "If I do, I've made a plan B."

"What is it?"

She took a deep breath. "I've saved enough to give myself a full year to travel and work. If Paris tanks, I'll figure out where I went wrong and spend the time tweaking my art. I'll take professional lessons and either stay in Paris or go to Italy. A place that inspires, where I can soak up everything history has to offer."

"It's a good plan," he said. "I believe in you. And since you've been brave enough to put your art out there, it's time I try to go deeper with my own work. Try a new outlet."

"You should. It's time we both take some chances."

He smiled, and warmth flooded her body. "Think we already started," he murmured against her lips.

She pulled back an inch. "But we can't screw up us," she said. "This friendship-with-benefits thing has been amazing, but the moment it gets wonky, we have to stop."

"We will. We've been clear with each other from the start. We can handle it."

She looked into his eyes and believed him. "Maybe me leaving this fall is a good thing. It will be healthy for us to live apart for a while. Figure our careers out."

"Just don't go falling in love with some lame French guy who thinks he's better than us because he eats smelly cheese," he warned.

She laughed and kissed him. "Deal. As long as you don't fall for some hippie, yogic chick who wants to teach you about the spirit of the earth while sleeping naked under the stars."

"Not my type. But now you're turning me on." He scooped her up, turned off the TV, and carried her to the bedroom.

"We didn't get to see the ax part," she protested, but the heat in his gaze and the way he looked at her made pure need explode within her until she was tugging him to the bed and wrapping her legs around him.

"'Here's Johnny,'" he whispered, lifting his brows in a crazy way that made her snort with humor.

"You're so weird."

"And you're hot." His hands ran up and down her naked form. She arched under him and moaned. "I should photograph you like this. I'd make a fortune."

"My breasts are too small."

He tweaked a nipple, then leaned down to suck it in his mouth, giving her a tiny, punishing bite. "Don't ever say that again. You're perfect." He stroked her hip, trailing fingers lightly down her mound. "You're a gift."

Her tummy tumbled and her heart soared, and then he was crushing her into the mattress. They made love with a hungry type of devotion reminiscent of their conversation, as if each physical motion was an imprint of their emotions.

Taylor surrendered to all of it, knowing that sometimes the sweetest, most precious things were the ones that could never last.

Chapter Thirteen

July whipped by at a record pace and melted into August. Pierce spent the height of the summer season working back-to-back weddings, restructuring his business to gain more creative freedom, and spending nights with Taylor. It was almost as if their lives were in pause mode. He needed to remind himself that she'd be leaving in a few weeks for the biggest opportunity of her life.

He wanted to have the same feeling about the new direction for his own career. He'd spent as much time as possible between his regular gigs trying to expand his contacts. He'd researched other photography niches and had messaged various friends in the business about other opportunities. His Instagram profile had been woefully inadequate, so he'd bulked it up and changed his sample work, showing more of a widened interest beyond weddings.

But each time he'd gotten a lead, he was blocked by his background. He'd queried some magazines, but they only wanted wedding photographs. His stock pictures hadn't made a sale. He scored more likes on Insta, but nothing ever came of them. Even the local news outlets he'd pitched only wanted his feedback on the top destinations to get engaged or married or go on a honeymoon.

His expertise in this niche was limiting his other options.

It totally sucked.

He'd just finished uploading a new set of images onto some photo sites when his cell rang. Pierce didn't recognize the number but picked it up anyway. "Hello?"

"Pierce Powers, please."

"That's me. How can I help you?"

"This is David Walker over at *Escape* magazine. I got your query and photo samples and wanted to see if you'd be interested in an opportunity."

Pierce tried not to reveal his rapidly pounding heart and kept his tone calm. *Escape* was a well-known online travel source with highly rated articles and top-notch photography. He'd tried a few times to get a contact there, but it was a hard business to break into. "Thanks for calling. I'd love to hear about what you have available."

The man snorted. "Well, to be blunt, I'm trying to fill a hole in our feature schedule, and my in-house photographers are unavailable. We're looking to do a full spread on Cape May, but I don't want the damn cookie-cutter stuff. Show me something I haven't seen a million times," he said, his voice brisk and gruff, as if he'd smoked for a number of years and was still pissed he'd quit. "Give me some unexplored territory and interesting reasons I want to spend my precious beach time there rather than the Hamptons or Ocean City, Maryland. I'm not as worried about the write-up as the pics—I have some talented writers in house that can do the copy. Can you deliver?"

Pierce wasn't sure, but he was determined to grab any opportunity that didn't have a wedding in it. "Sure can. When do you want them by?"

"Next week."

Pierce winced, but at this point, he didn't feel like he was in a position to be able to push back. "I can do that."

"Good. I'll send you the contract. Get back to me with any questions."

The brief call was over before he could think of anything to ask. Pierce thought about the hidden areas he loved so much in his hometown, but inspiration wasn't sparking in his brain. He only knew that he refused to document another dying sunset or a seagull that had been used to depict every other coastal beach in America a million times before. David wanted him to look deeper.

Which meant he needed to search for the unexpected.

Motivated by a tiny kernel of excitement for the unknown, he hurriedly finished up his paperwork and put a sign on the door that he was closed for the rest of the day. He stashed his various pieces of equipment in the car, then headed out to Sunset Beach in West Cape May, tucked away from the main flurry of activity on Beach Avenue. He drove out, enjoying the more rural atmosphere. Instead of houses squished together with a tiny fence separating them, farms took up more acreage, including the popular Willow Creek Farm and Winery. The beach was a magnet for tourists looking to investigate the lighthouse, watch the sunset, and hike. Since the shore was filled with pebbles, it wasn't as conducive to swimming, and the Delaware Bay side here had no waves.

Pierce parked, grabbed his bag, and headed to the lighthouse. It cost ten dollars to take the 199 steps to the top of the tower, so he paid his fee and climbed, needing a new perspective before he set out. At the summit, he caught his breath and stared at the stunning view of man and God fighting for space.

God won every time.

Water and sky dominated amid the houses and the people trying to crowd in. He thought about the balance of things and how a simple photo could evoke joy and wonder and rouse questions. He loved the idea of deepening his connection to an audience broader than a wedding couple's friends and family. This was a chance to explore bigger possibilities, and he didn't want to screw it up.

He took a few random shots, getting warmed up, and caught sight of a woman in a breezy, long skirt and white camisole. She hugged herself, her long dark hair blowing in the hot wind, her profile blurred from his perch far away. But there was something in her body language that called to him—a fragile loneliness that drew him. His shutter clicked madly, and he thought briefly of Taylor's woman on the cliffs.

He climbed back down and walked to where she still stood. He looked around, but she seemed to be alone. "Excuse me?"

She turned around, obviously startled. "Yes?"

He rubbed his head, feeling like an idiot. "Just wanted to make sure you were okay."

She blinked, as if not believing him. Maybe she thought he was either hitting on her or a crazy killer.

"Sorry," he said, lifting his hand. "Didn't mean to intrude." He turned to go.

"No, I'm sorry, you just surprised me. I'm fine. Thanks for checking," she said, a sweet smile curving her lips. Her eyes were dark brown, her skin a warm gold, and she was beautiful in that quiet sort of way: a woman who struck him as a bit shy and careful with her words. "I'm not going to throw myself into the water, if that's what you're wondering. Not that there's any moody cliffs to dive off anyway."

He laughed. "Good to know."

She reached out a hand. "I'm Samantha."

He took it and shook. "Pierce. Are you on vacation?"

"Oh no, I actually work at the taco place a few miles from here. When I'm on break, I like to drive here. It's peaceful. Quieter than the main beaches."

"Yeah, it is. I live here, too. I own Powers Studios in town."

She glanced at his cameras. "I think I've seen you around. Oh, your ad is in *Exit Zero* magazine, right?"

"Yeah—that's my big-time advertising," he said wryly.

"Are you taking pictures of anything specific?"

"No, I'm looking for inspiration."

"Oh, have you ever photographed that purple house on Perry Street? I always walk past it and feel like it's from a fairy tale."

He grinned. "That's actually a friend of mine's house. Avery Sunshine. She owns Sunshine Bridal."

"Oh my goodness! Well, please let her know I adore her house."

"I will."

She laughed again. "Well, I'm sure you'll find something inspirational. I'm new to the Cape—I just moved here."

He thought he heard a New York City accent. He'd know for sure if she uttered the word *coffee*. "You'll love it. Lived here my whole life and always found living by the beach to be a bit magical."

"I'm all for magic. Do you happen to have a card or something? I've been working so much, I'm not getting out to meet people. It'd be nice to know someone in town."

"Of course." He handed her a business card from his bag. "Contact me anytime."

"Thanks. If you need me, I'm at Key West Tacos—ask for Sam. It was nice to meet you."

"You, too."

He said goodbye and kept walking down the shoreline. Funny, he'd never thought of Avery's house as anything special because he was used to it. If he was going to photograph Cape May for *Escape* magazine, he needed to view the place through the eyes of a new person. Like Samantha.

Newly motivated, he spent the next few hours shooting with a new perspective. He stayed for the sunset celebration, one he'd grown up with and knew in his bones, but this time, he caught the wonder on people's faces as the music soared and the US flag flapped in the wind, and darkness teased the edges of the shoreline, exploding it into a thousand shades of rose and gold.

Pierce didn't need to capture the sunset. He needed to capture the emotions the sunset stirred, and that always led him back to people. As much as he loved natural shots, he was more of a portrait artist than a naturalist. But if he could combine the two, maybe the result could be what he'd been searching for.

When he finally returned home, he felt as if he'd unearthed a secret that would take him on a whole new route for his career. Excitement stirred within him, and he looked at the time, wondering if he could text Taylor.

Better not. It was late, and she was probably working herself.

Instead, he lay on his couch, ate a late-night snack, and watched a few episodes of *Impractical Jokers* before going to bed.

The moment he collapsed in his sheets, he turned his head and caught her scent.

And missed her.

♥ ♥ ♥

Almost done.

Taylor surveyed the workroom. Excitement nipped her nerves as she realized she had one last painting to do before she was done.

She'd talked on the phone with Luis after sending him some pics, and they'd discussed the different ways to stage her portion of the studio to best exhibit her collection. He urged her to come up with an overall theme, citing it as an important element to the success of her work. She had a hard time not laughing at that statement.

God, who would have thought her paintings needed a theme? She'd chased the nameless, faceless woman through her dreams, but Luis wanted a backstory—a way to explain to people what her thinking process was and the overall arc of the work.

At least she got to paint first, then come up with her theme. She guessed this was like writing a book before composing the marketing hook. The author needed the story, but the sales team needed to sell copies. Business and art working together.

Still, thinking of it as a body of work helped. Because she'd decided to put the woman in a red dress for consistency, in the ones where she was naked, Taylor had added flashes of red color in the mud earth, the crushed leaves, the flash of a squirrel, and other tiny touches to weave a thread of unity into each painting.

Taylor faced the blank canvas. The last painting was to be the culmination of the woman's search. She'd finally be face-to-face with her lover and allow herself to be truly vulnerable, opening her heart for the first and last time. Taylor just didn't know what the man's reaction would be. Or if it mattered. If it was the woman's journey, did it matter if he accepted her love or rejected it? The truth of the offering was the main message. That's what she needed to get across.

Somehow.

She groaned and stumbled out of her room, rubbing her eyes. A glance at the clock showed late afternoon, but time meant nothing to her anymore. She'd begun at nine a.m. and worked through lunch. Time to fuel up, stretch, and get back to it. She had to use every possible second she had left to finish this last piece.

At least she'd gotten over her awful creative block. After struggling for weeks, her muse had finally broken open and spilled her contents until Taylor felt as if she was channeling endless images onto the canvas, caught in an artistic frenzy. It was wonderful and filled her up from the inside.

Funny thing. It had also coincided with when she'd begun sleeping with Pierce.

An odd coincidence.

As if his ears were burning, her phone vibrated. She picked it up. **Finished with Hernandez wedding. Up for pizza?**

She hadn't seen Pierce in three days. They'd both been busy with work and on crazy schedules. Her heart squeezed in anticipation of seeing his face, especially if he brought a pizza box with him. She hurriedly texted back. **Hell yes. Get pepperoni.**

The thumbs-up emoji flashed.

She looked down at her messy clothes and paint-stained hands and laughed. Some booty call. Most men would run the other way, but Pierce wouldn't even blink. Another reason he fit so perfectly in her life—he knew she was different from most women and didn't try to change her. He never had, even back in high school.

She jumped in the shower and thought about their past. She knew it was probably odd that a boy and girl had connected so quickly without romantic intentions. They'd been stuck as lab partners, and Pierce had seemed awkward and shy, a bit nerdy, with his too-long hair, acne, and quiet demeanor. But she'd sensed a goodness in him different from the other boys. It was as if their creative souls recognized each other and decided to protect rather than destroy.

They'd eaten lunch together, gone to prom together, and raised hell together. Everyone thought they were a couple, but that had never bothered them.

So far, the friends-with-benefits arrangement had been working well. Taylor figured she'd go off to Paris, and their relationship could snap back to being strictly friendship. After all, everything else had been easy between them. Maybe that cursed pact wouldn't affect them. No one suspected they were sleeping together, and they only had a few weeks left to keep the secret.

She put on shorts and a loose tank, and then he was at her door. He'd changed out of his work clothes and wore faded jeans, a white button-down shirt, and loafers. His hair was loose and framed his face.

She took the pizza box and set it on the table, then headed to the refrigerator to grab him a beer. "How was the wedding?" she asked, flipping off the cap and handing it to him.

He took a long swig and nodded gratefully. "Not bad. No issues. Avery was at the top of her game, except when they said their vows—I caught her sobbing."

Taylor grinned. "Aww, I think she's picturing her own wedding, since it's so close."

"I had to send her to the bathroom because her mascara ran, and she hugged me."

"How did Nora do?"

"She's a mini Avery," he said, shaking his head. "No one can ever replace you, but she'll fill the position well."

"Good to know." Taylor put out paper plates, and they sat at the counter, munching out. "What have you been up to while I've been in Frankenstein mode?"

"Taking some pictures and exploring. I took the job with *Escape* magazine, so I've been perusing Cape May for original shots. They need them by next week."

"Well, you know the island better than anyone."

"Yeah, they want something different from the usual beach pics, but it's a good challenge. Met a woman who's new here. Her name's Samantha, and she works at the taco place in West Cape May."

"Did you score a date?" she teased, batting her lashes.

"No, but we exchanged info. She looked lonely."

He shifted his gaze away, and a shot of anxiety punched through her. Was he interested? If so, Taylor didn't want to block him from seeking out a relationship that could fit his needs. She ignored the lurch in her gut and asked him directly. "Pierce, if you want to ask her out, just tell me. It's okay."

Annoyance skittered across his features before clearing. "I appreciate the permission, but no. It wasn't like that."

"I just want you to always be honest with me. I don't want to hold you back."

"You're not. I'll tell you if there's someone else I want to fuck. Is that good enough for you?"

She jerked back in shock. "Hey, why are you getting pissy with me? I'm being understanding!"

He got off the stool and turned his back. "I get it, Taylz. You don't care. This is just a fun, casual thing to pass the time before you leave. No need to drill it in my head again."

Unease gathered inside her. What was happening? Did he really think she didn't care about what they were doing together?

Her throat tightened at the idea that he could be hurting from something she'd implied. "Hang on, I think I need to clarify something. When we decided to add sex to the equation, I wanted to be careful about blurring the lines so no one got hurt. I didn't want to hold you back, because you've always said you want a relationship—but I never said I didn't care. You're important to me, Pierce. I'm not having sex with you to pass the time. I'm doing it because it not only feels good, it feels right. But who am I to put demands on you when I'm leaving?"

He swore softly, then faced her. "What if I *wanted* you to make some demands?"

She froze. Searched his gaze for answers while tingles spread through her veins. A pent-up frustration sparked in those pale-green eyes, but she didn't know what he wanted from her. Her heart pounded in fear. "I don't know what you mean."

A muscle worked in his jaw. She held her breath as she waited for him to say something that would change everything, but then the moment passed, and the intensity drained from his gaze. His tone was falsely light. "Never mind. I get what you're saying. How about we just agree that until you leave for Paris, we won't see anyone else. Let's just enjoy each other and what we have. Okay?"

Relief loosened her muscles. "Agreed." All she wanted was for things to continue smoothly and for nothing to break their current bubble of happiness.

"Good. Now, tell me how much you got done."

She grabbed another slice and settled back in her seat. "I have one canvas left—the final culmination. I need to refuel and get back to it."

"Need help? I can mix paints. Clean your brushes. Inspire you."

She laughed. "Hmm, I always wanted to re-create that *Titanic* nude with a man. You good with wearing the jewel and nothing but a mysterious smile?"

"If it will impress your art curator, I'll do it. What are friends for?"

They smiled at each other. She grabbed a napkin and motioned him forward to dab at his chin. "Sauce. You always did eat pizza like a five-year-old."

"At least I don't leave my crust. It's a crime—bread is life. Give it to me."

She made a face and handed over her crust. Then went for a third slice.

"Do you still need the painting you gave me?" he asked. "I know Carter said it completes the set, but I wasn't sure what you'd decided."

"I'd like to bring it with me for the show, but I won't sell it."

"What if they offer you a million dollars for it?"

"I still won't sell it. I promised it was yours, and you loved it before anyone else—you believed in me before anyone else. I don't take back gifts."

He stared at her, a slow smile curving his lips. "That's one of the sweetest things you've ever said to me."

She rolled her eyes. "No, it's not. I called you hot. Said you had an amazing ass. I've termed you talented. The compliments go on and on."

"I think this one is the best, if you're saying I'm worth more than a million dollars."

"Duh. You're worth more than anything."

He blinked, obviously surprised by her admission, and she hid her flaming cheeks by busying herself with the plates and garbage and making the table tidy. Suddenly, he snagged her wrist and whirled her around. She fell against his chest, and he wrapped his arms around her, burying his face in her hair. "Well, I wouldn't trade you for the Hope Diamond."

"Show-off," she whispered.

He took her mouth and kissed her deep and long and slow. She surrendered full control and just let him take her away on a flood of warmth and arousal, her body molding perfectly to his. She protested when he finally stepped away, his hair mussed and his eyes bright with desire. "You have to work," he said. "Playtime is after."

She groaned. "You said you'd inspire me. How about a quickie?"

He laughed and backed up with his hands in the air. "Nope. I'm gonna crash on the couch and wait while you create magic. Think of me as a reward." He posed like a model, sticking out his chest and flexing his biceps. She grabbed a paper plate from the pile, tossed it like a Frisbee, and nailed him in the chest. He pretended to fall, groaning dramatically.

"You are such a dork." Shaking her head, she wrapped up the leftover pizza and poured herself a glass of white wine. "I'll give it another hour."

"Sounds fair. Aren't you going to recycle that?"

She looked at the box. "Later."

He actually twitched. "I'll get it." Pierce hated for any recycling items to lie around and needed to place them in the bins ASAP.

She was used to his quirks, but she still enjoyed teasing him now and then. "Great. Can you also take out the half-and-half cartons and the seltzer bottles?" she asked sweetly, pointing to the bulging bag where she temporarily stashed junk in order to save herself a walk to the curb.

He groaned. "Taylz, why is it so hard to walk a few hundred feet?" he muttered under his breath. He scooped up the rest of the stuff and marched outside.

"Thanks," she called out. Now, if only she could teach him to cook, they could practically live together.

Amused, she took her wine and went to her workroom. She spent the first fifteen minutes trying to get back in the mood. She fiddled with the music, mixed different colors, and nibbled at the end of her paintbrush, waiting for the woman to speak. She let her mind wander, touching like a bouncing ball on various memories and thoughts, and finally a garden took hold in her vision. A garden of roses, crushed on the ground by treading feet, broken petals strewn like tiny deaths. The woman felt all of it.

Following the image, she began to create the setting and build from there. Soon, she lost all track of time. It was only when she realized her bladder was about to explode and her wine had grown warm that she surfaced.

After stretching her muscles, she hurried to the bathroom, washed her hands, and walked into the living room. "I worked, so you'd better be ready for me to collect," she said loudly, following the sounds of the television. Then stopped.

Pierce was asleep.

Spread out on her sofa, he clutched a throw pillow under his chin and snored softly. She walked over and smoothed back his hair before lowering the volume on the TV. Poor thing was exhausted. She thought about waking him, but he needed the sleep.

She felt surprisingly awake, with adrenaline still buzzing in her veins, pushing her to ride the wave until she collapsed. Might as well work while he slept.

She grabbed a blanket from the chair and covered him, pressing a kiss to his forehead. He grunted and frowned, then settled back. Taylor watched him for a while, her gaze caressing his features, and she wondered when she was going to stop lying to herself. Since they'd begun having sex, her feelings had been changing. Growing. Morphing into a live, chomping beast, when before the beast there had just been a sleeping dragon.

Of course, there was nothing left to do except ride it out. Paris was her escape from the truth of her burgeoning emotions, and the end that was meant to be. Someday, he'd marry another woman. Settle down with children. Have the life he'd always intended.

And it would never be with her.

The smart thing would be to break it off now, but then she'd spend her last days being miserable and sad. No, better to go out on a high note and take everything he was willing to give her.

It'd be a hell of a ride.

Slowly, she turned and walked away.

Chapter Fourteen

He woke up dying of thirst.

Blinking, he took in his surroundings and realized he'd fallen asleep in Taylor's living room. A blanket covered him, and the TV droned in the background with low murmurs. Rubbing his head, he sat up and got some water, drinking in big gulps. Damn, why hadn't she woken him?

He glanced at the clock. Three a.m.

His little nap had turned into a four-hour snooze fest.

Yawning, he headed to her bedroom. The bed was unmade, but she wasn't there. Taylor subscribed to the theory that it was silly to make a bed each morning when she was just going to sleep in it that night. Shaking his head, he checked the bathroom, but there was only a deep hush blanketing the room, telling him it was empty.

Was she still working?

Frowning, he headed to the workroom. The music started faint, then grew louder, a grindy, sexy hip-hop with a growly voice like Barry White's. The lights were dimmed, and he walked past endless half-painted easels, containers, boxes, canvases, and various junk until he got into the main space where she painted.

He stopped still and stared.

She wore a tiny lace bra with red bikini underwear. Hair messily pinned up. Barefoot. The heat from the room was sticky—she was having ongoing issues with the central air in this back room, so it had probably crapped out again. Paint stained her fingers and dabs smeared her cheeks. She moved her hips to the music, muttering underneath her breath, attacking the canvas like she was at war and intended to win.

It was at that exact moment he realized their arrangement had backfired.

Taylor was right. Mixing sex and friendship had disastrous consequences. His entire body throbbed with a deep-seated need that transformed the physical and pierced straight through to his heart.

Dear God, he was in love with her.

She stunned him. The painting was still in its raw form, but he could spot the woman caught in the wild midst of vivid, broken blooms, her hands outstretched, knees half-bent in complete surrender to the shadowy figure before her. It was full of misery and pain, but in the lines of her face there was a joy in the abandonment of all she had, a freedom by offering it all, no matter what the consequences. Power beat from every brushstroke, the same power that exuded from the woman who painted it.

His body immediately hardened. He stared at her, his gaze hungrily taking in every inch of bare skin, the thrust of her small breasts, the intense concentration on her sharp features, the lush lip she nibbled on, the calloused hands that held the immense talent she was finally connecting with. She was like a caged bird finally ready to fly free, and Pierce knew he was the last thing holding her back.

He'd let her go. She'd be a big, beautiful light in the art world. She'd travel and have affairs with endless worldly, interesting men. And he'd remain behind, trying to pick up the broken pieces and come to terms with a life without her.

It had always been his fate. He'd been able to bargain for these past few years of having her to himself, but now it was time to pay. He accepted it with grace, refusing to fight for what would eventually kill her. If he begged her to stay with him, to give this relationship a true test, she'd never be able to follow her dream. She'd compromise once again, pretend it was what she wanted, and years later, she'd have regrets and resent him for all of it.

Brutal pain seized him, along with a sense of urgency. Right now, she belonged to him, even though she was still pretending their relationship meant nothing but friendship with an extra physical bonus. But he'd seen the way she looked at him. The boundaries had been crushed, and rules no longer meant anything. So tonight, he'd take what he wanted and burn his memory inside her so deeply that she'd always remember him and this night.

She paused, like prey sensing a predator, and turned to look at him.

Their gazes locked and held. The air thickened, and he noticed the sweat sheening on her skin, the damp strands of hair clinging to her forehead. She was half in this world and half in another, and he'd never seen anything so magnificent in his whole fucking life—this woman who challenged him and fought him and laughed with him. This woman who saw right into his soul and found nothing lacking.

"You were sleeping," she finally said. Her voice was half-drunk, and she swayed on her feet. He remained silent, and she seemed almost wary, her Bambi eyes wide while she waited for him to do or say something.

Slowly, he crossed the room until he stood before her. Her nostrils flared, and her pupils dilated. The pulse at the base of her throat beat rapidly, and he could almost scent her growing arousal in the sticky heat.

He took the brush out of her hand and placed it on the easel. With deliberate motions, he reached out and unsnapped the front closure of her bra. She sucked in her breath as the material dropped to the floor.

An animal instinct rose within him, pushing him to claim, mate, fuck, possess. Her eyes burned with the same longing, and she arched her back, her hard nipples evidence she was just as turned on as he was.

The music ground out a pulsing beat. He lifted her wrists and pressed his palms to hers, staining himself with the paint still gleaming and dripping from her fingers. When he withdrew, he reached out and cupped her breasts, smearing the paint over her nipples, down her stomach, and to the front of her underwear. A whimper escaped her throat, but she stood still, head tilted back, giving herself to the wild need to mark her beating through his very skin.

He dragged her panties over her hips until she stood completely naked before him. "I want to paint you," he said, his voice rough with barely restrained lust. "I want to cover your body like my own canvas, and then I want to fuck you with nothing between us."

Her lips parted. A shudder shook through her. "Yes. I'm on the pill. I'm good." She smiled wickedly and then added, "Plus, the paints are nontoxic."

"So am I." The thought of taking her without a condom made him want to roar in satisfaction. "I don't know if I can be gentle tonight." The edge of his control blurred, and for the first time in his life, he felt as if he were more animal than man, and he wanted to dive deep into the pool of desire he'd never experienced before.

She breathed out his name and reached for him. "Do it."

He took her mouth, his tongue gathering her taste, drowning in the sweet, spicy essence of her. He lowered her slowly to the hard floor, and she lay spread out for him, thighs parted, breasts and belly smeared with a gorgeous palette of colors like an artistic gift. He quickly stripped, dipping his fingers into powder blue, then knelt in between her legs.

He painted her with broad, brushing strokes, tracing intricate patterns over her legs and damp inner thighs, digging into her hips until she moaned, arching under each stroke like a cat begging for more. He worshipped every inch of her body and used colors that dazzled his vision—canary yellow, blush pink, deep violet—and then he spread her wide and dipped his mouth to taste her.

His name spilled from her lips in a chant. He licked and teased, sucking gently on her clit, savoring every dark, weeping secret of her pussy. He curled his fingers the way she liked it and thrust hard, his tongue flicking the throbbing nub, and she came against his lips, body writhing beneath his hands and mouth.

He moved up her body, dragging her hand over his front to gather the paint, then pressed her fingers against his chest. "Touch me," he commanded, wanting her own mark on him. "Show me what you want."

With a snarl, she was suddenly everywhere, squeezing his cock, sinking her nails into his shoulders, her teeth and tongue and lips covering him with her own brand, and when he was out of his mind, he grasped her knees, pushed them upward, and surged into her hot, tight channel with no barrier between them.

He pressed his forehead to hers. Breathing hard, he stared deep into her eyes and saw it all—the same expression that was on the woman's face in the painting: the ultimate surrender. The words came up from his very soul, but he pushed them back at the last moment, swallowing them back into the locked trunk to stay, but the truth was in his body with every thrust, with every locked gaze, with every whisper of her name.

He loved her.

He felt her breaking apart and let himself go, his mouth covering hers and capturing every sweet cry. As they came down, he refused to leave her, his mind furiously committing to memory the soft, loving look on her face as she gazed at him, the swollen curve of her lips, the wet silky clench of her body still holding him tight inside, the gentle strokes of her hand on his back.

He blinked furiously, feeling the sting behind his eyes, and without a word, slid out of her.

He eased her upward and turned off the music. After guiding her to the bathroom, he turned on the shower and stepped in with her. He washed her with gentle motions, rinsing the paint from her skin and hair, lingering over the tender parts where his body had marked hers.

When they were both clean, he took out a fluffy towel and dried her thoroughly. Then led her to bed, tucking her in like a child.

She said nothing, just lifted the covers to welcome him. He notched his body beside her in the perfect spoon position, then pressed a kiss to her damp hair.

He slept, knowing that tonight had changed everything for him, but the ending was still the same.

♥ ♥ ♥

Taylor woke up slowly and then stretched. Memories of last night flickered past her, and she turned to see Pierce still sleeping. With careful motions, she untangled her body from his hard warmth and then slipped on soft flannel pants and a tank. She padded out to the kitchen and made the strongest coffee possible to help her with a hangover that had nothing to do with alcohol.

She saw herself spread out on the floor, her body covered in paint, Pierce rising above her like a conquering warrior. They'd lost control and had taken the sex to a new level. Uneasiness stirred. The scene had meant more than some good orgasms. They'd connected in a way she hadn't thought possible—not with her boundaries. For so long, she'd just figured it was the way she was built—she was unable to give her all to anything or anybody but her painting. She'd made peace with it.

Now, she'd found the whole thing was a lie.

Because last night, she'd given her all to Pierce.

Biting her inner cheek, she analyzed how to handle him this morning. Would it be better to pretend it had been just a normal night of sex? What could she possibly say, anyway? That she'd cracked herself open like an egg and poured herself all over him in a messy, liquid spill? Better to move on and tuck the whole evening away in her mental vault. After all, she'd been deep in her work, and he'd been half-asleep. Things like this sometimes happened—they'd been in a vulnerable, open state and had taken advantage.

Satisfied with her analysis, she poured the two mugs, and on cue, he appeared before her.

God, he was sexy. And naked. Mussed dark hair spilled over his shoulders. Sleepy green eyes blinked in the morning light. A half-curved smile rested on his lips as if he, too, remembered the details of last night and was enjoying every single one. Lean muscles and toasty-brown skin on full display. Hips wide, stance powerful, comfortable in his nakedness in the middle of her kitchen.

A shiver shook through her, and his smile widened. Arrogant ass. She decided to take him down a notch. "Coffee's ready. Hey, did you end up carrying me to bed last night? I don't remember much."

He gave a husky laugh and took the mug she offered. "Too bad. We'll have to do it again, then."

She gave a little humph and slid onto the stool, concentrating on the hot brew.

"Want some eggs?" he asked, opening her refrigerator and sorting through the items. "I can make us a cheese omelet."

He knew she was a sucker for a hot breakfast someone else had made. She despised cooking and thought the entire production was a waste. Pierce wasn't good at it, either, but he could pull off simple stuff.

"Can you put onions and peppers in it, too?" she asked.

He chuckled. "Sure." He moved around the cabinets, grabbing the skillet and oil and then chopping up the veggies.

She drank her coffee and watched him, enjoying the view. "You know, you could make a lot of money being a naked chef. They hire them for parties."

"I don't have a cute apron," he said, beating the eggs with a fork.

"I'll get you one. Something frilly to show off your very fine ass."

He winked. "Since half of Cape May already saw my ass, I doubt people will want to pay for a second showing. Did you move the salt and pepper?"

She pointed to the upper cupboard. "There. Bella said all my spices were expired and I needed to behave like a grown-up, so she bought me a new rack."

"Ah, I should do that with my kitchen."

She snorted. "You barely have any spices. The only reason I do is because Bella buys them for me."

"That's true. Cheddar or mozz?"

"Cheddar."

"Your painting is extraordinary."

She froze, her mug halfway to her lips. "You think?"

He turned and gave her a look that stripped away her barriers and dove deep. "I know. There's so much there, Taylz. It will be a perfect final piece."

Lightness spread through her insides. "Thanks."

"Welcome." He paused. "You haven't had any artist's block lately."

"No. I guess my bitchy muse decided to finally behave."

He tilted his head, regarding her thoughtfully. "I love all your paintings, but the ones you've done the past few weeks are on another level. They seem to have more . . ." He trailed off, then ducked his head. "Never mind."

"No. More what?"

A tingle rose up her spine as he gave her the words almost reluctantly. "Emotion. You seemed to have tapped into this huge well of emotion that makes the paintings extraordinary."

Suddenly, she ached to hold him. To allow herself to soften against his hard muscles and let go.

She ducked her head, trying to hide her emotions. "That means a lot," she said gruffly.

When she looked back up, he was smiling at her, as if he knew she'd gotten shy over the compliment.

Taylor blew out a breath and fell back into her comfort zone. "I don't like mine burnt, remember?"

"I remember." He slid the omelet out of the pan, looking proud of himself. "I'm getting better."

"You are, but I think you need more practice. Maybe a few dinners under your belt."

He shook his head and began cooking his own. "You wish. As long as we have Bella, we'll never starve." Bella was the best cook in the family and invited him over regularly to eat with everyone. Taco Tuesday was his favorite night.

He plated his omelet, and they ate together in companionable silence, enjoying their food. She wondered if there'd ever be another man who knew her as well. Maybe that was why long-term dating was hard for her. All those new things to explore with another man intrigued so many women, but she'd rather be with someone who knew her quirks and what pissed her off, and liked her anyway. It certainly saved a lot of time, especially if you were crafting long, detailed summaries to impress strangers on dating sites. Bella had always said she'd be better off with a matchmaker because Taylor was too impatient to experiment.

"What are you thinking about?" he asked, refilling her mug.

"Thanks. Just how much I hate dating."

He grinned. "No one likes dating. But if we didn't do it, the population would die."

"I think people should just know right away how they feel and not waste time. All this compromising and angst and guessing if the guy is gonna call or not pisses me off."

"You date a lot," he pointed out. "Last year, you were out every weekend with someone different."

She scowled. "I'd decided to give it a real try. Figured the more men I met, the better the odds I'd meet someone I could stand for more than a night."

"Guess I'm the only one who succeeded," he said smugly.

She laughed. "Guess so, Mr. Arrogant."

"Hey, you're the one who keeps telling me how nice my ass is." He winked, got up, and did a little shimmy. "Plus, I got the moves."

He was so silly and nerdy and sexy that she began to actually giggle. Then she heard a sound, and the rest happened in slow motion.

"Aunt TT, Mama said I need fruit in my lunch box, but we ran out, so can I have a—Pierce! Hi, Pierce, are you here for breakfast?" Zoe's high voice echoed through the kitchen.

"Zoe, I told you to knock—oh my God!" Bella grabbed her daughter and turned her around, giving Pierce just enough time to duck behind the high counter.

Taylor froze, staring at her sister and niece in sheer panic, realizing she had a naked man hiding in almost full view in the middle of her kitchen.

Holy. Shit.

"Mama, look, Pierce is here!" Zoe said brightly, trying to wriggle out of Bella's arms.

Had she seen anything? Hopefully, Pierce had ducked in time, and her niece had missed an early biology lesson.

"Um . . . yes . . . isn't that great?" Bella stammered, eyes wild in her face as she glanced back and forth between them. "But, um, they're doing some grown-up things now, so we'd better go."

"How come Pierce doesn't have a shirt on?" Zoe asked. She swiveled her head, obviously wondering where he'd gone. "Pierce! Where are you?"

A lone hand raised above the granite countertop. "Hi, Zoe." His head bobbed up. A sick smile twisted his lips. "How ya doing?"

"Good. I came to get fruit for my lunch. Where are your clothes?"

Taylor suddenly came to life, springing from her chair and laughing a bit manically. "Pierce came over for breakfast and spilled food on his outfit," Taylor explained, giving her sister the stink eye. "He's waiting for them to come out of the laundry. Do you want strawberries or apples?"

"Strawberries, please. Once I got peanut butter on my pink sparkle shirt, and I cried 'cause I thought it was ruined forever, but Mama fixed the whole thing, so don't worry, Pierce."

"I won't, sweetheart."

Taylor shoved a carton of strawberries into her sister's hands. "Here you go! Well, you'd better get moving, or you'll be late for school."

"Okay. Bye, Aunt TT. Bye, Pierce!"

"Bye," Pierce called out weakly.

Bella pursed her lips. "I'll talk to you later."

Taylor winced at the threat in her voice. "Boy, I can't wait."

With one last lingering look, her sister escorted Zoe out and shut the door.

Pierce stood up and groaned. "We are in so much trouble."

Taylor tapped her lip in thought. "We can deny it. Say your clothes really were in the laundry."

"Are you kidding me? They're a bunch of sharks—they'll eat us alive."

"I can handle my sisters. The guys won't care."

Pierce arched a brow. "You're temporarily delusional. Carter and Gabe are worse than your sisters. They live for gossip. I'll be getting a call or text within fifteen minutes as the news spreads."

She covered her face in her hands. "You're right. Shit. We're doomed."

"Let's get our stories to match. They're all going to be mad we didn't tell them."

"I know! Okay, we tell the truth. We got super drunk one night, had sex, and decided to just keep having fun until I go away. It means nothing. We're still best friends, and this is just an extra bonus for a temporary time."

"Sure." His gaze drilled into hers. "Because that's the truth, right?"

Her chin lifted, and Taylor lied to her best friend. "Yes, it's the truth."

"Then we'll be fine. I'd better shower and get dressed. It's gonna be a long day."

She watched him walk out of the kitchen with a shred of regret, but she didn't know what to do or say to change it.

Better to leave things be.

She could handle her sisters.

Chapter Fifteen

"You lying little slut. Tell us everything."

Bella's usual calm demeanor had been replaced by an almost rabid need for information as she sat in Taylor's kitchen and drank her chardonnay. Taylor didn't even bother to look to Avery for help. Her oldest sister sat beside Bella and used silence as her way of torturing out the gossip. Her gaze was direct, probing, and a bit scary.

God, what a day. They'd both texted within minutes of Bella finding Pierce naked, demanding a meeting that night. Then Pierce had called and said the guys were taking him out for beers and to talk.

Another drawback from living in a small beach town—everyone cared way too much about other people's lives.

Taylor held back a sigh and decided her usual direct approach would work best. "It's simple, really. One night we ended up getting drunk, and I crashed at his place like I usually do, but this time we got physical and slept together. Afterward, we talked it out and decided to continue the benefits portion of our friendship until I leave for Paris. We both know it's temporary, and it doesn't mean anything. That's why we wanted to keep it a secret—both of us didn't want anyone thinking this had changed our relationship." Proud of her summary, she took a sip of wine and stared at her sisters.

"Bullshit," Avery said.

Bella regarded her thoughtfully. "Interesting. You're both in denial."

A sliver of uneasiness slid down her spine. "What are you talking about? I just told you the truth!"

"Your sanitized version of the truth," Avery said. "You and Pierce have always been like a married couple without the romance. You can't tell me introducing sex into your relationship hasn't changed anything."

Taylor blinked. "It hasn't. Everything has been exactly the same, in addition to some amazing orgasms."

Her sisters shared a look, then did something that horrified Taylor. They laughed.

Holding on to each other, they laughed uncontrollably until they both wiped tears from their eyes. Irritation bit at her like a snake.

She stood up. "I'm glad you think this is so damn funny. You're the ones who barged into my house demanding answers. If you want to make up your own stories to believe, go ahead, but leave me out of this. And leave me my damn wine, too."

Avery waved her hand in the air. "Sit down. God, you have the worst temper. I'm sorry, T, we didn't mean to make fun of you. It's just that you're so good about confronting both of us on our bullshit—it's amazing you can't call out your own."

Taylor sat down, her shoulders stiff. "Whatever. Pierce and I understand each other. I'd just appreciate it if you'd keep this to yourselves."

"Sure. How long has this secret affair been going on?" Bella asked.

"About six weeks."

"Wow, you guys were sneaky. I had no idea," Avery said, looking impressed.

"And you wouldn't have if Zoe listened to my constant requests to knock first."

Bella winced. "Sorry, that's on us. I had to deal with endless questions about what type of food must have spilled on him because all of his clothes were missing. Thank God she didn't say anything about his manly parts."

Avery raised a brow. "Impressive?"

Bella nodded. "Very."

Taylor snorted. "You have no idea."

This time, when they laughed, she laughed with them.

Avery spoke up. "Listen, we're not against some friendly hookup that's safe and consensual. But I think you're lying to yourself. There's not a lot of people you open up to, and Pierce has a special place in your heart. Though it may sound cool and manageable to add sex to the mix, I think you have real feelings for him. As more than a friend."

Her usual instinct to deny died on her lips. Her sister's words hit her like a sucker punch, driving the breath from her lungs. Images flashed before her eyes.

His hands all over her naked body, smeared with paint.

His fiery gaze burning possessively into hers.

The ferocity and tenderness of their lovemaking as she shattered in his arms.

Taylor shoved the memory aside and shrugged. "He's not. I'm gone in two weeks and plan to stay overseas for at least a year. He's staying in Cape May. We want different things. This is black and white here, and we both have our eyes wide open. Okay?"

She knew her sisters didn't believe her but were smart enough not to push. "Okay," Bella said. "But I have a caveat here you're going to listen to."

"What?" Taylor asked.

"If you find things have changed, and you're struggling with new feelings you don't know what to do with, you call me or Avery. Don't be alone in this. We've both gone through some rough transitions with the men we love, and you helped both of us. We deserve a chance to help you if you need it. Deal?"

She was touched by their obvious concern, and her irritation died. "Deal," she said.

"Good. Now that we've got the emotional stuff out of the way, it's time to share the other details," Avery said briskly. "Namely, on a scale of one to ten, how good is the sex?"

Taylor took a sip of wine and slowly grinned. "Fourteen."

"Now you're just bragging," Bella said.

"You and Gabe did it four times in one night," Avery reminded. "That's bragging."

A dreamy look came into Bella's blue eyes. "Oh yeah. I forgot. That's the night I threw away my vibrator."

Taylor laughed. "What about you, Avery? Do you think marriage will slow you and Carter down?"

Avery smiled smugly. "Not if last night was any indication."

Bella sighed. "Guys, we're all so lucky! Last year, we didn't have any of this, and now, look. We're all getting some, and it's first class!"

They burst out laughing and finished their wine.

Pierce met Gabe and Carter at the Ugly Mug for dinner and drinks. They sat at an outside table in the corner where they had some privacy. Thankfully, the conversation had been casual while they ordered a round of cheese sticks and beers, but after the waitress dropped them at their table, he noticed a weird vibe.

They both seemed hurt.

Finally, Gabe brought up the demon in the church. "When Bella told me what she saw, I was really surprised. I mean, I thought we were all pretty close." He shook his head and stared into his beer. "I just don't know why you kept this from us. It feels . . . dirty."

Pierce choked on his own brew and fell into a fit of coughing. He'd been expecting some lighthearted ribbing and high fives. Not this sense of betrayal his two friends seemed to be radiating like a nuclear explosion. "Are you fucking kidding me?" he asked, slamming his beer down on the rickety table. "*Dirty's* supposed to be a good word for us, man! Why are you trying to make me feel guilty?"

"We're not," Carter said. "I just think we expected you to tell us, since we've been asking how you really feel about Taylor for a long time. This is big news and you kept it quiet. You can't blame us for getting thrown off."

It was official. His gang was getting a little touchy-feely. When had this happened to them?

Pierce tugged on his ear in frustration. "I told you, this whole thing happened on impulse. We were drunk. We had sex. We decided to keep having sex until she goes off to Paris. Nothing's really changed between us."

His friends shared a pointed look, then refused to meet his eye. "Sure," Carter said. "We believe you."

"No, you don't. You're pulling some Oprah shit with me! Why don't you just say what you mean?"

Gabe cleared his throat. "You love that woman, dude. Always have. Now you're suddenly having sex and pretending nothing's changed, but I can already tell things are different. It's obvious when we look at you."

"Yeah, you look . . . happy," Carter said.

"I was happy before," Pierce grumbled, pissed off at this intimate exchange he wasn't prepared for.

"Not like this," Gabe said. "Maybe it's because you finally got what you want. Or *who* you want."

Ah, crap. His friends knew the truth he swore he'd never admit to anyone.

He loved Taylor Sunshine.

He thought of their lovemaking in her art room. The passion and connection. His hands painting over her while she fell apart with such a raw openness that he wanted to devour her whole. When she'd made that comment about the sex not meaning anything, it had stung worse than he'd expected. He sensed she'd also experienced a shift in the bond between them—the vulnerability and trust they shared—but he'd convinced himself there was nothing to do but let it go.

Admitting it to Gabe and Carter wouldn't change the outcome. In fact, it just might make everything worse. Denial was a beautiful thing, and he was going to wholeheartedly embrace it.

"Taylor is heading to Paris," he said firmly. "Even if the exhibit doesn't work out—which it will—she plans to travel and paint for a year. My business and life are in Cape May. We've both accepted we need to go our separate ways. Adding sex to our relationship is just an extra bonus. In two weeks, we'll break that off and remain close friends. I think you've noticed me being happier because I'm trying to make some changes in my own career. Decided to do some freelance work in a new niche for me. I'm feeling good about it."

"So it's work and not Taylor," Carter stated, as if he were a court stenographer and Pierce were on record. "She has nothing to do with that goofy-assed grin and the spring in your step?"

"Did you get brainwashed by some self-help guru?" Pierce asked, annoyed. "What am I, fucking Tigger?"

Gabe smothered a laugh. "I always pegged you as Rabbit."

Carter frowned and regarded Gabe. "You have Rabbit tendencies, too."

"Nope, I'm Pooh all the way. Kind of the leader in this crew," Gabe said.

"I'm Pooh," Carter said coolly. "You're really Piglet. Definitely the nurturer in the group."

"Fuck you. I'm no Piglet."

Pierce let out an annoyed breath. "Can we get off this ridiculous subject and all agree I've got this handled? I'm sorry for not telling you. Taylor and I decided it would be best to keep it a secret exactly for this reason. We didn't want anyone getting confused about our relationship."

"I don't think we're the confused ones," Carter said. "But we respect your decision."

"Thanks."

"You know, Luis found her a permanent place to stay rent-free, if they both feel the exhibit goes well," Carter said.

"Wow. Luis will really finance her to stay in Paris to paint?" Gabe asked curiously.

"Yes, if there's interest. He's got a lot of connections, and he's well known for investing in new artists with promise. Taylor's work is something fresh. I knew it the moment I saw that first painting." He narrowed his gaze on Pierce. "I'm just telling you, if all goes well, she'll be away for a long time. Luis has galleries in Milan and Switzerland. He'd make sure she becomes a household name overseas."

He nodded, his throat tightening. "What about New York?"

Carter's gaze sharpened, but his tone was mild. "Maybe eventually, but his plan seems to revolve around a European audience for a while. Lovers or friends, I'm just saying it's going to be hard to lose her."

Pain slashed through him, hard and fast and sharp, but he kept a smile pasted on his face. "It will. But she's been talking about this since college. It's what she's always wanted."

Their dinners came, and they dug into crab-cake sandwiches. Pierce dumped slaw on his, handing his tomato to Gabe, and they settled into easier dialogue based on sports, work, and good-natured ribbing.

"Bella was revved up tonight," Gabe said. "I feel bad for Taylor having to face their intense questions."

"Avery, too. She's like a drill sergeant."

"What do you think they're talking about?" Gabe asked curiously. "You don't think they're all analyzing their sex lives with us, do you?"

Carter shuddered. "Never."

"They're probably talking about emotions," Pierce said dismissively. "I guarantee they'd never discuss sex with each other."

"Yeah, you're right," Gabe said. "It's not like they'd rank us in bed or anything. That would be too weird, especially since I'd win."

"Sure, Piglet, you go on believing that," Carter said.

Gabe glared. "Have either of you ever been named Beach Bachelor? I didn't think so."

"You're officially retired now," Pierce said with a grin. "Why don't we just call it even?"

Gabe reluctantly agreed, and they finished their food.

Pierce thought of Taylor and her sisters' inquisition and hoped she'd been able to manage as well as he had, even though his friends' comments now stuck in his head like a mantra, pushing him to question everything he'd believed.

But it didn't matter. The stage was set, and he refused to change the rules now.

Even if his heart wanted to protest.

Chapter Sixteen

It was done.

Taylor put down her brush with trembling hands. Her body was slick with sweat from the broken central air and the final, brutal push to complete her last painting. She pushed her hair from her face and stepped back, surprised to find one word pop into her mind to describe it.

Disturbing.

She picked at her thumbnail and pondered the result. The past several days' worth of work had finally paid off. She could have sworn the features of the mysterious man would have been revealed in the last painting, but his face was still in shadow. The woman's face was completely clear, an odd combination of features that seemed not to fit—pointy chin, slashed cheekbones, and jet-black, fine, straight hair falling past her shoulders.

The woman was nude. Her high, small breasts and gently curving stomach were touched in silhouette. Her head was turned toward the onlooker instead of the man, as if to admit her weakness in love. Her eyes were dark brown, too wide, and filled with a begging humility that made Taylor squirm with discomfort. She was embarrassed for the woman. Upset that the female who'd haunted her dreams had stripped all her strength away to get on her knees to beg for the love of a man who might not return it. Taylor didn't understand how she could have transferred such raw emotion when, inside, she knew she'd never allow that type of vulnerability in her own life.

The background was a bedlam of broken flowers in a rich palette that immediately arrested attention. The vibrant colors saturated the canvas, almost blinding to the eye. Where before the settings had been dark, stormy, and bleak, this was an explosion of joy, madness, and raw passion.

Nothing she'd painted made sense to her, but on an instinctual level, she knew it was good. Very good. Somehow, she'd tapped into an emotion that had overtaken her consciousness, and that was where good art came from for her.

Her nerves jumpy with too much caffeine and the culmination of endless work, she cleaned her brushes and set her workroom back in order. After a shower, she got into real clothes and decided to treat herself to lunch and a walk by the beach. She craved sun, people, and noise in order to banish the tangle of feelings that simmered beneath her surface. Time to get back to the confident, badass attitude she was comfortable with.

She headed to Harry's and sat at the bar, sipping her favorite cocktail, the orange crush. The spread of beach and ocean made the perfect view from the upper deck, and she relaxed for a few minutes, listening to the mindless chatter around her.

"Taylor! Girl, I haven't seen you in a while. Where have you been hiding?"

She turned and smiled at the waitress, Kimmie. "In my workroom, barely seeing the sun."

Kimmie laughed. "Yeah, I can see that from your lily-white skin! You look like a tourist. What can I get you?"

"Salad with grilled shrimp, please. How's school?"

Kimmie was a part-time finance student. Her pretty features, gorgeous braided hair, and rockin' figure paired with a brain that solved complicated equations and pegged a stock report better than a Wall

Street executive could. Taylor knew Kimmie would be filthy rich one day, and Taylor intended to invest all her money with her once she got her official license.

Kimmie blew out a breath. "Hard. Last night, I had a dream that a bunch of numbers came to life and beat the crap out of me. It feels like I'll be doing this forever."

"You only have one year left, and then you can finally live the life you dreamed."

She shot her a grateful smile. "Yeah, I gotta concentrate on the end result and try not to hate the journey so much. When do you leave for Paris?"

"The fifteenth."

"And you'll be back for Avery's wedding?"

"Definitely. Then I'll head back and either stay in Paris or do some traveling."

Kimmie whistled. "Nice. About time you got out of here. Oh, hey, that means Pierce will be a hot commodity! I already have a girlfriend I'd love to set him up with."

She frowned with confusion. "Huh?"

"Pierce. You know, your best friend who's attached to your hip?" Kimmie laughed and shifted her weight. "Girl, no one else has a chance with you around. The last two women he hooked up with couldn't compete and gave up. I bet the day you fly out, he'll get hit up big-time."

"I don't understand. Pierce and I are just friends. We've always dated other people with no problem."

Kimmie arched a brow. "Says you, but the whole town knows how it really is. Hey, I think it's awesome you guys are so close. But a woman who's serious doesn't want to come in second to the best friend—you know? Anyway, this'll be perfect. You'll end up with some hot French guy, and I'll take care of our local man for you. Crap, I gotta get your order in—sorry! It was great to catch up."

She hurried off, and Taylor busied herself with her phone, trying to pretend her world hadn't just tilted upside down. My God, was this what everyone thought about them? She'd always encouraged Pierce to date, and vice versa. Apparently, they'd given off an entirely different impression.

At least Kimmie didn't seem to think they were sleeping together. She'd specifically used the term *best friends*, which they were. Maybe Kimmie was overreacting and others didn't think that way. Plenty of women had asked her straight up if she and Pierce were together, and she'd always said no, backed off, and invited them to give their luck a try.

How did that seem possessive?

Her thoughts spun out of control. Should she tell Pierce? He'd probably be just as shocked as she was. Or maybe they'd both end up laughing their asses off about it and toss the silly observation to the side.

She ate her salad, settled her check, and walked home, briefly wondering if she'd been the main obstacle to Pierce finding lasting love. He'd always been clear in his intention to settle down and get married. He wanted kids. Had she been subconsciously stopping him from those dreams, afraid she'd be left alone?

A shiver shook through her even as the sun burned her skin. Normally, she'd dig deeper into the theory, maybe even discuss it with Pierce. But with such a short time left, did it really matter? Soon he'd be free to pursue anyone and not have to worry about anyone else's opinion but his own.

Maybe this whole thing had been fated to happen to them. After all, something this good couldn't be real or lasting. It was just the thrill of temptation and secrecy, combined with being so comfortable with each other. There was no "getting to know you" period or awkward conversations about what one liked or didn't. Just great sex, trust, and perfect companionship.

It was easy. Too easy.

When she got home, Taylor was calm. She decided she wouldn't mention it to Pierce. The paintings would be sent overseas, and soon she'd be packing for Paris. It was silly to worry now. They didn't have much time left.

She wanted to make it perfect.

♥ ♥ ♥

"Ready for some touring?" Pierce asked.

Samantha shot him a sunny smile. "Definitely! I'm so happy you called and offered to show me around. I hope you're not taking time out of your schedule because you pity me."

He laughed and pulled away from the curb, heading out. "Of course not. Actually, you're helping me. I have to finish up a series of photographs I'm working on for a magazine, and I'm seriously lacking inspiration. Figured we'd hit the road and do some exploring together. You'll learn more about Cape May, and I'll get some new shots."

Sam settled in the seat with a sigh. "Sounds perfect. I was starting to take on extra shifts out of boredom. Plus, I'm worried about the smell."

"What smell?"

"Tacos. I go home and all I smell is tacos."

He grinned. "Well, I figured we'd grab lunch at a popular spot known for their organic, fresh food. You'll have to do without salsa and guac for a day."

"Thank God."

They fell into easy chatter as he drove deeper into West Cape May. Sam's personality was open and warm. With her long dark hair caught up in a simple ponytail, and her outfit of denim shorts, white cotton blouse, and Keds, she reflected a woman who was comfortable in her own skin. She'd been on his mind, and he'd reached out on impulse, figuring he'd enjoy her company and be able to help her feel more comfortable in her new hometown.

He turned onto Stevens Street, passed the sign that announced their arrival at Beach Plum Farm, and parked. They climbed out of the car, and he grabbed his equipment, hoping he'd be able to nail down his final selections for the *Escape* collection before deadline. He didn't want to lose his second paid gig that had nothing to do with weddings.

"This is incredible," she breathed, taking in the sprawl of farmland and the rustic brown Amish barn that held buckets of charm. "I had no idea this was here."

"There's a ton of hidden places on the Cape. Best thing to do is rent a bike and just poke around, but we need a car today for the other spot I want to take you."

"I can't wait to explore."

"Then let's hit it."

They took the walking path to the main farmhouse. Lush green lawns, sculpted shrubbery, twisted wood, and bright bursts of flowers led the way. Patio tables with umbrellas had been set up, with small groups of people hanging out, snacking on treats, and enjoying the day. Inside, long wooden tables allowed patrons to eat the farm-fresh produce of the day. The market displayed the wares of local vendors who made jams, honeys, pastas, and wine. Fresh fruit and herbs were held in baskets, and the two-level store boasted an array of vendors offering household goods, towels, signs, and body creams and soaps.

Sam squealed in pleasure, turning around with wide eyes. "I have died and gone to heaven," she announced. "I hope you don't mind women who like to shop, Pierce."

"I always encourage shopping local," he said with amusement. "Do you want me to show you the grounds first or eat?"

"Let's work up an appetite."

He greeted Emma, who worked the kitchen, and Anthony, who ran the farm, chatting briefly with both and introducing them to Samantha.

Then he led her down one of the walking paths toward the marshes. "The farm has sixty-four acres and provides food for the local restaurants," he explained, grateful for the cool shade of the trees from the sun's hot sting. The ground was soft and silent underneath their feet, but the air was filled with a musky, earthy sweetness and the sounds from the endless calls of birds and the scrambling forest creatures playing a lively game of tag.

"It's like a different world," she breathed in amazement. "The closest I've gotten to this is the Bronx Zoo."

"City girl, huh?"

"Born and bred, with the accent to match."

She didn't offer more, and he didn't want to pry. "Well, the Cape May Zoo is a great place to check out, too," he said, lifting his camera to zoom in on an interesting sprawl of wildflowers housing a gorgeous monarch butterfly. His skin tingled at the shot. The colors of insects and flowers blended together like one of Taylor's palettes in her workroom, blurring lines and boundaries. A few seconds later, the butterfly took flight and the moment was gone.

Sometimes, his work resembled magic.

Or at least, chasing it.

They explored the woods, then doubled back to the rear fields. Plots of land were fenced off with various herbs, vegetables, fruit, and flowers being tilled and nurtured.

Suddenly, Sam stopped and let out a cry of delight. "A swing!" she said, pointing down the hill.

He followed her gaze and saw the lone wooden swing swaying gently back and forth in the slight wind. It was tied with rope to a giant oak tree, whose branches hunched over like an old man, offering play and shade to whoever took a seat. He'd seen it before, and though charming, it didn't seem impressive. "Yeah. You can use it if you want."

She took off, springing across the hill toward the tree and then plopping her butt on the wooden plank. Her feet moved a few steps back, and then she launched herself into the air with a delighted laugh. "Oh my God, this is awesome!"

He shook his head, a smile tugging his lips, and moved closer. "Haven't you ever been to a park?" he teased.

"Tons. The city parks are epic, but not like this. Not a swing tied to a tree on a big-ass farm," she called out. Her ponytail bobbed behind her. Her feet pumped back and forth, taking her higher.

Pierce, overcome with a strange impulse, began taking her picture, moving to different angles, catching aspects of light as it dappled through the trees, trying to pin down Sam's playful, childish delight for a simple board tied with rope.

When she jumped off, her cheeks were pink and she was out of breath. "Sorry. I bet you think I'm pretty silly."

"Actually, I think just the opposite."

"Good. Your turn."

He jerked back. "Oh, I don't need to. I've seen this before."

She frowned. "Seen, yes. Swung? I bet no." She took his camera from his grasp, and suddenly he felt naked. "Go. Just for a minute. No one's looking."

He glanced around. She was right. It wouldn't hurt to do it once.

He trudged down the hill, sat on the swing, and began to move. The tiny flip in his belly yanked him back to his childhood, when slides and spinny things and swings ruled. When it didn't matter who was looking because you were always chasing the clouds. He closed his eyes and let himself go, pushing away his foolishness.

And thought about how much Taylor would love this.

When he returned to Sam, she winked. "Told ya."

"You were right. That was awesome."

They grinned at each other. There was no chemistry between them, but a pleasant ease and affection that reminded him of how a sibling would be. Even though she was a relative stranger, he sensed she felt the same.

Pierce showed her the chicken coop, where the fowl ran free. The chickens squawked and showed off and shook their wings, fat red jowls jiggling, making them laugh. Finally, they headed to the market and ordered veggie wraps with goat cheese, herbed potato salad, and mesclun salad with strawberries and walnuts. The lemonade was tart and cold, and they savored the crispness of the bread, the creaminess of the cheese, and the snap of the marinade. They grabbed a chocolate chip cookie to split for the road and headed back out.

He drove down Ocean Drive and spent the next few hours showing her his favorite hangouts and introducing her to everyone they met. Though Sam was shy, she was sweet. He'd already caught his friend Nick's lovestruck expression and figured he'd soon get a call, begging him for her number. In each new place, Samantha found something she loved that he'd either forgotten about or had taken for granted. Seeing things through her eyes helped remind him why the Cape was special.

The last stop at the end of the evening was Higbee Beach. It was a wildlife paradise with two miles of nature trails, dunes, scrub shrubs, and ocean. It was a sanctuary to various animals, especially a large variety of birds, depending on the season, but Pierce hadn't gone in a while. As he led Sam on the long track from the parking lot through the woods and dunes, he remembered why he loved it so much. There was an untamed wildness here that the other more civilized beaches on the Cape lacked.

"This seems more like a hiking trip than a beach," Sam commented, huffing a bit as they headed through the lush foliage.

"This place is unique. It's off the beaten path. There's no lifeguards, beach-tag checks, or crowds. You'll see."

He took a few photographs, allowing the setting to saturate him in order to guide him to the right shots. They came out from the trail and stopped.

"Oh my," she said.

Yes. It had that effect on people sometimes.

Dogs walked on leashes or bounded in the surf, playing with balls and sticks and various fetch items. A few beach chairs had been set by the water, some way back on the edge of the trees, and others close to the craggy, slick black rocks. A woman on horseback guided her filly through the mild waves, the horse's head bobbing up and down as she held her place in the saddle. An older couple with binoculars and muted-colored bird shirts wandered from the trails, engaged in a lively discussion as they pointed back and forth.

It was a haven for misfits, which made for the best type of environment because everyone fit in.

Sam squinted in the sun. "Is that guy naked?"

Pierce turned and nodded. The older man perched under an umbrella wore thick black sunglasses, lots of white suntan lotion, flip-flops, and nothing else. "Yeah. It's not officially a nude beach, but people seem to do what they want here. Everything goes, and everyone minds their own business."

"Interesting. While I respect his freedom, I don't need to see his business."

He laughed. "Got it. Let's go over here. There's interesting shells and horse crabs littered on the surf. We can check it out."

They walked down the beach in companionable silence. Sam found a starfish, and after confirming with him that it wasn't dead, she relaxed with relief and forced him to take a ton of photos. A giant flock of birds swooped down in a unified dance, screeching with glee. He watched a young couple caught up in each other, arms wrapped tight, foreheads pressed together, ensnared in an intimate moment of time that might never come again. He caught the shot, changing the focus and light a few times before capturing the magic. After a quick check, he confirmed he wouldn't need a signed release if he used it. The woman's back was turned, and Pierce couldn't see the man's face.

"God, it's all here, isn't it?" Sam murmured, tucking her hands around her stomach and rocking back on her bare feet. "We came from a farm with a forest and marshland. We got to eat from the land and get in touch with nature. Then, a few miles away, we're standing at the edge of the world—where ocean meets sky."

He jerked back, studying her profile. "I guess I never thought of it like that."

"Cape May is an extraordinary place," she said, turning dark, serious eyes on him. "No wonder you never left."

He shifted his feet, suddenly unsure. As much as he loved his home, lately he'd been wondering if his path was leading elsewhere. It wasn't about leaving because Taylor was—it was about connecting to a part of himself that had been too complacent to admit he needed a change. "Sometimes, I wonder if I'm missing out," he said wryly. "I never questioned my desire to stay here and build my own photography business. So many things have kept me stationary, but maybe I need to branch out more."

She nodded. "I've lived in the city my whole life. As much as I appreciated the sheer amount of opportunities I had, from the museums to restaurants to the arts, I always felt out of place. Crowds intimidated me. I craved a quieter setting to think and be me without being swept up constantly in the rat race—bigger, better, faster, now."

"Yeah, I can only imagine how that can burn you out." He tilted his head with curiosity. "What made you pick Cape May?"

She looked out at the ocean with a tiny smile. "I got on the Garden State Parkway and drove to the end. When I hit Exit Zero, I stopped. Found a place to rent. Got a job. Took one suitcase with me. I wanted to start new."

"Were you running from something?"

"No. But maybe I was running toward something. To figure out more about myself, you know?"

Watching Sam today reminded him of the things he'd been missing. The excitement and light of discovery in her eyes as she looked upon his childhood home made him want to experience it himself. It was time to cast his net wider and flourish in new ways. He'd played it safe for too long.

The sun sank. The ocean roared. The gulls screeched and swooped low. The dying light caught the tips of the foamy waves and glistened like fragmented jewels. In that moment, he realized that questioning where he belonged was integral to growth and change. But even if his photography led him away, he'd always come back to Cape May.

Eventually.

"Thanks, Sam."

She cranked her head around. "For what?"

"For helping me see things I couldn't."

She raised her hand with a grin. "Back atcha."

Laughing, he high-fived her, then rubbed his palm from the sting. "Damn, you city girls got some power."

"Don't forget it."

They watched the sunset, and then he drove her home, thinking about what he wanted his future to look like. He went directly to his studio and spent the evening caught up in his darkroom. Drunk on the chemical smell that was like pages to a book junkie, he fell into the experience of watching people and moments come alive before his eyes, a secret voyeur and treasure hunter looking for gold. As the pictures developed, he realized for the first time in a very long while that he was excited again about his work.

Chapter Seventeen

Several days later, Pierce stared at the various portraits he'd picked for the *Escape* collection.

Samantha gripping the worn ropes, feet high in the air, ponytail thrown back behind her as she reached for the stars, a delighted smile curving her lips.

A couple caught up with each other with quiet wonder while the sun sinks over the horizon at Higbee Beach.

Marcus's grandmother sitting on a bench, large eyes staring back at the camera without fear or apology—strong and proud—the darkness just a kiss of shadow shrouding her figure.

Zoe amid the vivid colored blooms in front of Avery's magical purple cottage, head bent, eyes closed, as she smelled a bunch of wildflowers, her pink dress billowing around her like a ball gown.

Yes. These were the ones that called to his soul. Parts of life that blended and blurred lines of emotion against the backdrop of nature.

Fierce satisfaction thrummed in his veins. Suddenly, he couldn't wait to go and explore more. The world cracked open with limitless ideas and opportunities, and he laughed out loud, freeing his burst of emotion.

"Never drink or laugh alone," Taylor drawled behind him. Her sandals flip-flopped against the floor as she made her way beside him. "You sound like a madman. What's going on?"

He turned with a grin and pointed to the photos laid out in a neat line. "Look."

She did. He watched her face greedily, both for pleasure and to catalog her reaction. He loved the hungry way she looked at his work. She always got him, needing no words, and a sharp ache hit him when he thought of not having her in his studio on a regular basis.

"These are extraordinary," she breathed, shaking her head. "Pierce, you're on a whole new level here."

Pleasure washed through him. "I feel it, too. This is for the *Escape* collection I'm sending over today. If David likes them, I may get more freelance work."

"I'm so damn proud of you," she said, her voice husky.

A shock of energy sizzled between them, and for a few seconds, he craved her naked body under his hands, his mouth on hers, his dick buried so deep inside her that she'd never question if he belonged there. The past week, they'd made love even more passionately, never skipping a day, using her departure as a sign to be greedy with one another.

The burning need for her was happening more often now, this knowledge that an innocent bargain had turned dangerous. Real feelings beat beneath the smooth surface, ready to break through. A tremble shook him, and he stepped back at the sheer intensity of it. So did she.

Taylor cleared her throat. "Wanted to invite you to Taco Tuesday tonight. Our celebration dinner before I leave."

"I'll be there. You have everything set?"

She shrugged, but he caught the worry lines on her face. "Yes. The paintings have been shipped, and I'm almost done packing."

"You never showed me the final painting."

Her cheeks turned a shade of pink he rarely saw. "I know. It kind of poured out of me and was a bit raw, so instead of second-guessing myself, I just packed it all up and sent it."

He understood. It must have been deeply personal, and he was happy she'd dug so deep. He wished he could have seen it. "Just remember my wall looks bare and pathetic now. Don't sell my painting," he teased.

"I promised, didn't I?"

"Yeah, you did." They stared at one another in silence. He felt her nervous energy and tried to help. "You know what they tell artists, right? The only thing you can control is the quality of your work. Of doing your best at the time—no more. Then it's out of your hands and doesn't belong to you anymore. Do you feel good about what you painted?"

Her body relaxed, and her slow smile was like the first trickle of dawn illuminating the darkness. "Yeah, I do."

"Then the rest is out of your control. It's time to enjoy the ride."

She jerked her chin toward the photographs. "I should say the same for you. Your point of view is changing. No more weddings."

"I'll finish up my commitments, but yeah, I'm taking a break from new clients. You know, I've been restless for a while. Couldn't figure out why. But yesterday, it was like I saw Cape May for the first time, through a clear lens, and I fell in love with this town all over again."

Her hand reached out and linked with his. He wondered at the strange look of sadness flickering over her face. "Because this is your home. It owns your heart."

He opened his mouth to share his newest realization—that as much as he loved his beach town, he was ready to explore other settings and allow his creativity to blossom; for the first time, he craved travel and new experiences, and wondered if he'd been so stuck in what he imagined his life would be that he hadn't given himself permission to change his mind and alter course. But before he could speak, she'd stepped into his arms. He sank into her, kissing her deeply, savoring her taste and texture, trying to show her physically how much she meant to him. God, he wished they'd made this agreement sooner, when they'd had all the time in the world to explore it.

The bell outside tinkled, warning of a visitor, and they stepped apart.

Samantha popped her head in. "Oh! I'm sorry, I didn't know you were with someone."

He smiled and waved her in. "It's okay. I want you to meet Taylor Sunshine. This is Samantha. She works at Key West Tacos and is new here. We met over at Sunset Beach, and she approved me using her as a model."

The women smiled and exchanged a handshake. "Then this is you," Taylor said, pointing at the picture. "It's so beautiful."

"Oh, I didn't do anything. I was just indulging in being a kid again," Samantha said. "He has amazing talent."

"Yes, he does." Taylor shot him an odd look but held the smile. "I'd better get going. I'll see you tonight, Pierce. Nice to meet you." She hurried out the door and left them alone.

Samantha made a face. "I'm really sorry I butted in. I came into town to pick up lunch and figured I'd swing by to thank you for yesterday. Oh my God, is this the rest of your work? It's stunning." She studied the lineup with obvious pleasure. "Are these for your collection?"

"Yes. We'll see if they sell."

"There's no doubt in my mind they will. You have this way of making me feel like I'm right there. How do you capture the light like that? In my picture, it looks like I'm almost ethereal."

"Each time the swing moved, the light danced. I was only chasing it."

"It's a lost art. Everyone uses their phones and computers, but I think we've forgotten so much of the creative process. It's sad."

"It is sad. Makes our lives both easier but also harder. Less pressure to think and dream and figure things out ourselves."

"Yes." She smiled, and he liked the way her entire face lit up. The easy energy between them calmed him. Already, he sensed she'd be a good friend to have. "Well, I'd better head out. Just wanted to tell you again how much I enjoyed yesterday. Let me know if you want to grab coffee or lunch this week." She hesitated, her body rocking back and forth slightly in obvious awkwardness. "I promise I'm not asking you out on a date," she said with a self-mocking laugh. "It was just really nice to feel like I'm a part of this town."

"Don't apologize. I'd love to hang out with you. Saturday works for me. Nine a.m. breakfast? Have you gone to Harry's yet? They have great omelets."

"No, that sounds good. Thanks. See you Saturday!" She bounced out, her ponytail bobbing.

He imagined how hard it would be to be new and need to make friends. Sam was easy to be with, though, and he still expected a text from Nick about asking her out. He'd make sure to try and introduce her to some of the waitstaff at Harry's, too.

The rest of his afternoon consisted of an engagement shoot on the beach. Then he had enough time to shower and change before heading to Bella's. The guys were already there, and he smiled as he crossed the threshold, enjoying the usual chaos of Taco Tuesdays.

Bella and Gabe were in the kitchen, chopping and grilling. Taylor was setting the table. Avery and Carter sipped red sangria and offered advice to Gabe, who wasn't comfortable in the kitchen but was open to Bella teaching him some skills. The scent of onions, peppers, and spicy meat filled the air, and Pierce's stomach growled. He'd forgotten to eat today in his need to put together those photographs.

Zoe rushed over and gave him a big hug. "Hi, Pierce! Did your stains come out of your clothes?"

He pressed his lips together and knelt in front of her. "They did. Thank you for caring—it was my favorite outfit."

"Which one?"

"The light-blue shirt and cool jeans with the holes in them."

"Oh yes, I like those, too. I made some new pictures today with the new coloring book Gabe got me. Wanna see?"

"Of course. One day, you'll be a famous artist like your aunt." Zoe was obsessed with all types of art and loved to practice with Taylor in her workroom.

"I'll get them!"

She rushed off, and he made his way to the kitchen to pour himself some of the homemade sangria.

"Ouch! That hurt!" Gabe yelled, jerking his hand back from the skillet. He glared at the sizzling meat. "How do you get the oil to stop splashing?"

Bella smiled and grabbed the wooden spoon. "Stir evenly and consistently. Do I need to kiss your hand and make it better?"

"Yeah," he huffed, sticking out the offended thumb.

She laughed and pressed her lips to his burnt skin. "There. All better."

Pierce groaned. "Do you even own a man card?"

"Hey, I'm trying, okay? I don't see you doing anything."

"Pierce, can you cut up the tomatoes?" Taylor called out. "I hate doing them. They get messy and pulpy and confuse me."

"Was that your only job for this meal?" he teased.

"No! I made the guacamole!"

He frowned. "That doesn't have tomato in it?"

"Not my kind."

Avery shook her head and handed over the tomatoes, knife, and a bowl to him. "Taylor, what are you going to do in Paris? You literally don't know how to make enough food to survive. We're going to be worried."

Taylor snorted. "Yeah, poor me. I'm stuck in a city where croissants, cheese, pastries, and wine rule the world. I don't think I'll starve."

"You're right. Bitch," Avery said good-naturedly.

"Aunt Avery! You need to put a quarter in the swear jar!" Zoe shrieked, racing in with her two drawings.

Avery winced. "Sorry, honey. Tell Uncle Carter to give you fifty cents."

Carter quirked his brow. "Why me? You're the money in this relationship."

She laughed and kissed him. "You're right. I forgot you were the pretty one."

He grunted, but Pierce caught the look of pure love in Carter's eyes when he gazed at his future wife. Taylor was also watching, and her face softened. Slowly, her gaze swiveled to his, and they stared at one another.

The connection surged and sparked between them. Her golden-brown eyes filled with a need he recognized, and he savored the open expression on her face, letting him know her desire.

An ache settled in his chest. He'd watched Avery and Carter go from cranky enemies to lovers. Then Gabe and Bella struggled to find their way to each other, fighting their own demons to finally accept love. He'd laughed off his friends' comments about his friendship with Taylor, but when he looked at her right now, he saw someone who was more than his lover. It had sneaked up on him so quietly that he hadn't seen it coming. But tonight, watching the other two couples in the room, he realized that he and Taylor had something just like theirs: the promise of a true, forever-love relationship.

If only she didn't have to leave him.

He jerked back and averted his gaze.

"Pierce, what do you think? Which one do you like better?" Zoe asked, spreading out the two pages. One was a princess with a sword, and the other was a dragon breathing pink fire.

He pointed at the princess. "Where's the knight who saves her?"

Zoe tilted her head and stared at him in confusion. "There's no knight."

"Oh. Who kills the dragon?"

She laughed and patted his hand. "The princess, silly. She has her own weapons, and the knight comes later. Gabe said women don't need men to save them—they can do it themselves. Then the knights come later to take them to dinner!"

"Damn right," Gabe said, giving Bella a wink.

"Gabe—swear jar!"

"Sorry, pumpkin. Get it from Mama. She makes all the money, too."

Pierce laughed, and they fell into work mode, finishing the food prep and finally getting everything onto the table.

Avery cleared her throat and stood up at the head of the table. "I'd like to make a toast," she said, her blue eyes serious.

"You don't have to," Taylor protested, seeming to sense what was coming.

"Shush, I want to, and you're just gonna sit there and take it. Lift your glasses, please."

Pierce held back a laugh at Taylor's cranky expression, but she obeyed her sister.

"Next week, Taylor will be in Paris at her first art exhibition. We've always known she was meant to be a great artist, and finally the world will recognize her talents."

"Okay, that's plenty, Avery. Thank you, but—"

"Don't interrupt," Avery growled. "Sunshine Bridal will never be the same without her creativity, energy, wit, and general snarkiness. But it's time for her to follow her dreams, because she helped us achieve ours. Sunshine is stronger and more profitable because of you." His throat tightened when he glimpsed the sheen of tears in Avery's and Bella's eyes. "We love you, we'll miss you, and we'll FaceTime you every Taco Tuesday."

Zoe sniffed. "And I will send you a drawing every week so you won't be lonely."

That did it. He watched Taylor's controlled facade fracture. She blinked rapidly to avoid tears and finally spoke in a husky voice. "Thanks, everyone. I love you, too. And I'm not going away forever, so let's not make this into a big thing where we all get weepy and sloppy. Cheers."

They clinked glasses and began eating in silence. A sad gloom hung over the table, the exact thing he knew Taylor didn't want. It was time to change things up.

Pierce cleared his throat. "Taylz, did you say you made this guacamole?"

She immediately perked up, likely sensing a compliment. "Yep. All by myself. What do you think?"

"I think it's truly . . ." He trailed off, a big smile on his face as he looked at her. "Awful."

She blinked. "That's a lie! I got the recipe from Food Network online! It had forty five-star reviews."

Avery cocked her head. "It does taste a bit funny. Almost like an Italian flavor rather than Mexican. Did you make any switches in the ingredients?"

"Well, only one. It needed cilantro, but I ran out, so I substituted basil." She shrugged. "No biggie. They're both green."

Everyone stared at her in horror. And then they began to laugh.

The rest of the dinner was spent engaged in their usual teasing manner. Gabe and Pierce occupied Zoe with a fun contest to get her to vote for the most charming man, which Zoe declared was a tie. They feasted on strawberry shortcake that Bella had baked—Taylor's favorite—and by the time they'd cleaned up, Pierce was happy to see Taylor looking relaxed.

Avery and Carter left, and Bella and Gabe began to get Zoe ready for bed.

Pierce stacked the last dish in the washer, loaded up the detergent, and started it. Then turned. "Do you want me to stay tonight?" he asked softly.

The rules of asking had blurred in the past weeks until they'd just fallen into a routine of being together. But tonight, he needed to hear the words from her lips.

She regarded him in surprise but seemed to sense what he wanted. "Yes. I want you to stay."

He smiled. "Good. I have a present I want to give you first. I'll meet you downstairs."

He dried his hands on the dish towel, then walked to his car to retrieve the package. He laid it on the coffee table, enjoying her curious expression.

"What is it?" she asked.

"It's a wrapped gift," he said seriously.

She hit him in the arm. "Pierce!"

"Just open it, okay? God, you really do hate surprises."

"True, but I do like gifts." She gave him a grin and pulled off the paper, lifting the book from the remnants. She caught her breath and stroked the fabric cover that read Taylor's Scrapbook.

"Oh, you didn't," she breathed, eyes wide with delight.

"I did. It's for Paris and wherever else your dream takes you."

Silently, she flipped through the pages. They told a story from past to present—a girl with big buck teeth at seven years old, an awkward teen through middle school, joyful Christmases with her sisters and parents, her prideful expression when she won the ribbon for track senior year.

Her hands shook as she got to the end and found a picture of them together at some event, their heads close, arms wrapped tight around each other, smiling goofy and happy as if the camera had been the first one to pick up their true love for each other beyond simple friendship. It had taken him endless hours to decide which pictures to choose, but he'd eventually gone with his gut.

The very last picture was his favorite.

Taylor sat on the yellow couch, knees up, head tipped back, pink hair like a punk-rock halo, laughing up at her sister with an open joy that made the world want to be part of their secret.

She closed the book and looked at him, those golden-brown eyes shining with a hint of tears. "This is the most amazing gift I've ever gotten," she said with a seriousness that shook him to the core. "When did you take that last picture of me?"

"At Zoe's graduation party from kindergarten."

"I look different. I'm not scowling."

He smiled, touching her cheek. "You don't scowl all the time."

"True." A frown creased her brow. "I think that picture is the most beautiful I've ever seen myself photographed."

His gaze locked with hers. "That's the way I always see you."

Her body jolted as if touched by an electrical current.

Without another word, he placed the book back on the table, stood, and took her hand. Their fingers entangled together. "Come with me."

He led her straight to the bedroom. This time, there was no mad rush or craziness to be with one another. He went slow, savoring every catch of her breath, gleam in her eye, and reaction of her body. Clothes fell away. His mouth and hands drifted over her skin. She melted against him, and he carried her to the bed, laying her out before him to worship. They made love with excruciating patience that only added to the need, softening all the edges between them, breaking down the final barriers he'd managed to keep erected. Knowing they had only a few days left added a bittersweet agony to the encounter, but Pierce didn't try to fight it.

When he slipped inside her, it was like coming home. She squeezed him tight, whispering his name, and he gently took her on a ride, refusing to let the sharp hunger take over and determined to accept every bit of pleasure and pain twisted together in one beautiful melody.

She broke apart beneath him, and he watched her face, treasuring the gift. When he let himself go, he gave her all of him in the quiet darkness, allowing the final denial to drift away as he realized that he had always loved her and would continue loving her even after she left.

Quiet, he tucked her into his arms, stroked her hair, and said nothing.

Neither did she.

♥ ♥ ♥

The night before she left for Paris, Taylor stopped at Pierce's house to say goodbye. She had an early-afternoon flight the next day and still had to finish packing and spend time with her sisters and Zoe.

Her mind was clear on the path they'd both chosen, but the idea of walking away with a hug, a farewell, and a decision to go back to being platonic friends made her stomach twist with nausea. As she walked through Pierce's door and he gave her his beloved lopsided grin, Taylor wondered if she could let him go in order to chase her bigger, shinier future. Last night had been earth-shattering—as if they'd stopped being two people and had melded into one. She'd had plenty of weekend flings and had never had problems walking away. She'd always been termed the "guy" in the relationship, because she easily separated sex from emotion. Sex was physical, an act enjoyed by both parties if they had consent and respect. She'd assumed sex with Pierce would be the same, but instead she'd been horribly wrong.

And now she was going to pay.

He handed her a beer and frowned. "You look upset. Are you freaking out about tomorrow?"

She swallowed back the impulse to ask if they could work something out. Maybe they could continue their relationship long distance? She wouldn't be in Paris forever. She'd visit her family often.

But the answer floated up inside her and quieted the urgent voice. *He doesn't want what you want.*

Pierce deserved to pursue his own happiness now. She'd no longer be there to block opportunities for him to find a woman to settle down and raise a family with, and to develop his photography business in a way that would excite him again. And she couldn't stay with him without wondering if one day she'd regret not chasing her own dreams, miles away from his beloved home.

No. This was the only choice they could both make.

"Taylz?"

She shook her head and walked toward the kitchen, taking a sip of beer. "Sorry. My mind's just all jumbled up. I promised Zoe I'd be home early to tuck her in tonight. Bella said she's upset."

"Don't blame her—you guys are super close. But she'll forgive you after her first visit to Paris and you feed her bread and chocolate."

She gave a half laugh. "That's true. At least I'll be back next month for Avery's wedding. Hell, maybe even sooner, if my paintings tank and Luis yanks my free ride."

"That's not going to happen," he said quietly. "You have your plan B, remember? And even though you're scared, I think you know this exhibition will change everything."

"Yes."

"It's what you always wanted." He paused. "Right?"

Her throat tightened. Why did she feel so raw and vulnerable? Pierce was acting perfectly. There was no pressure for her to stay or declare feelings for each other. He was supportive and encouraging of her art. He seemed poised and genuinely happy she was pursuing her dream. She had no right to change the rules at this point, and no idea if she had the guts to try. "Right."

He nodded, ducking his head to stare at his beer. When he looked back up, something flickered in his eyes but was gone in a flash.

Just a trick of the light.

He tipped the bottle up and clinked it to hers. "To the next great adventure."

She accepted the toast and drank. Shifted her weight. "Did you hear back from *Escape* yet?"

He set down his beer and stood with his feet braced apart, his arms tucked into each other. "Yeah, David loved it and asked me to do another spread. It's another beach theme, but flexible, to include portraits."

"For Cape May?"

"No, he wants me to expand, so I'm going to take a few days and do some road trips. Poke around. If something interests me, I may try to get my own collection together to sell. I like the possibilities now that I'm not tied to strictly weddings."

"Makes sense. I'm happy for you." Watching the excitement flicker on his face when he talked about his photography made Taylor feel a sense of joy, knowing how important it was to feel fulfilled. She had an idea he was only getting started with what he could do with his talent.

Just like her.

Too soon, their beers were finished. "I'd better go. They're all waiting for me."

"Don't forget your neck pillow, and take Advil with you in case you get a headache."

"I will."

He walked her to the door. "Text me when you land. I don't want to bother you while you're getting ready for the exhibition, so call me when you have time."

She touched his arm. "You're never a bother." She paused. "You're . . . everything."

His gaze crashed into hers. Suddenly, he was reaching for her, cupping her jaw, his mouth sliding over hers with a delicious precision and tenderness that made tears sting her eyes. She gave in to the kiss, the hot thrust of his tongue, the spicy masculine flavor and scent that swamped her senses. She tried to relay with that last kiss how much she'd miss him. How much she cared. How he was the most important person in her life.

How she loved him.

He eased away and ran the back of his fingers down her cheek. "We had a hell of a ride."

A sad smile touched her lips. "Yeah, we did."

He pressed his forehead to hers. "Bye, Taylz. Love you."

Her voice choked out the words. "Love you, too."

She left and wondered why the pain of what she was leaving behind seemed to override her excitement about the future.

♥ ♥ ♥

The next morning, Taylor was stressed and jumpy but figured she should have something with a good amount of protein before her long flight. After placing a call to Harry's, she headed out to pick up her coffee and favorite crab-and-avocado omelet—made without the basil. She shook her head and smiled as she walked in, thinking again about Pierce.

She'd grabbed her phone to text him a hundred times this morning before placing it back down. They'd said their goodbyes. Chasing him down for another emotional encounter wouldn't help either of them. Still, she craved seeing his face one last time.

Sighing, she stopped at the hostess stand. "Hey, Valerie, I called in a breakfast order and coffee."

The young girl nodded. "Sure, let me go get it. You paid already, right?"

"Yep, all set."

"Be right back."

Taylor leaned against the wall, lost in her thoughts, until a few steady bursts of laughter echoed in the air. Well, someone was happy this morning. Funny, too, the laugh sounded familiar. Almost like . . .

Her gaze swept the restaurant and landed on Pierce. He was at one of the tables behind the bar, engaged in a lively discussion with that Samantha woman he'd introduced her to. One of the waitresses stood by their table, giving a hoot and a high five to Sam, as if they were bonding. Pierce shook his head and said something that made them all laugh again.

God, they seemed so . . . close.

Then it hit her full force: Pierce was already moving on without her.

Her stomach clenched with nausea. She staggered back, desperate to hide her presence, and tried to get her shit together. Maybe it was a final slap of punishment for breaking their sacred blood vow.

"Here you go!" Valerie said cheerfully, giving her a bag and a cup of coffee. "Hey, good luck with Paris. We're all so excited for you."

She smiled sickly and retreated a few steps. "Thanks. So sorry, gotta go, don't want to be late for my flight."

Taylor ran out of Harry's without looking back, the sound of Pierce's laugh still ringing in her ears.

Chapter Eighteen

Paris was a feast for the senses.

Taylor was overwhelmed by the sheer energy and grace of the city. Luis had settled her into a quaint studio apartment near the Eiffel Tower. With a barely there kitchen, white walls, a small, glittery chandelier, and a bed that was also her sofa, it was everything she'd ever need. Luis had cleared one corner to stack a few canvases, easels, and paints. A window led to a small wrought-iron balcony, which held cheerful geraniums and a café table and chair. It overlooked a narrow Parisian street and faced a large yellow apartment building, so she could pretty much raise her glass of wine and toast her neighbor.

She loved every detail.

The first few days had consisted of visiting the gallery, approving the setup, and meeting the other two artists who would also be exhibiting at the show. The space was large and airy, and each of them had their own sections with various spotlights spilling onto their work, bathing it in a glow. The sleek and modern decor of black, white, and red was its own canvas to highlight each artist's specific display.

Luis had set up a dinner for them at a crowded café, where they sipped champagne, ate fish in a lemon-dill sauce, and talked about the art world and their individual experiences. They were all relatively new artists: one from Paris and one from London. Each had a niche that was unique, so there was no duplication of each other's work.

By the time Taylor got to bed, she fell asleep exhausted from the day. With the time change, anticipation, and general busyness, she didn't have time to touch base back home, other than a brief "I got here safely" text. She thought about Pierce a lot, but each time she'd wanted to reach out, something else had come up in her schedule. Besides, she reminded herself, he was now her friend, not her lover. It was best to transition back and not act like she had to check in.

Even though she wanted to.

Each of her paintings had been unpacked and tested endlessly in various display patterns and frames until they'd agreed on what looked best. Taylor learned a lot those next few days about the power of display and marketing, and the best ways to sell. The costs were exorbitant and made her choke the first time she saw them—it was definitely more than that first $250 she'd collected from Carter—but Luis told her the higher, the better. No one appreciated a bargain in art, especially when they were trying to position her as a high-quality artist.

When she finally stood and saw her paintings lined up on the giant wall, her signature scrawled at the bottom-right corner, a premonition rolled through her, almost as if she'd seen this exact scene in a dream. A mix of emotions tumbled through her. It was really happening. In two more days, this room would be filled with people drinking wine and judging her art. She'd be as naked as the woman in the portrait, begging them to love her.

A shudder racked her body. Panic licked at her nerves, but she fought it back, refusing to break now. She was strong, and even if her work was rejected, she had to honestly admit it had been the best she could do.

That would have to be enough.

When she got back to her room, she quickly FaceTimed her sisters, apologizing for the delay. She showed off her studio apartment with its amazing view and chattered about Paris, even though she hadn't been able to do major sightseeing yet other than the Eiffel Tower. She ached to walk the streets and get lost, let her muse take over, and simply surrender to Paris.

When she hung up, loneliness reared up inside, making her want to call Pierce. Her finger paused on the button. Should she, or shouldn't she? Maybe after the art show? He'd planned to fly out to see his parents this week, so he must be in Florida already. She didn't want to interrupt him, even though she knew Catherine and Carl would love to hear from her, too.

She was wrestling back and forth with her decision when suddenly her phone shook with a video call.

It was Pierce.

Smiling in relief, she hit "Accept."

"Hey, I was just thinking about calling you," she said, her gaze hungrily roving over his familiar face.

"That's why my ears were burning," he drawled. "I figured you were slammed this week and had no time. Am I interrupting you?"

"No! I've just been so tired after running around. There's so much stuff I didn't know about. Setting up the display took one whole day. Then they changed their minds on the framing and wanted a few more details cleaned up—it's been endless. But Paris is beautiful."

"I bet. Did you see anything good yet?"

"Just the tower. No time for anything else. Are you in Florida?"

"Florida?"

"Yeah, you're visiting your parents, right?"

"Oh, right, yep. I'm at their house right now."

"Why don't you put them on real quick? I'd love to say hello."

Pierce hesitated, looking behind him. "Um, they're not here right now. They . . . went out."

"Oh, okay. Tell them I said hello."

"I will. Tell me everything so far."

She sat back on her sofa bed and told him every detail since she'd stepped off the plane. He listened with his usual intensity, his gaze slightly narrowing, and he occasionally jumped in to clarify or ask a question. The loneliness that had struck before his call faded away under his gravelly voice and calm demeanor.

Finally, she wound down, breathless. "Sorry, that was a lot."

"No, it wasn't." He hesitated, staring intently into the phone. "I wish I could be there."

His words should have struck her as friendly, but instead, they seeped with intimacy. Need surged up like a tsunami, and she half closed her eyes, struggling not to tell him to jump on a plane and get here right now. "I wish you could, too," she finally said. "Have you taken any good pictures this week?"

"Some. I was in Delaware for a day, then Ocean City. Caught one with a little boy covered in blue cotton candy. His parents were scolding him, and he had this expensive-type short set on with a matching hat—looked like he should be on the tennis court instead of the beach. Anyway, the mother was fussing, the father was pissed, and the boy had this expression of pure magic on his face, like he'd just eaten the best thing ever created."

She smiled, picturing that exact moment. "Did the mom freak when you took the picture?"

"Yep. Then I explained it was for a magazine of candid photos—not posed—and she signed the release for me."

"Oh, good. You sound happy."

"Getting there more and more with each day."

They fell into silence, staring at one another, the words unspoken and lying between them lifelessly.

Taylor cleared her throat. "I'd better go. Call you after the show."

"Sleep well, Taylz." He clicked off.

She got ready for bed, pulled the sheet up to her chin, and wondered why the conversation hadn't made her happy. Had she been looking for something more? Had he been spending his extra time with Sam? She'd wanted him to say he missed her. A lot. That Cape May wasn't the same without her. But for God's sake, she'd only been gone a week! She didn't want to turn into a clingy female, moping over a man to want her.

No, she had to get used to the idea that their sexual relationship was over. They were friends who'd see each other at Avery's wedding, drink and party together, and go their separate ways. No reason to keep torturing herself over things that weren't meant to be.

She tried to sleep.

She dreamed of Pierce.

♥ ♥ ♥

Pierce stood outside the brightly lit Parisian gallery and stared at the window. Nerves nipped at his gut. What if this was a huge mistake? What if she didn't want him here?

He'd just gotten off the plane a few hours ago, then showered and changed at his hotel. He'd grabbed a bite to eat at a patisserie—and almost died when he tasted the buttery, crisp bread—and had taken a cab over. Now here he was, frozen at the entrance, half-tempted to go back to his hotel and call Taylor first to see if this was okay.

The line to get in had been long and snaked down the street. The people were well dressed and seemed elegant, probably all out for a weekend evening to enjoy some art and a nice dinner. He imagined Taylor in there, making nice with strangers, trying to pretend each opinion of her work didn't matter—that ripping out her heart and soul to put on display was no problem.

This past week, he'd been haunted with an instinct to be by her side. He knew Taylor would never ask for support—she was too stubborn to admit some things weren't meant to be faced alone.

Pierce straightened up. Enough of being a coward. He was going in as her friend, not her lover. As long as he remembered that, he'd be fine.

He strode through the door, nodding politely at the hostess, and then took a glass of champagne. The gallery was large, with giant walls sectioning off the different parts where each display stood. He meandered for a while, taking in the work of one of the other artists while he searched for Taylor. There were metallic sculptures made of interesting wire, scrap metals, and what looked to be car parts. The guy had a British accent and was deep in conversation with a patron.

Pierce slid by and found himself facing two murals—one of angels and one of demons. They reminded him of the age-old Sistine Chapel, a tangle of hundreds of figures gathered in a black, burnt forest where a tiny fire still flickered. The sheer sense of doom punched him immediately in the gut. The other painting was a complete contradiction, one of light and goodness, with angels singing and playing in a giant garden. He took a while to study the intricacies and noticed that the Parisian artist had an impressive crowd.

Pierce rounded the corner, impatient to get to Taylor, and stopped dead in his tracks. She stood a few feet ahead. A glass of champagne dangled from her hand. Her pink hair was slicked back and subdued. She wore a long, slinky black dress that emphasized her thin frame and natural grace.

A couple spoke to her, obviously fascinated by her work, pointing toward the paintings as if asking various questions. Her nose stud winked in the light. Her laugh was warm and rich, caressing his ears like thick velvet. He was struck in that exact moment by how well she fit within this gallery, an artist with every right to display her work in Paris. Pride rushed through him, and he took the time to turn and study her display.

It was magnificent. The paintings had been done in a series that built on the first. The woman on the cliff developed from a wispy, shadowy figure into the full light for the final reveal. The man, too, began in distant, barely there brushstrokes, then slowly revealed himself to the world and the woman who loved him. The settings were stark and brutal—the cliffs; the moody, roaring ocean; the desert; a balcony in a lonely, abandoned house. With each painting, the man grew closer to the woman, and when Pierce reached the final piece—the one Taylor had shipped before he could see it—he held his breath with anticipation.

He jerked back. The vivid, crushed blooms of endless roses attacked his vision—the bold, screaming mix of colors a complete contradiction to the previous settings. He stared at the painting, transfixed. The woman knelt on her knees, naked, one hand outstretched to her faceless lover, who stood before her, his face still in shadow. This woman had taken the ultimate risk, but an onlooker would never know if it was enough—if she was enough for him. There was no happy ending guaranteed to anyone. In its brutal humanity, Taylor's painting was simply brilliant.

"Pierce?" Her voice broke on his name.

He turned to her and smiled, trying to ignore his rapidly beating heart. Would she be upset he'd come? He swore he'd handle whatever reaction she threw at him. If she asked him to leave, he would. His breath got stuck in his lungs.

But her face reflected sheer joy and delight. She held nothing back, running the few steps over and flinging herself into his arms.

He caught her and held tight. Her musky scent drifted to his nostrils and made him drunk. He savored the few precious moments as his body pressed to hers, cradling each familiar curve, his hand stroking her bare back where the dress dipped low.

"What are you doing here?" she breathed out, her eyes wide.

"I didn't want you to be alone," he said simply. He got ready to explain that it had nothing to do with her not being able to handle herself, knowing Taylor would go nuts if she believed he thought her weak or needy.

A smile curved her lips. "This has been the scariest, craziest, most exciting thing that's ever happened to me, and this morning, I realized I had no one to share it with. I'm so glad you're here."

Relief surged through him. "Me, too," he said. He cupped her cheek, entranced by her face. God, he'd missed her more than he thought possible. She'd changed so much these past few months. Admitting her need for him without holding back showed him another layer of her surface being peeled back.

God, he was in so much trouble.

"Wait! You were supposed to be at your parents'."

"I told them you were a big-time artist in Paris, and they agreed I'd be nuts if I didn't come here rather than sit in Florida for early-bird specials and rounds of senior golf."

She laughed. "Good." She jerked her head toward the wall. "What do you think?"

"I look at these paintings and wonder how you have such a lion's heart in such a petite body, because only a warrior could be this brave and true to paint these."

She blinked, and her golden-brown eyes filled with a fierce emotion that seemed different from before. Not just gratitude or friendship or happiness. No, like her work, it was bigger and more real, but then she turned from him, and the moment to dig deeper was gone. "Thank you. That means more to me than selling them to a bunch of random people who don't know me."

"They do now. One look at your work, and they'll know. That's the beauty of it, Taylz." A touch of sadness flicked his voice. "You're going to be a star."

She opened her mouth to say something, but a small man dressed in a sleek, slim suit with impeccable gray hair and bright-blue eyes stopped before them. Taylor introduced Pierce quickly to Luis, and they exchanged pleasantries until he directed his next words to Taylor. "*Ma chère*, the feedback on your paintings is incredible. Everyone is simply buzzing, and there are many interested in buying."

Shock radiated from her form. "Really? You think we'll actually sell one?"

The man laughed and patted her shoulder. "All of them, I'm betting on."

"Except the third one," she said.

Luis frowned. "What do you mean? Some may be interested in buying the entire series!"

Her chin jutted out stubbornly. "I promised not to sell the third one. Remember I told you?"

"I thought you were joking," Luis said.

Pierce's jaw dropped. "Taylz, sell it! I was just messing around with you. I won't let you miss an opportunity to sell the whole series just so that one can hang in my office."

"I made a promise, and I'm keeping it. Luis, I'll be happy to paint another one on commission for whoever buys it. We can negotiate terms."

Luis glanced back and forth between them, as if trying to figure out their relationship. "Very well, *ma chère*. We shall see what happens." He shook Pierce's hand and headed toward the artist with the murals.

"Are you kidding me?" he hissed once Luis was out of earshot. "Why are you being so pigheaded? Just sell it and paint me another one."

She waved her hand in the air. "Carter would have never seen that painting if you hadn't hung it in your office and insisted it was good enough. You've been supportive of me from the very first time I confided I dreamed of being a big-time artist, and pushed me to take chances. That one belongs to you."

Staggered, he fought the impulse to kiss her cherry-red lips and tell her the truth. That he was crazy about her, that he didn't want to walk away or pretend they were something else, that he'd blow up his entire life at home and follow her around the world if she wanted him. But another patron came by, and for the next few hours, he watched Taylor discuss art and her work like she'd done this her entire life.

Pride coursed through him. She was in her element within this highbrow crowd. All her work and perseverance had finally paid off, and he was blessed to be the one standing beside her, watching her fly high. If only he could hold her hand, touch her, kiss her as her lover who had the right.

Not just be there as her friend.

Pierce knew that tonight, everything had changed.

He just didn't know how.

They walked to her apartment together. The night air was like a warm kiss, and their shoulders brushed, giving her tingles, like she was with her first boyfriend and dying for him to hold her hand.

Her heart danced.

He'd come for her.

The knowledge he'd flown to Paris to be with her for her big night went beyond friendship. It was an act she'd always treasure and remember, and once again, she was reminded of how, other than family, Pierce was the most important person in her life.

"Did you get a hotel room?" she asked, her heels clicking against the pavement.

"Yeah, I'm a few blocks away. How's your apartment?"

"Tiny. No real kitchen. A balcony, a sofa, and a place to paint."

He grinned. "Perfection." They walked in silence, each deep in thought. "When will you know how many sold?"

"Not sure. Luis will get back to me in a day or two. Whatever didn't sell he'll either decide to buy for his own inventory, or I can keep it."

"They'll all sell."

"Maybe." They reached her place, and he paused on the step. "You're coming in, right?"

His gaze searched hers. "To see your place? Sure."

Uneasiness unfolded. It was obvious he was wary she'd jump him. Was she reading the signals all wrong? Did he really come here just as her friend and with no intention of sleeping with her again? Why was she torn and confused when she was around him, yearning for something she knew they couldn't have?

Pissed off at her weakness, she climbed up the multiple flights of stairs, led him inside, turned on the light, and lifted her hand. "This is the whole thing."

He took a few steps, studying the decor and the little touches that added to the room. Then he opened the window and peeked out the balcony. "Taylz, I love it. Whenever I think of a real Parisian apartment, this is what comes to mind."

"I know, right? There's just enough space, and the sofa bed is actually comfortable. They even left me fancy satin sheets."

He stared at her, and she forced a laugh, fighting the flush threatening her cheeks.

"Um, want some water? Or some red wine?"

"No, thanks."

A heavy silence settled over the room. She shifted her weight and picked at her thumb. What was going on? Why was everything so damn . . . awkward? "When do you fly back out?"

He leaned against the window. "Two more days. I figured I'd get some sightseeing in. Brought my camera equipment to take some photographs. Build my portfolio."

"Great idea."

"You have time to show me anything, or will you be busy with Luis?"

"Of course I have time to tour with you. Why are you acting so damn weird and . . . tense?"

"I'm not! I'm getting the vibe from you. I don't know what you want."

She gasped. "That's the stupidest thing you've ever said. You flew across the ocean to be with me tonight, and now you're acting like we're casual neighbors who occasionally grab a cup of tea together."

A low growl emitted from his throat. "I'm trying to give you space, okay? It was hard for me to watch you surrounded by all those people and feel like I couldn't hold your hand or touch you the way I wanted. And I swore just because you didn't want what I want, I wouldn't act like an asshole."

"Well, you are."

"Are what?"

"Acting like an asshole! For God's sake, just tell me the truth—what do you really want? I don't like playing these games, especially with you."

Pierce was a force to be reckoned with when he lost his temper, because it was rarely seen. His nostrils flared, and his gaze narrowed, and his jaw clenched. He seemed to grow taller, stretching to his full height, and then he closed the distance between them with an edge that thrilled her to the core. "You want to know what I want?" he gritted out, eyes burning like jeweled jade. "You. Ever since I got off the plane, I've dreamed of kissing you, and stripping you naked, and fucking you senseless. How's that for the truth? And I know we agreed to go back to a platonic relationship, and it's supposed to be neat and tidy, but I don't give a shit anymore. I'm here till Tuesday, and I want you in my bed. I want you to be mine."

Satisfaction curled through her. She lifted up on her toes and grabbed at his shoulders, urging him closer. "That's perfect, because I want the same damn thing." She pressed her lips gently against his and whispered, "Now kiss me."

He did. He kissed her hard and deep, bending her backward so he could devour all of her. His slick, hot tongue thrust into her mouth, and she plunged her fingers into his long dark hair and hung on, thrilled with the ride.

He backed her up to the sofa, and they collapsed together, never breaking the kiss. In seconds, they were naked. She climbed on top of him, taking him deep, holding tight as he lifted her up, guiding her hips in a wild rhythm that took them both to completion. They came together, bodies shuddering, the sweet release warming her blood, and she dropped her head against his shoulder and tried to catch her breath.

"I'm glad we came to a mutual agreement," he finally said.

A tiny laugh escaped. "The moment I can move, I'll make up the bed with the fancy sheets."

He pressed a gentle kiss to her cheek. "Don't move. Not for a long time."

"I won't."

Taylor knew they needed to talk. Get serious about the future and how they wanted this new dynamic between them to play out. But right now, they were in Paris. They had a few idyllic days to just enjoy each other, away from Cape May, and let the city guide them in their heart and their pleasures.

Plenty of time to figure things out later.

Chapter Nineteen

"I can't believe this is happening," she whispered.

"I know. I just wish I could get closer. I thought it'd be . . . bigger."

Her eyes widened. "It's big in power, not size."

"Right." He squinted from the back row, trying to decipher the most mysterious expression in art history. "They said she should be looking at us no matter where we stand. Let's try it."

Taylor bumped into the person on her right and apologized. The large room was packed like a school of fish, all gazes focused on the famous *Mona Lisa*. The painting was behind a glass barrier, making it a little harder to see all the details. "How are we going to move?"

"We're from Jersey, Taylz. We got this."

She grinned, and they merged their way forward, like sharks amid minnows, until they reached the middle row on the right. Taylor gasped. "Yes—see how she's staring at us? This is amazing."

"Hmm."

"Why do you still not look impressed?" she demanded.

"I don't know!"

"Fine, let's get closer."

This time, people muttered under their breath, and some glared. A few deliberately bumped them back as they carefully maneuvered to the left. "She's still staring at me," Taylor whispered. "So direct. Gives me goose bumps. What do you think now?"

Pierce shrugged. "She's cool. You ready to go? I want to see the Winged Victory statue."

"Fine. I had no idea you were such a sucky art critic. It concerns me."

"I like *your* stuff," he said.

"That's why it concerns me."

He laughed and grabbed her hand, guiding her back through the mob. They toured some of the other highlights of the Louvre, torn on their favorites, then headed outside to explore.

The day was warm and bright. They darted in and out of shops, stopping at the occasional café for a champagne cocktail and nibbling on pastries from a patisserie, and snapped pictures to send back to Avery and Bella. The treats looked like fine art: almond croissants, thick and buttery; macarons in beautiful pastel colors; eclairs filled with rich cream; and sponge cake dusted with sugar. They washed it down with strong noisette, the hazelnut flavor and cream a dessert in itself.

They took a ferry to walk past Notre-Dame, solemn as they stared at the fire-ravaged cathedral, which was now a construction site, with the hope of saving the historical building. Taylor studied the dual south bell towers that had been saved, the lonely, graceful columns shooting high into the air, reminding the city of hope. She murmured a quick prayer for restoration, her heart tinged with sadness from the loss.

They worked their way back to the Eiffel Tower and scored a small table outside one of the cafés. Jammed between chattering groups of French students, they ate juicy steak frites in bordelaise sauce and drank a bottle of dry red wine that sparkled on the tongue and lingered with the taste of blackberry.

They stopped at Pierce's hotel to get his camera equipment, then headed to the tower.

"I may be a while," he warned, setting up his tripod.

She smiled at the look of banked excitement on his face. The crowds swarmed the square. Street vendors hawked their wares—flashing mini towers, glow sticks, and fresh bouquets of flowers. Music played softly in the background, and as the sun's rays seeped from the sky, they were replaced by the tower's sparkling lights.

She sat on one of the wall ledges, completely content. "I'm in no rush. I love people-watching. Plus, I can be the snack runner."

He laughed and knelt down, pulling attachments from his bag. "I'm so stuffed, I don't think I can eat again."

"Within one hour, you'll be asking for a baguette."

"Maybe two."

She fell quiet and just watched him in his element. Strong, tapered fingers were gentle with the lenses, and he moved his equipment with a sense of respect for the tools of his trade. Once, she'd made the mistake of asking how he chose all his equipment, and half an hour later, her brain was spinning with information overload. In her mind, it wasn't his equipment that made a real difference. It was his vision, creativity, and endless hours of practice to find the best way to capture an image.

He looked through the frame over and over—adjusting, resetting, mumbling to himself—while the city of Paris thrived and exploded around him against the regal backdrop of the black iron tower that rose to a mighty height above them.

"Is it harder to do night shots?" she asked curiously.

"Sometimes. The tower is illuminated, but the background is pure black, which makes this a particular challenge. In order to see the buildings, people, and statues in the distance, I'll need to bracket the shot."

"What does that mean?"

"I take a few pictures with different exposure levels, then combine them to create the perfect shot."

"Cool. Bet a picture of the tower will bring in some decent money."

He shook his head, still focused on the lens. "Nope. You can't sell a picture of the Eiffel Tower illuminated—the French government doesn't allow it. It has to be for personal use only."

"Damn, I thought all important monuments could be photographed for profit."

"No, but I can use it to impress my friends and clients."

She grinned. "Envy. That's even better than money."

He laughed and sank back into his work. It took him a good hour to get all the shots he wanted. He moved the camera to different angles, capturing the row of statues as if they were looking at the tower, then did a few with the monument straight out, highlighted against the sky. He danced around his equipment, seeing something through the lens she was incapable of. It was almost as if photography was consistently chasing the idyllic picture in a vision, which was exactly how her artwork evolved.

Maybe it was another reason she felt so close to him. They understood each other's creative souls and goals, and with that came a certain respect. She could have easily watched him for hours at his craft, finding peace in his purpose.

When he began to pack up, she asked, "Did you get what you wanted?"

"I did." His features took on a satisfied, almost blissful look. It was so very familiar, and her body immediately responded, softening and melting in anticipation. He seemed to notice, and suddenly the air sparked around them, bringing that delicious sexual tension to the forefront. "Why are you looking at me like that?"

"Because you have the exact same expression on your face that you do after you orgasm."

He stilled. His pale-green eyes filled with a fierce hunger that drove the breath from her lungs. "Photography and sex have many similarities. First, the pursuit—a seduction of sorts to remove all obstacles to get to the target."

A husky laugh escaped her lips. "Sexy."

"Hmm, it is." He moved a step closer. "Sweet anticipation takes over your mind and body. You can practically smell victory. Knowledge of the pleasure that's about to come shakes through you."

She licked her lips, caught up in his seductive gaze. "What's next?"

"All of the focus and effort chasing that one perfect moment suddenly explodes through you. With the click of the shutter, you're released, and it feels so damn good, it's like you're flying."

She yanked his head down and kissed him in the Paris square, with the Eiffel Tower beaming a thousand lights from behind. A scattering of applause sounded around them, obviously celebrating young lovers grabbing a fleeting moment in time to always remember.

"Let's go home and take some pictures," she whispered in his ear.

He laughed and grabbed her hand, and they ran the entire way back.

♥ ♥ ♥

The next day, they visited the catacombs. Traveling down the tight spiral staircase consisting of 130 steps, it was as if they'd reached the bottom of the earth. They silently walked through endless, twisted rows where hundreds of skulls were displayed, stacked on top of one another in a horrifying art exhibit. When she reached the children's section and the stoic, stamped brass signs declaring its innocent residents, shudders racked her body.

By the time they'd climbed back up into the light, Taylor was clinging to him, desperate to celebrate life again, so they headed to Versailles and steeped themselves in opulence at the king's palace. Room after room of gilded gold treasures, exquisite tapestries, rich paintings, and antique furniture took their breath away. They took selfies in the Hall of Mirrors and walked the elaborate gardens, videoing the water shows and getting lost in the tangle of mazes stretched out for endless acres.

Time stopped. They became caught up in details of each other amid the glorious background of Paris. Taylor knew she was in a temporary time warp of their making, and she refused to waste a moment worrying about the real world.

Until the real world called

It came later that afternoon, while they were eating french onion soup with gobs of cheese and home-baked croutons in a crowded café.

"It's Luis," she said, putting down her spoon to take the call. Her palms were sweating, knowing this was the news that would set up her future. She wondered if by failing, she could still win. If Luis had bad news for her, then she could go back to Cape May and tell Pierce she wanted more than friendship. They'd settle together in their beach hometown. He'd return to portraits, she'd work at Sunshine Bridal, and their future would be stable and secure. With him by her side, maybe a life of home, hearth, and family would satisfy her.

The image punched her straight in the solar plexus. She knew deep within that she'd slowly wither and die if she was stuck in Cape May in a traditional marriage and life.

But that was the only way she'd get Pierce.

He watched her across the table with a frown. "You have to answer it, Taylz," he said as she sat there, caught in a panic. "Whatever he tells you, it will be okay."

She dragged in a breath and hit the button to answer the call.

"Ma chère," Luis greeted her warmly. "I have fantastic news for you. We have officially sold all of your paintings. The show was a complete success, just like I believed."

She blinked, wondering if she'd heard correctly. "You . . . you sold them all?"

A chuckle spilled into her ear. "Yes. Except the one you refused to let me sell. As you requested, I told the buyer you'd be willing to work with him on another to complete the set, but he pushed back hard. If you change your mind, I can double the price."

Her throat dried up. She croaked out her next question. "How much?"

"A hundred thousand dollars for the entire series. We have much to talk about. Can we meet tomorrow morning?"

One. Hundred. Thousand. Dollars.

Holy. Shit.

Her hand trembled violently. "Yes. Tomorrow morning is good."

"I'll pick you up at nine a.m. Now you must go and celebrate. See the city. Drink champagne. Engage in wicked, wonderful activities. Your life is about to change!"

The phone clicked.

"What?" Pierce asked, reaching out to grab her still-shaking hand. "What did he say?"

"I sold them all." Her voice sounded high and faint. "I sold them for one hundred thousand dollars."

She recognized the shock, but it was the other emotion she saw in his eyes that hit her deep: *pride*.

The man sitting across from her had always believed in whatever she wanted to do. The sheer joy and pride reflected in his gaze were the confirmation of a love she didn't know if she was strong enough to deny any longer.

Because she loved him right back.

"I knew it," he whispered fiercely. "I knew you'd do it. Taylz, you're going to be rich and famous."

They sat in that café, gripping each other's hands and laughing full force, drawing a bunch of looks from other patrons and the French waiters. Pierce lifted his hand and motioned them over. In clumsy French, he asked for the best bottle of champagne they had, and they toasted to her success.

As Taylor drank her bubbly, her heart filled with both excitement and regret. Because as she was finally reaching her lifelong dream, she was letting a different one go.

Chapter Twenty

The window was open, and a warm breeze drifted in, fluttering the cream curtains. The faint sound of French music faded in and out, along with the occasional chatter of Parisians as they strolled back and forth on the street below. The lamp was dimmed, and the room was shrouded in darkness. The luxurious satin sheets were a tangled mess around their limbs. They lay naked together, her head on his chest, her fingers stroking his face.

"We're not meant for this, you know." Her hand dropped to rest on his upper arm. "Us."

He pressed a kiss to the sensitive curve of her shoulder, letting his teeth sink in. The shudder caused a rush of satisfaction. She was so responsive, never hiding a reaction or the animalistic need in her eyes when she wanted him. If only it was just that.

Sex. Want. Lust.

Instead, it'd become so much more. He loved her. Wanted to claim her as more than his buddy or lifelong friend. He wanted to officially date and be exclusive and not hide their relationship. He wanted to try. But did she?

Pierce knew she was falling just as hard. It was in every look and touch and kiss. Those few seconds when she'd caught sight of him at the art exhibition, he'd seen the naked love in her eyes. He didn't doubt her feelings any longer.

But he doubted if she wanted him enough to risk it all.

"We've done pretty good for ourselves so far," he said lightly. Her nipple pebbled when he teased the peak with his lips. Her fingers clutched him tighter. "Best friends since high school. An easy transition to lovers. We've done all the hard work already."

Her pink hair fanned out on the pillow when he gently pushed her back. Her lips were swollen, her skin warm and flushed with razor burn. "What happens when the bubble bursts?" she asked at the same time she lifted her arms to welcome him closer. "I'm probably staying in Paris. I'll find out tomorrow what Luis thinks is the next step."

He hated the touch of guilt in her voice. He'd never think of changing her mind. His feelings may have morphed to something bigger than they'd imagined, but this was her time and her opportunity. He wouldn't let her blow it over guilt for leaving him back home. After all, it was his choice to stay in Cape May. But these past weeks, he'd realized he had his own dreams to pursue. He just hadn't known exactly where they'd lead him.

Until now.

He'd been playing it safe for long enough. These past months of feeling a bit lost and unsatisfied suddenly made sense. All this time, he'd wondered if he was limiting himself by staying in Cape May. But being with Taylor these past few days had made him realize he'd been wrong all along. It wasn't about the place.

It was about the person.

Taylor Sunshine was his true home.

Once the thought took form, a sense of peace and acceptance overtook him. He finally knew all the answers. He'd live in Paris. Explore the countryside and people. Steep himself in the culture and fill up his well. And be with the woman he truly loved.

Pierce opened his mouth to tell her, then shut it. No, it wasn't the right time. She needed to talk to Luis and focus on the next steps that would be best for her career. But afterward, he'd present his plan and how they could move forward as a couple.

"We'll work it out. And as for us not being meant for this, I'll have to disagree." With one quick movement, he parted her thighs and slid inside her hot, wet channel. She gasped, her nails digging into his shoulders, and he swallowed the sound with his mouth. "I think we fit perfectly," he whispered, keeping his thrusts slow and controlled.

Sweat dampened her skin, and she pressed her heels into his ass, urging him on. With each jerk of his hips, he pressed a gentle kiss to her face, dragging her right to the edge and keeping her there with a ruthless precision.

"We were always meant to fit like this." He increased the pace, and she sank her teeth into his bottom lip as her body shuddered. "No one will ever fit me like you, Taylor Sunshine. Now come for me."

She did, crying out his name. He studied each beautiful feature as she broke apart, committing this moment to his memory. And as he orgasmed, spilling his seed and holding her tight, he swore everything was worth it for this—no matter what happened.

It was only after she was sleeping that he uttered the words to the empty, dark room. "I love you, Taylz. I have always loved you, and I always will."

He listened to her steady breaths. It was hours later when he finally fell asleep.

Chapter Twenty-One

Taylor sat next to Luis in his office. They perched on the leather couch. Two cups of espresso sat on the breakfast tray. He'd brought in croissants, thin slices of cheese, and an array of jams. The air was full of delicious smells like coffee, wood polish, and lemon.

A giant desk was near the window, and the decor was luxurious yet masculine. Thick wine carpeting, a stately black chandelier, and mahogany cabinetry filled the space. Normally, she'd be a bit intimidated, but she'd already spoken at length with Carter and her sisters last night. Carter reminded her that although Luis was a businessperson, he was more interested in helping talented new artists rather than turning a large profit. Luis held long-term relationships with the clients he'd helped, and Carter trusted him.

They discussed the terms Luis might offer and helped her flesh out what would work for her, and what deals to avoid. After doing some additional research, she felt more confident in her negotiation skills.

"We had a bidding war for the series," he said briskly, "which means we should have even more success with your next exhibit. Now my vision is to secure a solo show rather than combined, and plan your official debut."

"I thought this was my debut."

"No, that was strictly introductory to see if your art resonated. I have instincts, but until I put out the bells and whistles before a wide audience, I never truly know. Do you have an idea of what your next projects will be?"

She hesitated. "I'd like to say yes, but most of my work comes from hours in front of the canvas until I'm drawn to paint. It's a bit of a meandering process, I know, but I can assure you I don't take it as permission to goof off for long periods of time. It's through the discipline of sitting and waiting that I get there. So no, I can't give you a neat, detailed outline of what you'll see, if that makes sense."

"It does, and work ethic is critical, which you've shown. You delivered the first time; you shall deliver the second. Which will be in your contract anyway," he said with a twinkle in his blue eyes. "What I'd like to discuss is your vision for your career. Where you want to work. Time schedule. I want both of us to be satisfied that we're moving forward but not draining the well too fast. I've seen many young artists burn out in a glorious rush, never to paint or sculpt again. I will not let that happen to you."

She smiled. "I will not let that happen to myself," she said firmly. "But I do appreciate the intention, and I'm open to your guidance since you're the expert."

He nodded, respect gleaming in his eyes. "Very good. After your debut, I was thinking we could go to Italy. I have another successful gallery in Milan I think you'd do quite well at."

"It sounds wonderful, Luis," she said. "The more I explore, the more inspiration I get. But my family is in Cape May, and I also can't imagine myself not seeing them for a year at a clip."

"You can work anywhere you'd like, *ma chère*. I'd like you to stay in Paris, though, for the next six months. We need to work on your connections and build your business résumé. I think some art classes will also help, so I'll arrange some private tutoring with some of our masters. Think of it as an apprenticeship. By the time of your debut, we'll be ready to launch your career, and you'll have more flexibility in your schedule."

Excitement stirred in her gut. This was everything she'd ever wanted, worked for, and dreamed of. But in that moment, she was thinking of one person—Pierce—and the confession he'd whispered in the dark last night, thinking it had gone unheard.

He loved her.

It had taken all her control not to reach for him and tell him she loved him, too. That she didn't care about the obstacles or distance between them. That she wanted to try.

Instead, she'd remained silent, sensing a choice ahead: her career or Pierce.

She couldn't have both.

She'd be in Paris for six months, then Italy, then maybe return to Cape May. Yes, she'd visit her sisters and spend long weekends and holidays there—maybe even a few weeks in the summer, maybe a few months if she wanted. But Pierce was tied to his photography studio and his home. God, he'd openly admitted that he'd rediscovered his true love for Cape May during his pursuit of the *Escape* collection. Trying a long-distance relationship, where he sacrificed his own dream of a settled, long-term relationship that led to marriage and kids, was a recipe for heartbreak.

The end of their friendship.

They could hurt each other in the quest for love. If she sacrificed her lover, she'd still have an opportunity to salvage the friendship. Right now, they were lucky. They still remained in the safe zone.

It was crucial they stay there.

"Taylor?" Luis frowned. "This is a big decision. You need to be a hundred percent committed. I am going to put all my efforts and resources into making you a successful artist, but it will take all of your time and focus, too. Is there something I need to know? Something holding you back? This is the time to discuss, not afterward, when too many people are counting on you. Do you understand?"

She did. Funny how she could reach her dream while her heart slowly crumbled in her chest. How she could achieve one stunning success yet lose what was most precious to her. The angles and sharp curves of life lay before her. It was up to her this time to choose the road she wanted. This time, it wasn't like that frantic middle-of-the-night phone call in college. She didn't need to return home to save the family business. This time, nothing could stop her except herself.

Hadn't she waited long enough?

Taylor squared her shoulders. "I understand, and I'm completely dedicated to my career. I'd like to go over the details of the contract. As for the schedule, I love the idea of getting business savvy and taking classes. Whatever will help make me a stronger artist, I'll embrace."

He nodded, obviously pleased. "Then we'll go over the contract."

"I'll need to send it to Carter's lawyer, who will be representing me now."

"I would be upset if you didn't," he said with a touch of humor.

"One other thing." She took a deep breath. Her heart begged her not to utter the words, but it was the only way she could think of to show Pierce she was putting her career first and leaving him behind. "I'd like to sell that painting in the series, after all."

He stared at her, looking surprised. "Really? You were quite stubborn about keeping your promise to your friend. Are you sure?"

She thought back to the conversation with Kimmie and knew she didn't want to be the one to continually hold Pierce back from finding love with a woman who better matched his own goals. Agony speared her, but she only saw one road left to take—one way to set him free. She prayed they'd heal with time and space. It was a gamble she had to risk. "I'm sure."

"Then I shall reach out and secure an outrageous price that will make the sacrifice worth it. Yes?"

She forced a smile, even though her bottom lip trembled. "Yes."

It was done.

♥ ♥ ♥

Pierce hummed to himself as he sat on the balcony, waiting for Taylor to return.

He'd been up all night, excited to finally tell Taylor his decision. He was done worrying about pushing her too hard, afraid of her rejecting him as a lover in order to save their friendship. Why were they both lying to each other, pretending nothing had changed? Why were they trying so hard to ignore the fact that they were in love with each other?

Their friendship had been the reason that love had bloomed in the first place. It was the foundation of everything and could never be ruined. Now that he'd made his decision about his career and moving to Paris, there were no other complications.

It was time to chase their dreams together.

His plan was solid. He'd keep his studio to have a home base and spend a few months a year in Cape May, then travel the rest of the time. He'd exhibit his work and freelance. His savings were padded nicely, and money was no longer a problem. He'd been living simply for a long time.

Of course, it also depended on what Taylor wanted to do, but they could easily make it work. She could keep her place downstairs from Bella, and they'd visit whenever possible between her painting classes and shows. Maybe they'd end up going to Milan, where he could steep himself in the rich history—a place where a million stories breathed, ready to be told.

The future lay before him in all its dazzling possibility. Most of all, he'd finally be able to say the words that had been bottled up for too long, because he was no longer afraid.

He heard the door open and left the balcony to greet her. "How did things go?" he asked. "Tell me everything."

When she turned, he immediately sensed that something was wrong. There was a stiffness in her shoulders and a distance in her golden-brown eyes that made his gut clench. He tried to remain calm, waiting to hear her next words. "It went great. Luis is excited about setting up another show in six months. He wants me to stay here and work, take some lessons, boost up my business contacts. It'll be a lot of work, but I got everything I ever wanted."

His throat tightened. He was so damn happy for her. "Good for you, Taylz. I always knew this would happen. Now, tell me, what's making you sad?"

She jerked at the direct question. Pierce knew going on the offense was the best way to plow down her defenses. "I'm not sad. Just . . . overwhelmed. It's all wonderful news, but it will take endless work and effort. I'm only going to be able to fly back for Avery's wedding, then come straight back."

He nodded. "Everyone understands. The beginning is sometimes the hardest, to be able to launch something big. Plus, Paris is a wonderful place for you to work. You've wanted to travel and steep yourself in the culture. I think everything Luis has been offering you is perfect. Don't you?"

This time, she looked him in the eye. His breath caught at the raw fragility he spotted in her gaze and realized there was something bigger he was missing. "Yes. It is perfect. For me, Pierce. Not you."

He kept his voice mild. "How do you know? I haven't told you my plans yet."

"I didn't want this to happen to us," she suddenly whispered, pressing her hand to her mouth. "But we can't keep pretending nothing's changed."

"I don't want to pretend, either," he said with a smile.

Her eyes were wide and pleading. "Then can we just agree we went too far and try to get back to the way it was? You return to Cape May. I stay in Paris. We take a break from . . . this. Get our bearings. Then, when we see each other again, we have our normal friendship back. Right?"

The words sounded terrible in his ears, an awful truth she was spinning in order to push him away. His jaw clenched, and he tried to calm the rising panic that told him she'd already made up her mind. "Wrong. I don't care about our original agreement, and neither do you. Because we're more than friends, Taylz. Don't deny it. I'm in lo—"

"No," she practically screamed, shaking her head. "Please don't say it."

He stared at her in shock, speechless.

Her voice broke. "If you say it, we can't take it back. Listen to me, Pierce. You are the most important person in my life. And I will never forget this time in Paris together, ever. But we can't go forward like this. I need to focus on my work, with no distractions. And you need to be real with yourself and what you want in life. I will never be the right woman for you long-term. I can't pretend to be her, and then tear both of us apart when it's too late. Don't you see? If we walk away now, we can salvage us!"

He staggered back and tried to sort through her speech. My God, she didn't want to deny as much as she wanted to ignore. Pretend the summer and Paris were just temporary, magical chapters in their story, never to be repeated or spoken of. Did she really believe he could ever look at her and not crave her naked beneath him while he buried himself in her tight, wet heat over and over? Was she imagining polite chitchat when she introduced him to her new lover, thinking he wouldn't want to tear him apart and bury his body?

He had to make her see. Somehow.

"There's no way to salvage what we once were," he said quietly. "You know that. But we can move forward in a different way. Won't you even let me tell you what I truly want, instead of not trusting me to know? I want—"

"I sold the painting."

He stopped, trying to understand what she meant. "What painting?"

She lifted her chin, stared directly into his eyes, and said the words that changed everything. "The painting I promised to keep for you. I sold it."

The trembling happened deep inside his core and radiated outward. The ground underneath his feet shifted. He was the same physically, but inside, something had broken, ripping apart the last segments of hope he'd clung to with a passionate intensity. He asked the only question he could. "Why?"

Pain flickered over her face, then a terrifying sort of resolve. "For money. I'm truly sorry, Pierce. I didn't do it to hurt you, but I had to choose. And I choose my work. I choose this life, a brand-new one, not the one I left behind." She paused and closed the final door. "Not the life I had with you."

Agony shredded through him, but he took it stoically, wondering when the numbness would come. Later. Definitely later. Maybe he'd never be able to feel anything again after this. It would be a good thing.

"I understand." His voice came from far away, as if he were in another dimension. "My flight leaves tonight. I'd better go now. Check out of my hotel, get there early."

She didn't say anything. Her arms wrapped around herself as if seeking comfort.

He got his camera bag and tripod, not caring if he left anything else behind.

"Pierce?"

He paused at the door. "Yeah?"

"We'll be okay. We just need time to let each other go so we can make our way back to friendship."

Even now, he wanted to reassure her. Hug her, stroke her back, and remind her that a crazy leap was just like a creative element. Sometimes you failed spectacularly. Sometimes you won spectacularly.

But this was a cop-out, a lie to keep from jumping at all. And that move, out of all of them, had completely destroyed them both.

He didn't answer. Just walked out the door and out of her life.

Chapter Twenty-Two

Taylor stared at the canvas in front of her. She'd been at it for hours, but nothing made sense. The meandering mess of lines and colors tried to come together as a whole but was falling flat. Better to take a break and try again later.

She put down her brush and stretched out her cramped muscles. Uncorking a bottle of red, she climbed out to her balcony and sat on the wrought-iron chair, staring out at the crumbling yellow building across the road. A woman three stories down to the right was also outside, drinking a glass of wine, flipping through some type of magazine. She lifted her head, saw Taylor, and raised her glass of wine in a toast.

Taylor smiled, mimicked her movement, and drank.

Paris was everything she'd ever hoped for, but the city was now teeming with ghosts. The sight of the Eiffel Tower brought nothing but agony and images of Pierce in front of his camera, then kissing her while the crowd clapped. The streets were haunted with the cafés they'd eaten in and the sights they'd shared. But most of all, her apartment had become a tool of torture. She went to bed every night clutching the shirt he'd left behind, trying to wrap herself in his scent to soothe the pain.

After he left, her multiple texts went ignored the first few days. Then he'd finally responded.

Taylz, I can't talk to you right now. I need time. This is not a
punishment, but I can't pretend to chat like a friend. Not for a
while. I'll see you at the wedding. Hope you understand and
that you're doing well in Paris and with your painting.

Each word was like a slash of a knife, cutting through her skin.
She'd read it over and over, trying to decipher every emotion and
nuance, until she lay on the sofa, exhausted and clutching her phone.

Another full week passed before she finally got herself together.
After all, she'd been the one to send him away. She couldn't waste any
more days grieving and torturing herself over what-ifs. She'd come here
to achieve her dreams, and that took work. So Taylor forced herself in
front of the canvas every morning and didn't stop until late at night.
Slowly, images began to take hold, misty at first, then emerging from
the background. She remained patient with her muse and her broken
heart, putting her entire focus on the only thing she had left.

As the weeks passed, she fell into a routine. Lessons three times per
week. Regular meetings with Luis. Appointments at galleries, meeting
wealthy business owners and other artists, broadening her circle. She
studied French every morning for an hour with a private tutor. Anything
to fill up the empty spaces inside that Pierce had left behind. And though
she loved every new experience, something always seemed to be missing.

Late one night, Taylor sighed and stared up at the full moon. At
least the wedding was in three days. She'd been on the phone with her
sisters almost every night, going over all the details. Her parents were
there, and hearing their proud voices praising her for all her accomplish-
ments brought silly tears to her eyes.

She also used those conversations to squeeze out every kernel of
information she could about Pierce. She pretended that they'd decided
to return to a platonic friendship and were both happy and satisfied
with their mutual decision.

Lying was so much easier over the phone.

But right now, in this instant, she craved the sound of his voice. It was like a sickness crawling through her—this desperate need to make contact. What or who was he photographing lately? What did he have for dinner last night? Had he seen the latest episode of *The Witcher*? Did he miss her?

She looked at her empty glass of wine and buckled under the loneliness.

Taylor dialed his number.

One. Two. Three rings.

It was going to go to voice mail. He still refused to speak to her, even when they'd soon be walking down the aisle together as grooms-man and bridesmaid.

Click. "Hello? Is this Taylor?"

The feminine voice caught her by surprise. She stared at the phone, trying to find her words. "Um, yeah. Who's this?"

A light, tinkly laugh responded, like one of the Disney princesses Zoe loved. "It's Samantha. I'm sorry, Pierce is in the restroom and left his phone. I didn't want him to miss your call, so I figured I'd pick up. How's Paris? Pierce filled me in, and your art show sounded so exciting! Congratulations on your success!"

Taylor's stomach clenched into a hard knot. This was the woman she'd met at Pierce's studio. The one he was eating breakfast with the morning she'd left. The one who seemed super friendly. Had they hooked up? Was this his new girlfriend? How could he dive into a relationship so soon after their breakup?

The questions circled her mind like a merry-go-round, but she was desperate to get answers while she could. "Thanks so much—I appreciate it. Paris is amazing! How are you guys doing? Where are you eating?"

"We're all doing great here! Tonight, we're at the Blue Pig."

She stiffened. They rarely ate there due to the gourmet food and high prices, preferring to only go on special occasions. Pierce always loved casual dining and bigger plates. "Oh, fancy."

Another laugh. The sound grated on her nerves. "We wanted to indulge for a change. And Pierce had a great day—did he tell you yet about the big sale?"

Taylor smothered the pain and lied. "Yes, isn't it wonderful! What were the final details? He was going to tell me later since we didn't have time to chat."

"Oh, well, after he did so well with his collection at *Escape*, they offered him a monthly blog. He's supposed to do a kind of photography-in-the-wild column, which I think he's perfect for. It's only a three-month contract, but if it goes well, they'll extend it. I'm so happy to see both of you succeeding—it gives me hope I won't always be at Key West Tacos! Oh, Pierce is back. I'll hand you over."

"No! I'm sorry, Samantha, someone's, um, knocking at my door and I have to go. I'll call back—thanks."

She hung up quickly and threw the phone on the table like she'd been burned. The realization that Pierce was already moving on shook through her. Samantha was her replacement—a friend who could turn into something more. Yes, she wanted Pierce to be happy and eventually settle down with a woman who could give him everything she couldn't. But not so soon after they'd experienced a joy and passion she used to believe was only possible in the movies.

She'd given him up for the greater good because she loved him too much to hurt him later. The sacrifice had taken all her strength. Yet he'd happily picked up the pieces without even grieving her.

Bastard.

The betrayal ate at her insides, like a mouse gnawing on a piece of string, and she dropped her face into her hands, overwhelmed and lonely and terrified that she'd lost not only the love of her life, but her beloved best friend.

For the first time in a long while, she cried.

"You're home!" Avery screeched, throwing her arms around Taylor's neck. "We missed you!"

Bella was right behind, getting in on the hug, and Taylor laughed. "Guys, I love you, too, but you're strangling me."

They jumped back. "Sorry," Avery said. "I just got excited."

"Where's Mom and Dad?" she asked, dropping her bags.

"Out with Zoe at the beach. We're having a big dinner tonight, though, to celebrate your amazing art-show success, and everyone will be here."

Taylor's heart pounded, and she turned away so her face was hidden. "Oh, was Pierce able to reschedule to make it?" she asked casually.

"No, I'm sorry, babe. He called and said he's out of town, and there was no way he could get home in time."

"Yeah, he told me," she lied. "I was just double-checking." She forced a smile and walked into the kitchen. "I can't wait to catch up with everyone. Are you set for the rehearsal dinner tomorrow night?"

Avery's eyes sparkled. "Yes. I put Nora in charge of all the outstanding details, and she's done amazing. I'm not even stressed. I thought about what you guys said and really began to enjoy the wedding planning again instead of looking at it as a job. It's going to be perfect."

Bella sniffed. "We know it is."

"Oh no. You will not start crying before the ceremony," Taylor warned, jabbing her finger at her sister. "Seriously, I'll kick both of your asses. We will not be one of those weepy, wimpy families that blubber over a bride in white. We have a reputation to uphold!"

They laughed. "You're right," Avery said. "We're professionals and will act as such. We can cry later in private—a happy cry, of course."

"Deal." They stuck out their pinkies, made the swear, then sat in the kitchen, catching up.

"Avery, are you sure you don't want a crazy bachelorette party with strippers and dancing and cocktails?" Taylor teased. "I hope you know Ally gave us a hard time about you refusing to celebrate." Ally was

Carter's younger sister and Avery's best friend in college. They'd dubbed themselves the double A's, which Carter had disapproved of back in the day, when he believed Avery was too wild. Avery and Carter had fallen in love with each other while fighting throughout planning Ally's wedding last year. Which was hysterical, since it was right out of one of those rom-coms her sisters adored.

Avery waved her hand in the air. "I swear to you, I've been to enough of those things over the years and don't want it. I'm looking forward to our pajama party tonight. I want to watch romantic movies and eat goodies and do shots at home!"

Bella laughed. "Simplest wish to fulfill. It's almost embarrassing how easy you're making it on Taylor and me."

"I think Ally was craving some time to cut loose since she was the first one married. She wanted the double A's to ride again," Avery said.

"Well, Carter chose her as his best woman," Bella said. "She could go to his bachelor party if she wants."

"Carter's just hanging with the guys tonight, too," Avery said. "I guess we both wanted to enjoy some special downtime with family and friends."

"Fine with me. I'll concentrate all my spectacular bleach-worthy bachelorette party ideas while planning Bella's," Taylor said.

Her sister widened her eyes in horror. "God, no. Just . . . no."

"We'll see. Now, did I tell you what Luis said about the next exhibit?" she asked, deftly maneuvering the subject.

Taylor filled them both in on her work and routine in Paris, then prodded a bit to find out more about Samantha. "I called Pierce this week, and Sam answered his phone. Do you think they're dating?" she asked breezily.

Avery frowned. "I'm not sure. They've been out and about a lot together, but it looks like they're strictly friends to me. Babe, are you holding out on us? Did anything else happen between you and Pierce?"

She looked at her sisters and felt the resolve inside begin to crumble. God, she just wanted to tell them the truth and ask for their opinion. She felt so isolated, trapped in her own lies, but she didn't want to ruin Avery's wedding with the selfish problems she'd brought on herself. But she'd made a vow to tell them if she needed advice. Maybe during their pajama party there'd be a good opportunity to open up.

She forced a smile. "No, we're both good—just been very busy. We'll have plenty of time to catch up this weekend. I was just curious."

Avery breathed out in relief. "Oh, good. I got scared. What a nightmare it'd be if you two were having issues during my wedding, right?"

She kept her smile and hoped it didn't look frozen to her face. Thank God, she hadn't said anything. She'd wait until her sister returned from her honeymoon. Avery didn't need any additional stress. "Right. That'd be just . . . awful."

"I've always admired the closeness you both shared," Bella said. "And you proved it again to us! You were able to have amazing sex, then flip right back into friendship. I'm so happy you've achieved everything you want, Taylor. It's finally your time." She jumped up and glanced at the clock. "Now, I'd better get started on dinner, and aren't we lucky you're back? You can set the table!"

She shook her head, enjoying the familiar teasing, and settled back with the people she loved.

Chapter Twenty-Three

"Hi."

Pierce froze on the path the moment he spotted her a few feet in front of him. The rehearsal dinner was being held at the famous Peter Shields restaurant, known for its impeccable food, charming atmosphere, and impressive bar.

Taylor smiled shyly and closed the distance, and just like that, all his good intentions shattered around him.

Damn her. Why did she have to be so arresting? The woman would never be called classically beautiful—she was too bold for such a polite type of word. But the short, glittery black dress she wore was both elegant and unapologetic. It dipped low in the front and back, emphasizing the tilt to her small breasts and lean figure. She'd slicked her pink hair back away from her face, showing off ruby-red lips, her nose piercing, and sexy, dangly earrings. Her shoes were a kick-ass mingling of combat boots with high heels, somehow matching perfectly with the fancy dress.

He locked his muscles in place to keep from attacking her right there and throwing away weeks of discipline. God, he'd missed her. But every time he'd reached for the phone, which was hundreds of times per day, he'd reminded himself that she didn't want him. Not like he did her. She'd sold the painting as a symbol of rejecting what he wanted to offer.

Seeing her now, he wondered if there'd be enough time in eternity to get over her.

"Hi," he said with a nod.

She picked at her thumb, her telltale nervous gesture. "Can we talk?"

"Of course."

She motioned him to the side of the restaurant, tucked away from the arriving crowd. Her gaze probed, searching for something he didn't have to give her anymore, so he kept his own gaze hooded, hoping he'd get through this weekend without a mental breakdown. "How have you been?" she asked.

"Good. How about you?"

Taylor gave a shrug. "Okay. Busy. Painting, taking lessons, studying French. Making business contacts."

"It's everything you wanted, right?"

She flinched.

He muttered a curse. "I didn't mean that as a jab," he said stiffly.

"I know. I've just missed you. I understand you need time, and I didn't want to pressure you. I called once, and Samantha answered."

"She told me."

Taylor waited for more, but he had nothing else to offer. He stayed quiet, refusing to explain or detail his and Sam's relationship, which was just a simple friendship. She'd gone out with his friend Nick, which had fizzled after two dates, but yesterday, he'd introduced Sam to Rob Livery, a local cop, and sparks immediately flew. Pierce bet they'd be dating soon.

"Oh. Well, this wedding is really important to everyone, and I don't want it to be awkward between us."

He looked at her coldly. "For you or them?"

Those Bambi eyes widened. "For all of us. Pierce, please understand— I didn't know what else to do, but I don't want to lose you." Her bottom lip trembled, and he caught the raw pain stamped on her features, the misery cloaking her. "I think about you all the time. Not talking to you for so long has been like losing a limb. I hate that I hurt you." Her voice finally broke. "I didn't know what else to do," she repeated.

Calling himself every curse word in his mental bible, he reached out and squeezed her hand in comfort. Watching her in pain was his own special torture, and though he was still angry and hurt as hell, he couldn't blame her for making a choice. "I know, Taylz. It's just hard for me, that's all. I hope one day we'll work our way back to each other, but I think, right now, it's important for both of us to structure our lives alone. We need that. That's the reason you went to Paris—to discover who you are separate from all of us back here. Including me." He dragged in a breath. "I need to do the same thing for myself. I can't depend on you anymore. Maybe, if we can both build ourselves back up on our own, we'll be able to be friends again, in a new way."

He looked deep into her eyes and saw a certain hope slipping away—one he didn't understand, because she'd already made her choice. "Yeah, I know I can't go back and change things. I just never thought this would happen to us."

He slowly released her hand. "Me, either."

"I'll try to give you space, but I didn't tell anyone what really happened between us. My sisters think we just decided to return to a platonic relationship."

"So do the guys."

"I don't want the wedding to be awkward."

Pierce hated to hear the aching sadness in her voice. "I promise it won't be. Let's keep the focus on Avery and Carter, and everything will be okay."

"Okay." She offered him a smile, and they walked back to the restaurant. She paused briefly on the pavement, turning to look at him. "Pierce?"

"Yeah?"

"Even with the fallout, I won't ever regret what happened between us."

And then she was running ahead inside, greeting her family, playing her role in a sparkly evening dress while she pretended not to hurt like he did. It took him a few more minutes before he felt strong enough to follow.

Pierce had almost made a clean exit after the rehearsal dinner, but then he heard his name bellowed down the street. Shaking his head, he turned and saw Carter and Gabe coming toward him.

"Have one beer with us at Barefoot Bar," Carter said, slapping him on the back. "I didn't really get to talk to you guys during dinner with so many people needing attention."

Gabe grinned. "Yeah, it'll be his last drink as a single guy."

Pierce laughed. "Does that give you cold feet, Romeo?" he teased.

Carter waved a hand in the air. "Hell no. I can't wait to marry this woman. I just figured we'd talk."

At his friend's sharp gaze, Pierce stiffened. *Oh no.*

And there it was. The gleam of sympathy in Carter's blue-gray eyes. Gabe had the same look, as if trying to pretend this was a casual beer and not a grilling session.

In one whoosh, his breath exited his lungs, and he was suddenly too tired and sad to lie anymore. "You know, don't you?"

"Not everything. But we're not stupid, dude. You have misery and lovesick pain written all over your face."

"I acted normal, though, right?" God knew, he didn't want anyone to recognize that his relationship with Taylor was a mess during this important wedding.

"Yeah, no one would know but us. Come on, I'll buy," Gabe said.

They walked to Barefoot and settled at the corner of the bar, tucked a bit away from the partying crowd. "Tell us what happened," Carter said.

Pierce rubbed his face. "Man, I don't want this to be about me and Taylz. This is your time."

"You're one of my best friends," Carter said simply. "When one of us is fucked-up, we all feel it. It's not about separating someone's happiness from misery—that's not what people who care about each other do."

Gabe looked alarmed. "Um, can we fart or do something manly, please? This is getting way too emotionally intense."

Pierce took a long swallow of beer, then let out a satisfying burp. The guys looked a tad relieved, and then they all started laughing. Already, the sense of heaviness in his chest had lifted.

"Seriously, consider your confession my wedding gift," Carter said. "You can't fuck up my day by keeping a secret like this—I'll worry."

This time, no one tried to make a joke. And then he told them everything. He went back to the beginning, to the lies they'd spun to their family, friends, and each other. He opened up about his time in Paris, his plan to move and be with Taylor, and how she'd sold the painting and sent him away. When he was done, the beer was gone, and his friends remained silent.

Carter slowly shook his head. "Well, fuckity fuck."

It was the perfect answer.

"Dude, that's brutal."

"I know." He tugged at his ear. "What really sucks is I'm mad at her, but I'm also not. How can I be for not wanting me as badly as I want her?"

Carter tapped his chin thoughtfully. "That's what's weird about this whole thing. Taylor has a really hard time opening up—she's always been the most difficult of the Sunshine sisters to crack. But when she's with you, she lights up from the inside. Are you sure she just didn't get spooked? Maybe she sold that painting because she was terrified of taking that final leap?"

"I don't know. But she's so damn stuck on me not wanting the same things as her. Kids, a home here, a steady gig. As long as I have her, I have everything I could possibly want. She's all I need."

The guys nodded in unison, and Pierce finally felt understood. They sat for a while, listening to the revelry of the crowd, just processing everything he'd dumped in the ancient way guys communicated.

Beer and sympathetic silence.

"You're gonna be okay, man," Gabe finally said. "And maybe in time, you'll be able to circle back. Maybe she needs to live on her own for a little while, in order to come back."

"Maybe. But I need to move forward. I just booked another piece with *Traveler* magazine's website, so I'll be heading out for a while."

"Best thing for you," Carter said.

"We got your back, dude," Gabe said.

"Thanks."

Emotion filled him up, but he just nodded and let the comfort of his friends soothe the jagged edges.

Chapter Twenty-Four

The soaring church music fell silent, and Avery stepped up to Carter, her hands shaking a bit as she reached out to take his offered hand. Bella fussed with her train, then slipped back into line. Taylor glanced at Zoe, who was a showstopper in her mini bridal dress, holding tight to her basket of rose petals, her young face shining with excitement and awe.

Lucy remained perfectly quiet and well behaved in Ally's arms, her big brown gaze trained on her people. The dog wore her usual pink glittery collar but had been fitted in a pink shirt sequined with the words BEST CANINE. Her stroll down the aisle had elicited almost as much buzz as Zoe's.

The service passed by in a blur with various readings and a stirring speech by the priest regarding love. And then it was time.

"To have and to hold . . ."

"From this day forward . . ."

"For better, for worse . . ."

"For richer, for poorer . . ."

"In sickness and in health . . ."

"Till death do us part."

Taylor watched her sister radiate a glow that was almost otherworldly. Avery gazed at Carter with tear-filled eyes, her face beaming with the type of love Taylor had never truly believed existed. The kind that made you want to be better for the other person. The kind that broke your heart in the same way it filled you up, because it was consuming and raw and beautiful and real. Watching them together, the rings sliding over their fingers, she finally came to a new truth she'd always refused to see.

A love like this was possible.

She'd watched endless couples recite their vows, but deep inside, she'd always questioned if it wasn't just for show. A way to explain passion and lust, gain security in a scary world, and dazzle society with a fancy party to distract from the likelihood the relationship would break apart at the first sign of a true challenge.

Not anymore. Her sisters had shown her another path. Love seemed to be an adventure all on its own, full of ups and downs but also happy endings.

Or, in this case, happy beginnings.

Avery and Carter were pronounced man and wife.

They kissed. Carter whispered something in Avery's ear, and she threw back her head and laughed with delight. Taylor's gaze landed on Pierce, who turned a fiery glare at the photographer, as if he was itching to have been the one to grab the shot instead of the guy Avery had insisted on hiring so Pierce could be a groomsman at the wedding.

The couple walked up the aisle, and Bella ushered Zoe to the front, her toothy grin gaining oohs and aahs from the guests as she smiled broadly and threw the rest of her flower petals down the aisle. Taylor watched Ally walk with Lucy still tucked in her arms, then Bella and Gabe; and finally she stood next to Pierce, temporarily stalled from the backlog of getting into the proper line.

She stiffened beside him, trying not to turn her head and stare. He was perfection. The sleek black Tom Ford tuxedo molded to his body, emphasizing his muscles and broad shoulders. His hair was caught in a black tie at the nape of his neck, accenting his angled jaw and sharp cheekbones. Had he lost weight? He smelled of spice and soap and the whiskey they'd been sipping on the way over for an early celebration toast.

Her fingers brushed his, and she half closed her eyes, wishing they could laugh and talk and tease the way they had their entire lives. Instead, there was a heartbreaking distance that nothing could erase, unless she was willing to give up on her dream and fight for the man she'd fallen in love with.

But she'd done it for him, too, so he wouldn't compromise his wants for hers.

They began to move up the aisle, and she plastered a smile on her face, nodding to the familiar faces crowding the pews.

The next few hours flew by in a rush of photos and cocktail hour. She visited with second cousins and aunts she hadn't seen in years, and she checked in with Nora to make sure she was keeping a close eye on all the details swarming around them. Taylor had been worried Avery would have a hard time enjoying her wedding as the bride rather than a planner, but every time Taylor checked on her sister, she was dancing, socializing, or managing to actually eat something between the festivities.

She grabbed a glass of champagne and eased toward the open doors for some air. The ocean breeze caressed her face, and she watched the dying embers of the sun dot across the skyline, exploding into muted, glowing colors of umber, blush pink, cream, and tangerine. She took it all in, thinking about Pierce and what he'd said to her before the rehearsal dinner. Her brain understood and accepted that they needed to be apart for a while. Her heart rebelled against the rules, determined to find a way they could still have it all. Knowing she was no longer the one who he confided in pierced through her very soul. Maybe she should try to talk to him one more time. See if they could try to spend some time together before she flew back to Paris. Maybe they just needed some time alone together with no pressure. Maybe—

"Aunt TT! Aunt Avery needs you now!"

She turned to a breathless Zoe tugging at her gown. She ignored the panic, set her inner dial to calm, and followed her niece, already thinking of creative ways to attack any problem her sister threw at her.

She reached Avery, stunning in her A-line bridal dress, which cut low in the back and had a gorgeous pale-pink underskirt peeking out from beneath the glossy, stark-white satin. Taylor swept a gaze over her sister, checking for any issues. Hair still coiffed into perfect curls, makeup set and not smudged, white lace Tieks subbed in for the wicked stilettos. Nothing seemed out of place.

"What's the problem?" she whispered to her sister.

Avery gave her a pained look. "I gotta pee!"

Taylor shook her head. "You gave me a heart attack. Why am I taking you? Bella's your maid of honor."

"Well, she disappeared with Gabe, and I can't wait another moment—I need a tow truck to lift this five-hundred-pound skirt, stat."

"Fine. I'll do it, but you owe me." Taylor guided her out of the reception hall and into the luxurious bathrooms with large-enough stalls to contain a bride in all her finery. Taylor took stock of the gown and train, making a quick mental plan of attack. "Okay, I'm going to get under the skirt and lift it up. Then you pull down your underwear and pee. Got it?"

Avery stood stock-still, touching her lower lip.

Taylor slapped her hand away so she wouldn't ruin her lipstick. "Stop that. Now, let's get this over with."

"I can't."

"What do you mean? I thought you said you had to pee."

"I do! But you know my problem," she hissed.

Taylor blinked. Holy shit, she'd forgotten.

Avery had bashful bladder syndrome. Ever since she was young, her bladder would freeze up if she thought anyone could hear or see her use the bathroom. She needed full privacy in order to go.

"Are you kidding me? You have to get over it, Avery! You can't pee without help, and if you don't go, you'll wet the dress. I'm your sister, for God's sake. I've seen your boobs."

Avery groaned. "This is my worst nightmare coming true!"

"You have to try. Look, stop thinking about it, and let's just do it, okay? I'm going in."

"Wait!"

"Avery, you have to try! Think of your happy place."

"Fine!"

She didn't pause, just knelt down, shoved both hands under the mass of crinoline, and lifted the heavy material. Avery wriggled, trying to get her underwear down, but Taylor's balance wasn't the best, so she ended up toppling over, and the skirts came crashing down.

A distressed cry filled the stall. "You suck at this! How did you manage to help so many brides pee?"

"I don't know, I just did. Oh God, I don't want to think of the germs on this floor that just got all over me, or it'll ick me out. Let's do this again. Ready?"

"Yes."

This time, she managed to keep her balance and lift the weighted mass.

"Are your eyes closed?" Avery shouted.

She winced. "Dude, don't scream, I'm right here. Yes, I'm not looking. Now go."

Silence. And . . . nothing.

"I can't. You're listening to me, and it won't come out."

Taylor cursed, sweat popping on her brow from holding up the dress. "Fine, I won't listen."

"Sing something so I know you're not listening."

"But you always say I'm tone deaf." She gritted her teeth and swore she'd get revenge on Bella for not doing her maid-of-honor duties.

"For God's sake, I don't care right now. I need noise—now sing!"

She searched her head for a song, any song, and finally belted out the first lyrics she remembered loud enough to keep her sister distracted. "'Got me lookin' so crazy right now!'" she screeched, praying it would do the trick. If anyone could help them right now, it was Queen Beyoncé.

She kept singing "Crazy in Love," and finally, the sound of trickling came, so Taylor sang even louder, hoping to get her sister to empty out her entire bladder.

She was *not* doing this shit again.

It felt like forever before Avery called out to stop. Taylor's hands shook slightly from holding her arms up for so long. Avery's underwear in place, Taylor unfolded herself from the floor, staggered back, and dropped the gown.

Avery grinned. "It worked. Thanks, babe."

Taylor glared. "That was definitely a PITA moment. Congratulations. I knew you had it in you to be a pain-in-the-ass bride."

"Love you, T!" She flushed the toilet, bounced out of the stall, washed her hands, and disappeared.

Taylor limped to the faucet, washed her own hands, and tried to blot the excess sweat from her face. By the time she got back out to the reception, the DJ was in full force, and the dance floor was packed.

Zoe grabbed her hand and dragged her out, and Taylor laughed, allowing herself to get lost in the moment of happiness with her family. Eventually, a slow song broke out, and she lifted her niece up in her arms, swinging her gently around while Zoe laughed hysterically. Bella and Gabe drifted by, and Zoe joined them in a tight circle while they danced together as a new family, making Taylor's throat tighten.

She turned to ease off the floor and came face-to-face with Pierce, who was dancing with his mom. Wreathed in smiles, Catherine Powers greeted her in delight, then insisted she needed a break, forcing them to dance together.

In the past, they danced like they did everything else—effortlessly. They knew each other's bodies and movements, the songs they both liked and disliked, the way Taylor liked to try to lead, resulting in Pierce's insistence she follow since he was the man, which made her want to lead even more.

This time, they held each other at a distance, their hands stiff, their gazes averted. Tension seeped between them along with something else, something much more dangerous, as the low embers of sexual chemistry stirred. In moments, her body had a will of its own, softening against him in full invitation. A curse drifted to her ear. He shifted his weight, and she knew in that moment, he was just as turned on as she was.

With a resolute gaze, he seemed about to release her and run, so the words fell desperately from her lips, a last-ditch attempt to keep him with her for a little longer. "I heard you got two big jobs," she said. "A monthly blog and a feature? What's that all about?"

His shoulders relaxed slightly. "Yeah, *Escape* liked the last spread I did, so they hired me for a monthly column. The blog will combine photographs with my personal thoughts on the places I'm exploring. We'll see how it goes. If it's successful and I like it, I can do more. And then I booked a feature with the *Traveler* magazine website."

His words caused a burst of surprise. "Have you stopped doing wedding photography completely?"

"For now. I have a few I previously booked, but I made arrangements with Jackie from Shore Photography to transfer my client list. I'll be officially free by the end of the year."

Free. All this time, she'd believed he'd wanted to stay exactly where he was. Yes, he'd mentioned he wanted to travel more to expand his creative vision, but was he actually committing to a whole new lifestyle? He'd never said anything to her about dumping his entire business.

An odd resentment stirred. She'd given him up so he could get married and have kids like he always said he wanted. What was going on?

"I guess I'm confused," she finally said. "Are you saying you're leaving Cape May, or that you're doing more weekend and day trips to new places for the magazine features? I mean, you can't be thinking about giving up your studio, right?"

His face was set in stone. "I'll keep my home and studio here for now, but I'll be traveling extensively, probably for weeks or months, depending on the location and if I feel it's right. For the first time, I have a clean slate to explore and follow my creativity."

She shook her head. "But you always wanted to settle down in Cape May and get married, raise a family. You never talked about craving travel or being gone for months on end."

His gaze narrowed. "What does it matter?"

"Because that was always *my* dream! I'm the one who wanted to get out—you wanted to stay. God, Pierce, it's one of the reasons we couldn't continue after Paris."

He stopped dancing, staring at her with a mix of anger and disbelief. "Are you serious?"

"Of course I'm serious. Unless it's Samantha? Is she going with you? Is she the new *me* in this scenario? I guess I'm trying to figure out why you don't want to continue our friendship when you seem to be quite happy with the way things turned out anyway."

He breathed out in a long rush of air and dropped his hands, taking a step back. "Samantha is just a friend."

"Funny, that's exactly how we started out."

His jaw clenched, and his eyes burned bright, like jade fire.

Oh, crap.

His voice came out like a whip's lash. "Since I don't want to cause a scene at your sister's wedding, you'd better follow me right now, where we can get a few things straight."

"Fine." She marched after him, threading through the crowd, and locked them in the private wedding-party room, where it was quiet and they wouldn't be interrupted. Simmering with multiple raw emotions, she embraced the only one she ever felt truly comfortable with when challenged.

Anger.

She spun around and jabbed her finger in the air. "I don't understand why you're punishing me when this entire time you planned to be this new free spirit, jetting around the world."

"And I didn't know your new talent is rewriting history," he said. "You made the choice to send me away. Hell, I tried to have a conversation about our options, but you didn't want to hear it."

"Because I wasn't about to ruin your future!" she said with a touch of bitterness. "You always said we wanted different things, and I didn't want to be selfish."

"Lie."

She flinched. The word was flung at her like a bullet. "No, you lied to me. Why didn't you tell me in Paris that you planned to leave Cape May?"

"You never gave me a chance. You sold the painting and locked the door behind us without ever asking me. Do you know how badly I wanted to tell you how I really felt? What I craved from our relationship? The words I'd been swallowing back for weeks because I was terrified I'd spook you?" The surge of fury had tempered into a bleak resolution, and it made fear curl through her. "Did you actually believe we'd go back to our old dynamics, being best buds, without any consequences? Because I can't do it, Taylz. I can't pretend I don't love you when I do."

The breath left her lungs in a whoosh. The words should have been celebrated—the final admission they'd both tried to deny but knew as truth—yet the man who stood before her was like stone, his face carved into a blank slate.

"Pierce," she whispered, "don't you see I had no choice? Was I supposed to pretend one day I'd feel differently about getting married and having children and giving you a picture-perfect life in the beach town where we both grew up? I was trying to be a realist."

He stared at her for a few moments before he spoke. "Did you really believe that? Or were you just terrified about gambling on an uncertain future, preferring to keep what was safe and controlled and orderly—a friendship that had lines and rules and stayed static?"

"It worked for us our whole life!"

"Yes, it did, until it changed and became more. We had the opportunity to embrace a new relationship, but instead you tore it apart. Don't pretend it was to save me—that's not fair to either of us. You didn't let me choose. If you had, you would have learned one thing, Taylor Sunshine."

He closed the distance between them and tipped her head back, forcing her to meet his gaze. She fell into the blaze of green fire and tried to regain her footing, tried to defend herself from the rip of her heart and the realization she may have been horribly wrong.

"You're my home—you've always been my home. It was never about settling in Cape May or getting married or being a father or having a goddamn white picket fence. It was about feeling like my best self. All I ever wanted or needed was you. Can't you see that? I was going to move to Paris to be with you. I had big dreams for myself, to study photography and travel and steep myself in a world I wanted, a world I chose. But you refused to let me even say the words. You shut me out completely."

Her voice broke. "I was trying to protect you."

He leaned in and spoke deliberately against her mouth. "You weren't protecting me. You boxed me in and picked out my future based on what you wanted to see." He paused in the terrible, aching silence. "But the only future I ever dreamed of was with you."

Then he kissed her. His lips moved over hers in frustration, anger, and finally, passion. Her body exploded under his familiar caress, and she grabbed his shoulders, opening her mouth to the sweet thrust of his tongue, drowning in his muscled heat and musky scent and taste, and for a few glorious moments, there were no barriers between them, only the truth of how they both felt.

He loved her.

Suddenly, he broke the embrace and stepped back. She waited for him to smile or reach out his hand or say he wanted to try again. Instead, he turned and headed for the door.

"Wait! Where are you going?"

"Back to the wedding."

Shock barreled through her. She squirmed with vulnerability and a growing panic. "I thought—I thought we were going to talk. See if we can . . ." She trailed off, waiting for him to finish.

His gravelly voice held a resolution that made her want to drop to her knees and beg, just like the woman in her paintings. "No, Taylor, there's nothing left to talk about. Saying I love you doesn't change what happened, or the fact that you're not ready for this type of change. Not between us. Maybe not with anyone. Like I said, I can't pretend to be happy going back to friendship when I found so much more. It's best we keep things the way they are. Take the time and distance to build our own lives apart. I can't offer you anything else right now."

He left.

Taylor stared at the closed door.

She'd made a terrible mistake. She'd believed their friendship could withstand any type of hurt or abuse, and she'd taken advantage. She'd stripped away his choices and opportunity to show her what they could be together. She'd sold the painting in a final symbol that had destroyed their very foundation. All because of her need to protect . . .

Herself.

Maybe Pierce was right. Maybe it had never really been about him.

Her mind whirling, she dragged in a breath and gathered her composure. No way was she falling apart at Avery's wedding. She'd sit and analyze the entire encounter with Pierce later.

For now, she'd let him go.

Chapter Twenty-Five

"No, hold the brush like this, sweetheart. See, if you want looser, lighter lines, you keep your fingers toward the middle of the handle—away from the bristles. Yep, like that." Taylor watched Zoe create long, sweeping lines of sky, her sweet face furrowed deeply in concentration. "Now, when you do the trees and need finer detail, you hold it here—close up, so you have more control."

It was as if the light had broken through a thick, soupy mist. Zoe gasped, gazing at her with wide blue eyes. "Yes! That's it—I couldn't figure out why it didn't look right. Thanks, Aunt TT."

"Welcome, honey."

She watched Zoe paint for a while. Her niece had talent. Maybe she should talk to Bella about putting her in private art lessons to give Zoe a head start. Her family hadn't been able to afford them for her when they were building Sunshine Bridal, but now, with the business booming, they could all afford to give Zoe many more options.

She'd return to Paris tomorrow. She and Pierce had gotten through the rest of the weekend like polite strangers. Taylor had put all her efforts into making sure her sister's wedding was perfect, and enjoying family she hadn't seen in too long.

Her phone still remained silent, a reminder of their final break. She'd almost driven over to see him but had stopped herself at the last minute. What would she say? Did she want to take the risk and try to turn a lifelong friendship into a lasting love? Yes, he'd said he didn't want all those things she believed, but what if they got together, and later, he realized he'd made a terrible mistake?

Or, was it just an excuse, as Pierce had accused? She hadn't given them a chance to even try to work it out. It had seemed so much easier and cleaner to let him go, but now she was haunted by endless regrets.

"Aunt TT, I don't want you to go back to Paris. I miss you too much."

She refocused on her niece. "I miss you, too, Zoe. But I was thinking—maybe you could watch my workroom for me while I'm away? I'll leave my canvas and paints here, and when you need some quiet time or want to do some painting, you can use it. As long as your mom says it's okay."

"Yes, I'd love that! When I'm ready, can I have my big art show with you?"

She laughed. "Of course. I bet you'll sell out the place."

"Are you happy in Paris?"

"Yes."

"Are you more happy in Cape May?"

She frowned at the odd question. "I'm happy in both places. When I'm here, I get to be with my all-time favorite niece and my family. When I'm in Paris, I get to paint and explore new things and meet new people."

"Oh. So you can have a home, and be somewhere else, and not have to choose?"

"That's right. Home is a place you can always return to if there's people you love there."

"Like Mama and Gabe, and Aunt Avery and Uncle Carter, and Pierce?"

She jerked, staring at her niece. A shiver of awareness trickled through her. "Yeah, just like them."

"Good, then I can go away to places like Disney World until I get lonely and want to come home."

The words echoed in her head over and over like a haunting mantra. *You're my home.*

Pain exploded within. Tomorrow, she'd be safely in Paris, where she could bury herself deeply and hide her wounds. No one knew of her suffering, since she'd carefully kept everything from her sisters. But the loneliness washed over her like the ocean waves, dragging her under, and in that moment, she made a decision.

She needed help. Someone to talk to and confide in.

She needed her sisters.

"Hey, sweetie, you keep painting, okay? I'm going to get your mom so I can talk to her for a minute."

"'Kay!"

She grabbed her phone and sent a text. Can u come down?

Within minutes, Bella walked through the door. "Tired of babysitting already?" she asked cheerfully. "Wait till she's old enough and I can send her to Paris. You'd better start saving—my girl has designer tastes already . . ." She trailed off, staring. "What's the matter? You look . . . sad."

"I am."

"Sit down. Is Zoe in the workroom?"

"Yeah, she's fine for a while."

Taylor settled next to her sister on the couch, trying not to avert her gaze from Bella's probing blue eyes.

"Uh-oh. It's bad. And you've been keeping it from us."

Taylor tried to find the words to explain the crap show that was her current life. She came up empty.

"It's Pierce, isn't it?"

Taylor nodded. "Yeah. I lied. We never politely agreed to go back to just friends. We were sleeping together in Paris, but things got way too intense. After Luis told me I'd be in Paris for the next few months working on a new exhibition, I decided it was best to break the whole thing off. I thought I was doing a good thing for Pierce."

"For Pierce, huh?"

She blew out an annoyed breath. "Why does everyone always question my motives?"

"Because it sounds too familiar. I broke up with Gabe to protect myself, while I told myself the whole time I was doing it for him so he wouldn't be trapped here in Cape May with a single mom. In fact, you were the one who called me out on my bullshit, remember?"

"Yeah, I remember. But Pierce has always told me he wants stability. His studio, his home, a wife and kids. It's everything I don't want. Suddenly, we were this new thing together that came out of nowhere, and I was afraid if I tried to change him to be something I needed, we'd end up resenting each other. What if we regret giving up our dreams to be together?"

Bella nodded with sympathy. "I get it. And it does make sense. But it seems to me you guys are already experiencing regret. Go back to the beginning, and this time, tell me the truth of how things went with you two. All of it."

She did. She told her sister everything, refusing to hold back. When she was done, her entire being felt lighter. "Is this how you felt after you told me about Gabe?"

"Like a giant weight was lifted off my shoulders? Yeah. 'Cause I was finally being real with myself."

"Cool."

Bella smiled. "Before we go any further, we need to get Avery on the phone. I really want her input on this, too."

"Absolutely not. She's on her honeymoon, and I'm not bothering her with this junk. She doesn't need to hear about my emotional baggage."

"That's not very fair, is it?" Bella asked quietly. "Why should you make the decision about what we get to care about? We both love you and want to help you, like you helped us."

"Nope. I don't need to FaceTime her and get an eyeful of bleach-worthy moments. I was already under her skirt at her wedding, remember?"

Bella sighed and shook her head. "Just be honest with yourself, babe. You didn't want to tell us because you wanted to bury your feelings. Pretend everything is fine. How's that working for you?"

She groaned and picked at her thumb. "Dammit, don't use that old Dr. Phil line on me. It's probably trademarked anyway."

"Well?"

"Fine. It's all shit, okay? I've been a mess since Pierce left Paris. I was the one who chose to send him away, and now I'm devastated he's moving on. I'm fucked-up."

Bella raised a brow. "Yeah, you are, but so are all of us. That's why we need to stick together and help each other."

They got Avery on FaceTime. Their sister was wearing a wide-brimmed, obnoxious hat and seemed to be in a giant field. "Hi, guys! Check this out!" She waved at the camera, then moved it so they could focus in on the group of giraffes walking gracefully past. "Isn't this amazing? We're on a safari. We've seen so many amazing animals in their habitat."

"We're so happy you're having a great time," Bella said. "Please send pics. Where's Carter?"

"Talking to one of the safari guides, trying to find more ways to help stop poachers. If he could cart the elephants home, he would, even though it would piss off Lucy."

"He's such a softie," Bella said with a laugh. "Listen, do you have a few minutes to talk? Taylor is having a crisis."

"I knew something was wrong! It's Pierce, isn't it?"

Taylor's jaw dropped. "How did you know?"

"I sensed this new tension between you, but I also know how you refuse to talk about things until you process them. Now, catch me up."

Taylor began talking, and Bella jumped in now and then to flesh out the problem. Avery nodded, her gaze completely focused, while giraffes moved in and out of the frame from behind.

"You fucked up," Avery finally said. "You assumed Pierce wouldn't want you if you didn't change, but meanwhile, he fell in love with who you are. Babe, I hate to say it, but I bet Pierce was already planning to make some changes for the benefit of his career and your relationship. You just didn't give him the chance, or a choice, and that can be devastating."

"I know. How do I fix it? I can't lose him."

Bella sighed. "Are you willing to put yourself out there? Tell him you love him and want to make it work? There's no reason he can't be in Paris with you while you pursue a relationship."

"Agreed," Avery said. "The logistics are doable. But you need to convince him you're ready to do this with him and apologize."

Taylor nodded. "I get it. I need to do something big in order to convince him to forgive me and understand I'm really committed now."

"Exactly."

"No problem. I'll sneak into his house, get naked, and be waiting for him on his bed. Who knows? Maybe I'll bring some rope with me."

Her sisters exchanged a pointed look. Bella cleared her throat. "Um, babe, I think that's not going to be enough. Remember when I was going to lose Gabe, and I decided to use the Beach Bachelor article to show him I was all in?"

"Yeah?"

"That was big. It was a huge risk for my heart, because it was scary as hell. Do you get it?"

"No."

Avery jumped in. "Okay, I know you remember when Carter was a big asshole and broke up with me because he was terrified, right?"

"Sure."

"Well, he used Lucy to bring me a note and said something in the restaurant that was romantic and epic. Think big, like a rom-com. Not erotica."

She frowned. "But sex is so much easier."

"For you it is," Bella said. "But what will show Pierce you're offering him the most vulnerable part of yourself? Where does your heart really come from? How will he know it's for real?"

And then she knew. She didn't like the answer, but she knew. It was where she shared all the things that terrified her—the only safe place in the world she'd found and created for herself.

Her art.

"I think I know," she said slowly. The idea took hold. It would take great planning and faith. It would take a leap and expose what she'd been hiding the most from him. And he could reject her anyway. She probably deserved it, the way she'd turned him away, refusing to give him anything.

But for God's sake, she was no coward. It was time to be real—with herself and him—and she was done with her old bullshit wrapped up in lame excuses.

It was time to bring it.

"Good, then my work is done here. Are you going back to Paris?" Avery asked.

"Yes. I'll need to do some work there before I'm ready to come back for him. And to be honest, I think he was right about one thing. We both need a little bit of time apart. Some breathing room."

"Agreed," Bella said. "Sometimes, space makes people realize nothing is worth losing the person they love."

They said goodbye to Avery and clicked off.

"Do you need help with anything?" Bella asked.

"No. This is something I need to do on my own. But thanks for being here for me, Bella."

"Anytime. That's what sisters are for."

And though Taylor usually avoided big displays of sappy emotions, this time, she hugged her sister tight.

Chapter Twenty-Six

One Month Later

Pierce looked at his new collection. Satisfaction surged through him. It was a good start to his current theme: the effect of setting on mood. After developing the set of photos of the Eiffel Tower, he'd been struck not only by the glory of the structure itself but by the reaction of the crowds looking on.

He'd shifted his attention and discovered that couples became closer and families bonded, and that the instant of studying something either beautiful or ugly or shocking stripped the civilized surface of a person to expose the real stuff. The treasure. He was on a journey now where he knew what he searched for, and the quality of his work had jumped to a new level.

He shuffled through the pile of discarded prints that weren't up to the new standard he required, then froze as his hand slid one across the table. He studied her face, noting the light dancing in her golden-brown eyes, the curve of her cheek, the stark pink of her hair against the encroaching night.

Pierce ran a thumb over the purse of her red lips and remembered that perfect day in Paris. The night he'd realized he loved her too much to walk away. This time, the pain tumbled through him a bit slower, a tad duller. It was there every day—a knowledge that the woman who owned his heart and mind was across the world, making her own life away from him.

Just like he'd requested.

He snatched back his hand and turned to look at the empty, mocking space behind his desk. He still hadn't been able to put another painting up on the wall. Perhaps it was good to be reminded on a daily basis that he needed to stay away from her.

In the past month, he'd worked hard to focus on his career. He liked writing the blog for *Escape* and found peace in the days spent searching for that one picture that would help him understand things—to connect with humanity and the good parts while struggling with an intense loneliness and grief he feared had become a permanent part of him. But he embraced it all and found he was a bit stronger in himself.

He sighed and began straightening out his desk. It would be hard not to see Taylor for Thanksgiving. She was supposed to arrive Wednesday, and though he always spent the holiday with his parents and the Sunshine family, he'd convinced his parents to stay in Florida this year. He'd fly out and be there for the week. He just couldn't bear to sit next to her at the dinner table and pretend he was okay.

Not yet.

The bell tinkled.

Muttering a curse under his breath, he called out, "Sorry, I'm closing up!"

Silence.

Pierce shook his head and trudged to the outer waiting room to get rid of his five-o'clock walk-in on a windy November evening.

He stopped cold.

"It's me."

Pierce stared. His throat dried up and his skin itched, every part of his being crying out to touch her. At the same time, a helpless frustration and anger rose up. Why was she here? Did she want to torture him by offering more excuses of why they couldn't be together?

His voice sounded like gravel and grit. "What are you doing here?"

She gave a half laugh, then began to pick at her thumbnail. "I . . . I flew home early. I wanted to see you. I brought you something."

"I can't, Taylz." He shook his head, his insides raw with the effort to pretend she didn't affect him. "You have to go."

"Please, Pierce. Let me show you this."

Before he could say anything else, she propped the door open and dragged in a large canvas wrapped in a sheet. She laid it against the wall and faced him. It was the naked fear and vulnerability on her face that made him pause. The air thickened and stirred. His breath strangled in his throat as he waited for her to continue.

"I have stuff to say. I'm asking you to listen." She tucked her hair behind her ear, stood tall, and lifted her chin. Her nose stud winked in the lamplight. "In Paris, I thought there was no chance for us. I'd convinced myself we not only wanted but needed different things, because that's what we'd been saying for years. But those were things we said when we were young and naive. When we were children. I just never had the guts to even ask myself if I wanted something different."

He understood, even as sadness leaked through him. She'd come here to present her case, but she still didn't realize it made no difference. He didn't need explanations or rationalizations or an apology. He needed her to confess her real feelings—to give him everything she had inside and offer it to him with no strings. It was an act he knew Taylor couldn't do, and trying to change her wasn't fair to either of them. "Taylz, you don't have to—"

"Please listen. When you left, I figured we'd fix it. Give us some time, and we'd go back to the way it was. But after I saw you at the wedding, I realized how badly I needed you—not as a trusted buddy, but as a partner. A soul mate. My better half. But you said it was too late. I hadn't proven to you that I was strong enough in what we'd found together to know it was greater than anything we had originally planned or thought we wanted."

Suddenly, he sensed what was behind the sheet. He shook his head, raw at her speech, still wondering what she was trying to prove. "You didn't have to get the painting back."

"I didn't. Because we're past that painting. In fact, I learned something else about myself and my artwork. My paintings were most powerful when I connected with my emotions and let you in. The more I pushed you away, the more I was blocked—like looking at the world through a glass wall. But by loving you, I'm able to smash right through that barrier, and now there's nothing left holding me back."

Her voice shook. "I'm ready for anything, as long as I have you by my side. I love you, Pierce Powers. As a man, a friend, a lover, a confidant, a partner. I want to travel and make glorious art and watch you light up the world with your beautiful photographs. I want to go where you go. Sleep with you every night and wake up with you every morning. I'm not looking for halfway; I'm looking for everything you are. If you can forgive me." She ripped off the sheet and slowly sank to her knees in front of him. "If I'm enough."

He took in the magnificent painting before him. It was reminiscent of the final picture in her series for the art show—a retelling of the woman on the cliffs. The woman was kneeling in front of the man, but this time she faced him with clear, determined eyes, the love and longing carved out in every line of her features, every muscle in her body, hands reached out in supplication and surrender. Her message was bright and clear to the world who viewed it.

Love me.

And this time, he recognized the woman immediately, because her beloved face was in the woman who knelt in front of him.

Taylor had painted herself.

There were no gardens or flowers or broken roses or thorns. Instead, they were on a beach, and she knelt in the sand as the sun shone down on them, the ocean waves roaring in the distance.

The man was no longer in shadow, either. His long dark hair was tied back at his nape. Green eyes stared straight at the woman with determination and a raw type of victory, as if he'd been demanding her surrender over and over, only to be turned away over and over . . .

The man was him.

Everything he'd ever sought or dreamed of radiated out at him from the canvas. His hands shaking, his gaze flicked back to her, where she held out her hands just like the woman in the painting.

"I love you. I have always loved you."

He crossed the room, yanked her up into his arms, and crushed her with trembling arms that refused to let her go. "I love you, too," he said against her lips, and then he was kissing her, hard and deep and long, claiming her in the way he'd always wanted—as his partner, his love, his heart.

His best friend.

"I'm sorry it took me this long," she whispered against his mouth. "You can hold it over my head forever."

"I'll take you up on that," he said, smiling, pressing endless kisses to her plump red lips, his hands running up and down her body. "But you've always been worth waiting for."

Epilogue

The Christmas tree sparkled with ropes of multicolored lights that Zoe had generously applied. Outside, snow dusted the sidewalks and roads, crusting the trees and cloaking Cape May in a winter wonderland.

Taylor handed out the mugs of hot cocoa. "This one's for Zoe," she said, sliding it down the table. "Extra whipped cream."

"Thank you!"

"Welcome, honey. Avery and Carter—whipped, shot of espresso," she called, deliberately handing her sister the Grinch mug.

"Thanks—hey, you know I like the Disney one!"

"Tough, that one's mine. Be happy with the Grinch, or Santa will put coal in your stocking."

Zoe burst into giggles, especially when Avery stuck out her tongue.

"Irish cream shot, whip, and peppermint stick?"

"Me," Bella called out, scooping up the two mugs for her and Gabe.

"And for us, Kahlúa, whip, sprinkles, and a peppermint stick," she said, winking at Pierce as he claimed his *Witcher* mug.

"Thanks, babe," he muttered, giving her a kiss.

Avery arched her brow. "Hmm, for someone who's always complaining about all the lovey-dovey affection around here, it seems like you're the worst," she declared cheerfully.

Taylor shot her a warning glare. "There's mistletoe over us," she explained. "And I do hate that stuff."

She tried desperately to assume her usual cranky face, but it was harder with Pierce grinning and blowing her air kisses in his adorable way. God, she was happy. Down-to-her-bones happy. Who would have thought she wouldn't fight the feeling anymore and would just embrace it?

She took a seat on the couch, and Pierce settled on the floor at her feet, leaning against the cushion. The song "Frosty the Snowman" chirped from the speakers. Zoe drank her hot cocoa and chattered about snow and if she'd finally get the puppy she dreamed of for Christmas. Taylor had gotten a sneak peek at the sweet, mischievous golden Lab puppy Gabe and Bella had already picked out from the local rescue shelter. Santa was going to blow Zoe's mind when she opened up the red box Christmas morning. Taylor couldn't wait to see it.

"What's the plan for you guys?" Carter asked, holding his wife's hand, his thumb sliding over the shimmery wedding band on Avery's finger.

"I'm going to finish up this new series, which is going well," Taylor said, her hand dropping to Pierce's shoulder. "Luis already booked the gallery for the March exhibit."

"Which is solo," Pierce said, his voice full of pride. "She's already got a long client list waiting for inventory. I bet she'll sell out within the first few hours."

"We'll see," she said with a laugh. "Then Pierce wants to spend a few weeks in Italy for his next blog piece. And we'll be back to spend the summer here. Who knows, maybe I'll even help out with a wedding, for old times' sake."

"Funny you should mention that," Gabe said. "We may need an extra hand around here. Things are gonna get nuts next summer."

"Oh no," Taylor groaned, shooting a look at her sisters. "Did you guys overbook again? Honestly, am I the only one in this family who has no problem saying, 'Hell no'?"

"I couldn't say no to this one," Bella said with a sigh

"My bleeding-heart sisters. What's this one gonna be? Another Dr. Seuss–themed wedding? Or did some sappy bride get you all teary, begging to fit her in so she can marry the love of her life?"

"The last one," Avery said firmly. "Don't you think, Bella?"

"Absolutely. Zoe, honey, why don't you tell Aunt TT about the summer wedding we're going to plan?"

Zoe lit up, clapping her hands and jumping up and down in her seat. Her nose held a dollop of whipped cream. "Mama and Gabe are gonna get married!"

Taylor blinked, stunned. She turned to Bella, whose cheeks turned pink. "Seriously?"

Bella nodded. "Gabe asked me this past week. I wanted to wait to tell you in person."

Gabe grinned. "Zoe helped me with the whole thing. The ring, the proposal, the flowers—"

"And I told you not to be nervous because Mama was going to say yes!"

Everyone laughed. Taylor hugged her sister and grabbed her left hand. "No wonder I didn't know—you're not wearing your ring!"

"It's being adjusted at the jeweler's."

"So I was the last one to know?"

"Yep," Avery said. "Now I'm the most important sister."

Taylor sighed. "Fine."

"But I'd like to ask you to be my maid of honor, Taylor," Bella said.

Taylor tried not to whoop with victory, but she ended up doing a happy dance while Pierce laughed. "You're so bad," he said to her, eyes lit with humor and love. "It doesn't matter who the maid of honor is. It's an honor to be in the wedding party."

"Absolutely," Carter said. "So, Gabe, I'm going to be best man, right?"

Pierce frowned. "Hell no. I've known him longer. I'm going to be BM. Right, Gabe?"

Gabe stuck his face in his mug and doused himself in whipped cream.

Pierce and Carter continued arguing until the girls broke up the fight and said Gabe would give his final decision at a later date. Pierce's face reflected determination to win the nomination. There was nothing better than some wedding fights, and this one was going to be epic.

As the night wore on and the hot cocoa was drained, Taylor snuggled up with Pierce and realized that sometimes the things you pushed away the hardest were the things you loved the most. Whether it was a career calling or a family member, friend, or lover, she was happy she'd finally learned to embrace it all, even if it wasn't in the original plan.

Sometimes the roughest side roads led to the most magical, hidden treasures.

It didn't matter where Pierce and she ended up, as long as they were together.

Because that would always be home.

AUTHOR'S NOTE

I feel as if this series is an ongoing love poem to Cape May.

The moment I hit Exit Zero, I always feel something inside shift, as if I'm being welcomed home.

I hope you all have enjoyed the journey and that I've done justice to my beloved beach town.

I left a piece of my heart with the Sunshine sisters, like every writer does when she completes a series that makes her laugh and cry and feel alive.

I hope we will have many more adventures together. As always, thank you for reading.

ACKNOWLEDGMENTS

I'm so lucky to be able to have a tribe of people to thank!

Big thanks to the amazing Maria Gomez and the Montlake team for supporting and loving the Sunshine sisters through every stage. I'm grateful to Kevan Lyon, my talented agent, and my team behind the scenes: Nina Grinstead from Valentine PR, and my assistant, Mandy Lawler.

Special thanks to Anthony LeDonne for helping me with the ins and outs of photography and allowing me a peek into his art.

A big shout-out to all the businesses and people in Cape May who make it such a special place full of inspiration. Some of my mentions are real, some are fictional—all mistakes are always mine.

ABOUT THE AUTHOR

Photo © 2012 Matt Simpkins

Jennifer Probst is the *New York Times* and *USA Today* bestselling author of the Sunshine Sisters series, the Billionaire Builders series, the Searching For . . . series, the Marriage to a Billionaire series, the Steele Brothers series, and the Stay series. Like some of her characters, Probst, along with her husband and two sons, calls New York's Hudson Valley home. When she isn't traveling to meet readers, she enjoys reading, watching "shameful reality television," and visiting a local animal shelter. For more information, visit her at www.jenniferprobst.com.